Love Notes
Bishop

BLUE SAFFIRE

Perceptive Illusions Publishing, Inc.
Bay Shore, New York

Blue Saffire/Perceptive Illusions Publishing, Inc.
PO Box 5253
Bay Shore, New York 11706
www.BlueSaffire.com

Publisher's Note: This is a work of fiction. Names, characters, places, and incidents are a product of the author's imagination. Locales and public names are sometimes used for atmospheric purposes. Any resemblance to actual people, living or dead, or to businesses, companies, events, institutions, or locales is completely coincidental.

Ordering Information:
Quantity sales. Special discounts are available on quantity purchases by corporations, associations, and others. For details, contact the "Special Sales Department" at the address above.

Love Notes/ Blue Saffire. – 2nd ed.
ISBN 978-1-941924-27-3

There is a flame that burns from soul to soul. Find the soul that matches your flame.

—Blue Saffire

CHAPTER ONE

Back to Work

Bishop

"Are you listening to me?" Jag says.

I tear my eyes away from the brown legs that have had my attention since their owner walked into the door. Jag is always worried about something. Although he may have something to worry about this time.

I need to finish my album and my muse is gone. I just don't have it. Nothing has sparked that place inside where I want to create. I don't want to write another album about random sex.

I want more.

"They'll have their album," I say, knowing it's a lie.

I need to have songs written by the end of this tour. I've got a month left and nothing. I turn back to the ebony beauty sitting alone with a stack of papers and slips in front of her.

That sexy haircut makes me want to shove my hand in the front of it as I ride that juicy ass of hers. I love how the longer front feathers into curls that cover her right eye. She stands out in this place and not because she's Black.

Those red bottoms don't belong in a place like this. Not on these sticky floors. The only reason my crew stopped here was because I was craving a greasy burger and fries.

Those heels and that face have a story. The more I look at her, the more I want to know it. When she pouts at the papers in front of her, I have to shift in my seat. Those lips are sexy as fuck.

"*Bishop*," Jag growls.

I turn back to him, annoyed he won't leave me to my fantasies. It's been two years since I've had sex. Yup, that fucking long.

I've grown tired of random pussy. The next pussy I fall into is going to be mine. I'm going to own that shit. My balls swell just thinking about owning gorgeous over there.

"I said it will be done," I reply and stand to close the distance between me and the first spark I've felt in four years.

She's so engrossed in what's before her she doesn't notice me standing over her. She smells so fucking good. My mouth waters and I can't tear my eyes away from her.

Saga Walden.

I read the name printed on all the documents. Pretty name for a knockout woman. I have to shake my head clear as the sound of my voice groaning it fills my head.

Oh, yes. This is the one. I'm not leaving here without her number. As a matter of fact, I need to hear her voice to see if it's as beautiful as she is.

I bet it sounds like warm honey. Sticky and sweet. A sound to pour all over my damaged and lost soul. Fuck, I might be losing my mind.

However, when she speaks, I know I'm not because her voice is sexier than I imagined. Even as she mumbles to herself under her breath. Time to make my move.

I lean into her ear and answer her muttered words. When she looks up at me with those big brown eyes, I feel like I fall right into them. Holy shit.

Saga

It's been six months and I've run through my savings way too fast. The chunk I have left will pay off most of my bills, but I'm going to have to get a damn job.

Unfortunately for me, Tom had me blackballed. I should have flipped his fucking desk. Entitled bastard.

Once again, I shuffle through the receipts and bills in front of me, hoping something changes or money magically appears from somewhere.

"Fuck me," I mutter, pushing my hand into the front of my hair.

"I would love to, but first, we should get to know each other," a sultry voice whispers in my ear.

I startle and look up to find the most gorgeous blue eyes I've ever seen. I mean, they're vibrant and so blue they're electrifying. I'm sucked right in.

"Excuse me?" I say just above a whisper.

"Nothing," he chuckles darkly. Reaching for the bills before me, he lifts a few in his hand, still leaning over me. "Now, I was imagining you studying this whole time I watched you. You ruined my fantasy."

I snatch the papers back from him as my cheeks heat. I gather my things and start to shove them into my bag. I'm still stunned from looking into his eyes.

It's not until he claims the seat across from me my brain starts to fire again. I glare at him as he waves the waitress over. He sits back in the booth as if he owns the place.

His presence is magnetic. It's like he's sucked all the air out of this tiny booth. At least, it seems tiny now that he's seated across from me.

"Excuse me. Why are you sitting here? Who are you?"

"That"—he points at me—"is the reason I'm sitting here. You have no idea who I am and I want to know who you are."

I lift a brow. "Should I know who you are?" I say with no small amount of attitude.

"Not necessarily. But I aim to change that," he says slyly.

"If you don't mind, I just want to be left alone. Thank you."

"Oh, come on, love. Don't ruin our first date."

The waitress stops at our table before I can respond. I shift in my seat uncomfortably. She's been giving me the eye since I walked in here. I guess ordering a coffee wasn't enough for her.

"You look like a french fry kind of girl. Bring us a basket of fries to share and I'll have a chocolate shake. You want one too?" He pauses for a second before continuing without my answer. "Make that two. You know what, I'll have a platter of the buffalo wings as well. Those looked really good."

"No problem. Coming right up," the waitress says with stars in her eyes.

Maybe she knows who this character is supposed to be. The way she's tripping over herself, you'd think he were royalty or something. I stare at his handsome face. He does look a little familiar now that I'm looking at him.

"You used to work for Carmichael, Pike, and Jeffreys Advertising and Marketing?" he says.

I stiffen and narrow my eyes at him. Blackballing me is one thing. If Tom has sent this guy to harass me, that's an all-new ball game.

He points to my bag. "Your termination letter was on top of the pile."

My cheeks heat again. He needs to mind his business, but it's still embarrassing. I still haven't wrapped my head around all of this.

"Do you always go around getting into people's business?" I say.

"No. I just couldn't stay away from you. What did you use to do there?"

"I don't know you. I'm not about to tell you my life story."

"I'm not asking for your life story, gorgeous. Not yet, at least. My name is Bishop. Bishop Love," he says.

I burst into laughter. He can't be serious, but as I swipe at my tears, I see he's very serious. Something about the name tickles the back of my thoughts.

"Your parents named you that?" I ask.

The waitress arrives with a basket of fries and a huge platter of wings. Another waitress is with her. She sets down two tall milkshakes in front of us.

My stomach growls, announcing to the world it's been hours since I ate a grilled cheese sandwich that did not hit the spot. The fresh-looking fries make my mouth water. I don't realize

I'm looking at them longingly until he pushes the basket toward me.

"Go on, dig in," he says, popping a fry into his mouth. "And yes, my parents named me Bishop Love Moran. People think it's just a stage name, but it's who I've been since I was born."

Suddenly, it clicks. Bishop Love, the singer. He does rock or something like that. I was supposed to put together a proposal for a campaign involving him just before the fiasco.

"What's a big shot singer like you doing in a dive like this?"

"Ah, so you do know me. I could ask you the same thing, Miss Red Bottoms. Those are some nice shoes for a place like this," he replies.

"I asked first."

"I was craving some greasy shit. We pulled into the first place that looked good." He shrugs.

"My car died," I say, not knowing why I'm telling him this.

He sits up straighter, concern clear on his face. I tilt my head a bit. He doesn't know me, but he's feeding me, and he looks concerned about my transportation.

"Where's the car?" he asks as he gestures for one of the guys from a few tables over.

"Why?"

"I want to have one of my guys take a look. I'm not going to leave you stranded."

"Who says I'm stranded?"

"Baby girl, the address on those bills tells me you're a long way from home. If your car broke down, chances are you're stranded," he says.

"I'm not your baby girl."

He gives me the sexiest crooked smile I've ever seen. "Not yet," he says.

I look at him, really look at him. He's gorgeous. Those eyes are just the beginning. His lips are full, but his bottom lip is plush, giving him a sinful-looking mouth. He has a soft face with just the right hardness to his jaw to give him a masculine look.

His lashes are extra long and thick. If he were a woman, I'd think they were false. I still question them as I stare at him. His dirty-blond hair is piled on top of his head in a man bun. Something I normally hate, but it looks damn good on him.

His body is a sin of another kind. I'm not even going to linger there. It's been too long for me to get lost in thoughts of his well-toned, chiseled body. If I go there, I might climb across this table.

"Where's your car, Saga?" he asks.

I blink a few times. He just said my name. A name I never gave him. This one is a quick one. He downloaded all of that information in a matter of moments.

I like men who pay attention to details.

I'm not even going to go there. The last thing I need in my life is another man. The last one didn't do me any good.

"It's in the lot. I made it here before it gave out," I murmur.

"Keys," he says, holding out his hand.

I eye his long fingers warily. I don't have many options. I can't afford to call a tow.

Reluctantly, I reach into my purse and retrieve my key. I hand it over and his smile broadens. He looks at the emblem and gives a whistle.

"Mercedes. Nice. Jared, can you check out her car and see what's going on?" he says to the guy he called over.

"Got it, boss."

"Do they all wait on you hand and foot?" I ask as the guy rushes off with my key.

"Nope. We're a family. I take care of them. They take care of me," he replies.

"Must be nice," I say, looking over to the group watching us.

I mean it. I haven't had family to look out for me in so long. I wanted to live the big life in New York and I ran off to do just that. I don't know how to go home with my tail between my legs.

I mean, that's where I'm headed, but I don't know what I'm going to do once I arrive in Cali. Daddy will be so disappointed. He never wanted me to leave in the first place.

"The wings are getting cold. Come on. Let's eat. Then we can talk some more," he says, watching me.

I stare at the food before us and get ready to decline, but my stomach tightens and warns me not to pull any stupid shit. Fixing my car may leave me starving for real after tonight.

"Thank you," I say, reaching for a fry.

Soon, I've placed food on one of the extra plates and I'm devouring fries and the wings he offers me. It doesn't take long before I notice he's not eating much with me. I pause and push my plate away.

"Why'd you stop? You're adorable when you eat," he says with a smile.

"Why aren't you eating?"

"I had a burger and fries. I'm good for now," he says.

"So why order all of this?"

He sits back, assessing me. Those eyes, probing and searching for more. I look away, not sure what I might reveal.

"I watched you before I came over. I could tell you were hungry. Now eat up," he says.

"I'm fine."

"No, you're not."

"Hey, boss. Her ride is busted. It's not moving anywhere without some major attention. I wouldn't be able to patch her up, not out there anyway," Jared says as he returns.

That's it. That's the final straw. I cover my face and start to silently sob. I feel the weight of the last six months deep down in my soul.

"Hey," he whispers in my ear as he wraps an arm around me. I can feel his warmth seep into me now that he's seated beside me. "It's going to be fine. We'll take care of it. Don't worry."

"I'm not your problem," I sniffle.

"It's no problem at all. Where were you headed? Maybe we can drop you off," he says soothingly.

"Cali."

"All right. My tour ends in Cali. We're a ways out from the end, but we'll figure something out. Let's go get your things onto the bus," he says.

"What? I can't just get on your bus. I don't know you," I say through my tears.

"Give me your phone," he says.

I look at him curiously. He has that hand out again. I hand over the phone and watch him.

"Unlock it," he says, handing it back.

Dummy.

I chide myself and unlock the phone for him. He takes it back, grinning at me. Reaching up with his free hand, he wipes the tears from my cheeks.

"Ah, look at this. You talk to your dad. I'll just call him and let him know you'll be with me—"

"Oh, hell no," I say and go to snatch my phone back.

"Okay, okay, not your dad," he chuckles and looks back at the phone. "Is Isha a safer bet?"

I bite my lip and think for a moment. Isha was my first friend in New York. We lived together for my second year there. We've become best friends.

"Yes, she's safe," I reply.

He dials the number and places it on speaker. I don't realize I'm holding my breath until Isha picks up. I look up into those blue eyes and they're twinkling at me.

"About time you checked in. How's the drive going?" Isha answers.

"Hey, Isha. This is Saga's new friend. My name is Bishop Love—"

"What the fuck? You're lying. Where's Saga?" Isha gasps into the phone, cutting him off.

"I'm right here," I say.

"You're not with *the* Bishop Love. There's no way you're with *the* Bishop Love," she squeals.

"It's him in the flesh," I reply.

"What the fuck is going on? I thought you were going back home. Did they give you your job back? Tom's a fucking douchebag. I hope they fired him and gave you your job back," she rambles.

"No, I didn't get my job back." I sigh. "My car broke down. I'm in some diner. I happened to run into Mr. Bishop."

He gives me a pointed glare and shakes his head at me. Turning his attention back to the phone, he pulls out his wallet. I tilt my head as I watch him. He takes out his ID and takes a picture with my phone.

"Isha, I just texted you a photo of my ID. I'm also going to text you my number and my manager's number. I'm going to have Saga check in with you daily until she reaches her destination," he says.

"What's going on?" Isha asks, sounding concerned now.

"I'm taking Saga on tour with me. I'll make sure she makes it to Cali. It will just take a little longer than she planned," he says.

"*You're going on tour with Bishop freaking Love. Oh my God.* From being blackballed to being on tour with a freaking superstar," Isha practically yells through the phone.

My face fuses with heat. I can't believe she just blurted that out. As if I'm not already embarrassed enough.

Bishop's eyes home in on me. Again, he has that concerned look in his gaze. As if he plans to find a solution to that problem as well.

"Maybe we should keep this quiet for now," I say.

"Oh, right. Okay. I'll keep my mouth shut even if it kills me. It's totally going to kill me," she says. "Oh my God. I have Bishop Love's phone number. I must be dreaming."

"Not dreaming at all, sweetheart. If you don't hear from Saga, feel free to call me," he says.

"Oh, I will. You be safe, Saga. And don't do anything I would do," she says and giggles.

I roll my eyes. "Later, Isha."

Bishop ends the call and hands the phone back. I stare at him, trying to figure him out. No one is this nice. He has to want something.

"Come on, let's get your things. I have a tune I want to get down when we're done," he says as his eyes grow a little distant.

I had an ex who was a writer. He would get that same look when his muse hit. I gather my things and get up after he slides out of the booth. I don't want him to lose whatever has started to call to him.

I must be going insane. Am I really getting on this tour bus?

Looking around the diner, I know this is my best option. I never would have stopped here if my car hadn't broken down. I don't get the most welcoming vibe.

I'm not trying to get hacked up and placed on the menu. Besides, I didn't see any place to get a room or anything nearby. I say a prayer and roll with it.

The tour bus it is.

Bishop releases a loud whistle and the guys with him all start to get up from the tables they're sitting around. Bishop then pulls out a wad of cash, peels off a few bills and drops them on our table.

One of the other guys seems to handle the other tables before following us out. I walk beside Bishop, leading him to my car. I unlock it and open the trunk while trying not to pout.

"You want to move all this stuff from the back seat into the trunk? I don't think we should leave it on the seats. Someone might take that as an invitation to break in before we get her towed away," Bishop says.

Between my luggage and the few things I packed to carry with me, I didn't have enough room in my trunk. I place the excess on the back seat of the car for the ride. However, he has a point and I wouldn't want to have to replace a window on top of fixing the car.

"Good idea. You're right."

"Hey Ed, come here," he calls out as his crew mills around the parking lot in front of two buses.

I keep telling myself this is the best option as I grab my suitcases from the trunk to take with me and make room for the things on the back seat. My chest starts to tighten. This is so unlike me.

Never in a million years would I take a ride from a stranger—let alone a stranger and his crew. This screams stupid when I'm anything but. However, it feels dumber to stick around here.

My father's voice rings in my head, telling me there is a safer option. Calling him to swoop in to the rescue. That's the last thing I want.

"Hey, you all right?" Bishop asks, pulling me from my spiraling thoughts.

"Um, yeah. I'm fine."

"Here, let me get that," he says and takes my suitcases. "No laptop bag?"

"No, I didn't think I'd have time to use it, so I shipped it ahead. Not like I need to check work emails or anything," I murmur the last part under my breath.

"Cool, did you need anything else?"

"No, I think that's about it."

"Come, I'll introduce you to the guys. I think you'll be more comfortable once meeting everyone."

I nod and bite my lip. I don't believe anything is going to make me more comfortable with this. That is until we walk over to the group of guys joking and horsing around.

Bishop stops in front of them and I stop at his side. He places a hand on my back and it's like my entire body comes alive and I'm hyperaware of him.

I don't take it as sexual tension. I don't know this guy and have barely given attention to his physical presence. Okay, maybe I have just a little.

However, his touch has a comforting feeling I'm a little thrown by. I almost want to turn into him and snuggle into his side while whispering the word safe. I shake the feeling off. I'm probably just in my feelings because he's saving me.

"Guys, this is Saga. She's going to be joining us so I can get her back home to Cali safely. She's having a rough go, so be nice," Bishop says.

"You sure you want to ride along with this bunch?" One guy says with a mischievous smile.

Not dangerous, just teasing. He's handsome, with dark-brown hair and light-hazel eyes. I notice he's not as tall as Bishop, but still a lot taller than me.

"That's our drummer, Thrush. Totally harmless and will talk your ear off if you let him."

Thrush tips an imaginary hat. "Nice to meet you, Saga. I have all the good snacks in my stash and the movie collection when you're bored."

"Good to know. Thanks. It's nice to meet you too."

"That guy over there with the shaggy golden-blond hair is Bop, our rhythm guitarist. Not a man of many words, but when he speaks, it's sure to be some smart-ass remark."

Bop lifts his head from his phone and smiles, his green eyes twinkling with mirth. He gives me a wave and a wink, then goes back to his phone.

"And that's Fendi, our bass player," he says, pointing to the guy with all the tats and the crew cut.

Fendi is another tall and muscular guy. I chide myself again about how stupid this is. These guys are huge and it's all of them and just little old me.

Bishop continues with his introductions. "Dwayne over there is our other bus mate. He's the head of my security."

"Hi," I say and wave.

Dwayne gives a small salute. I can't tell what color his hair and eyes are because he has on a baseball cap that's pulled low. What I can see is that he's huge. I get why he's security. He probably just chucks fans aside if they get out of hand.

I notice most of the others have all loaded onto the other bus. I don't take offense. Maybe this happens all the time and they're over it.

That thought makes me feel self-conscious and a bit foolish. If I call my dad, he'll send in the calvary, but at what cost? And is it safe to wait here for help to come?

"Come on, I'll get you settled on the bus. You look exhausted," Bishop says, placing a hand on my back.

Again, his touch brings me a sense of comfort. My feelings are so conflicted. There's what I would have done yesterday—heck, an hour ago—and what I'm talking myself into doing now.

Bishop pauses and turns back to the others. "By the way, lay off the pranks while she's on the bus and definitely no shitting on the bus. I mean it," he grumbles.

The others groan and start to grumble. I don't know whether to laugh or feel bad that I'm ruining their fun. Although, I'm not going to object to the no-shitting rule. I opt to stay silent and make my way on the bus.

After all, I don't think I'm sticking around to make it back to Cali. I step one foot on the bus, then exhale. Well, I guess I'm getting on this bus. Here goes.

CHAPTER TWO

Muse

Saga

"Okay, hold on a sec," he says as we step into the back room of the tour bus.

I look up at him. He's twice my size, even with my heels on. Not just tall but broad. It would be easy for him to pin me to that bed and take advantage. Yet, I feel safe with him as I did before stepping onto the bus.

Turning from him, I look around the room. It's a lot more spacious than I thought it would be. The big king-size bed is tossed—sheets and pillows all over. Bishop places my things in the corner before he starts to pull the linens from the bed. I'm frozen as I watch him; not sure what's going on here.

I'm not sleeping with this guy. He has to be out of his mind if he thinks I'm lying down with him in exchange for this ride.

I fold my arms over my chest, feeling like it's the only thing I can do to protect myself.

"I'm not the best at making a bed, but I'll change the sheets to give you a fresh place to lay your head," he says.

His cheeks pink a bit and it's adorable on this big, sexy man. Okay, yes, now that I'm looking him over in this tight space, I'll admit he's fine. Like fine, fine. *I might drool a little while staring fine.*

His presence and that endearing look also allows me to calm my nerves a little. He has been nothing but a gentleman, helping me with my bags from my car and having one of his guys move the things on the back seat into the trunk.

I'm still not sleeping with him though. I shake my head to clear it as I think this situation through. I chew on my lip as I have a million things running through my head.

"Where are you going to sleep?"

"Don't know if I will. I'll be up front with Lucie for a bit," he replies.

I sag my shoulders in relief. That's good. They have a female member of the crew. That makes me feel a whole lot better.

"I didn't see her with your guys. Was she not in the restaurant?"

Bishop pauses, looking up at me with a sexy grin on his lips. My mind wanders to questions of who this Lucie is to him. Is she his girlfriend or something?

"Lucie is my guitar. I didn't have her in the restaurant with me, but I have a feeling she and I will be busy tonight," he says as his eyes roll over me appraisingly.

I fight not to shiver as his blue eyes caress me with his glance. When they return to meet mine, I see that distant look again. He shakes his head and returns to changing the sheets.

I move to help. "Thank you," I whisper.

"It's not a problem at all. We'll take care of it," he says and winks.

I lower my eyes to the bed. I'm not going to get invested in staring at this guy. I need to find my way home. I appreciate his offer for me to stay on this tour with him, but I'll be finding a way to get to Cali on my own.

I'll figure it out once I've had a moment to sleep and think clearly. He starts to hum and bop his head as we work together to get the clean linens on the mattress after he pulls them from a secret compartment under the bed. I have to admit this bus is pretty nice. Nicer than what I thought it would be.

It looks like an actual bedroom back here. I look up at the mirror on the ceiling and can't help wondering if the sheets are the only thing that needs changing. I push that thought aside when I feel a sting of jealousy jab at me.

"That should do," he says once we have the bed made up. "Make yourself comfortable. What's mine is yours. There's a shower right through there."

I turn to look as he points at the wall behind me. It's then I notice the latch to reveal the room beyond the barrier. I see others that I assume are for closets and storage.

"Thanks again," I say, not knowing what else to do.

He nods and heads for the door. "Sleep tight, gorgeous."

Sitting on the bed, I sigh and place my head in my hands. How is this my life? I went from having it all to watching it all slip through my fingers.

This situation burns so much because I don't deserve any of it. I did my job and I excelled at it. They'll be regretting it, I was the best they had, but that doesn't fix what's done.

Bishop

Those eyes. I can't get them out of my head. They've brought the muse back. I strum my guitar and sing the tune that's pouring out of me.

Giving a nod, I jot it all down. It feels good. The music is back. This is the best shit I've had in… I can't remember.

Returning to my guitar, I play through the entire song this time. I'm loving it. It makes me feel alive as I croon it out softly.

Most of the guys are tucked away in their beds. I don't want to disturb them. Or should I say her? The guys are all pretty used to this by now. When I finish the song, I put Lucie aside and peek back toward my bedroom.

The lights are still on. I can't help wondering if it's because I've been at it for the last… damn—it's been four hours. I lift to stretch. Not able to take my mind off the beauty in my bed, I start for the back of the bus.

I walk my hands against the roof of the bus to steady myself as I move my feet toward my target. I'm just going to check on her. That's what I tell myself.

Sliding the door open, I lean on the jamb. Once again, she's so engrossed in the papers before her she doesn't realize I'm standing here. I take a moment to watch her.

I stand, truly studying her. She has a black silk scarf tied around her head, revealing her neck and cute ears. I've never known ears could be so sexy.

From this angle, her lips are still as enticing as they were at the diner. I'd love to suck and lick on them as I push inside her. *Damn*, I've never had a woman make me want to fuck them so bad.

Her toes are even sexy, painted a pretty blue. What I'd do to suck her toes into my mouth while she screams for mercy. My cock swells just thinking about it.

Just as I go to adjust myself, she lifts her head. I push off the doorjamb, not bothering to shield the bulge tightening the front of my jeans. Instead, I climb onto the foot of the bed and lie across it in front of her.

"Did I keep you awake with my playing?"

"No, that didn't bother me at all. It's more my thoughts and all of this keeping me up," she says, waving a hand at the papers around her.

"What can I do?"

She snorts. "You've done enough. I'll take care of this. I should have enough to settle all of this and still find a cheap flight home from your next stop. Detroit, right?"

"Yeah, Detroit. But didn't I tell you I'd take care of getting you to Cali?" I say, searching her eyes.

"Why would you want to carry me along on tour? I'm taking up your bed and I'm an extra mouth to feed," she replies.

"Actually, I have selfish reasons of my own," I say and shrug.

"Can you clarify that?" She shifts on the bed as her face takes on an uncomfortable expression.

"I've written my first song in four years. I… I was missing my muse until you walked into that diner. I want to keep you around so I can finish this album."

She tilts her head, narrowing her eyes at me. Those brown eyes are so pretty as they slant slightly upward. Their almond shape and deep-brown color are just right for her heart-shaped face.

"You're saying that you wrote your first song in four years because of me? Now, that's a first. Probably the most creative line I've heard," she says with a small smile.

"It's not a line, gorgeous. It's the truth."

"Um… okay. If you say so," she says.

"Listen, I have to finish writing this album by the time I finish this tour. That's in four weeks. I was hoping you'd stay. I'll get you to LA and you can be my muse," I say, watching for her reaction.

"I don't know about that," she says hesitantly.

My mind rushes for something more enticing to offer her. I'm not willing to give up so easily. I can feel it in my bones. I'm going to get this album done with her here with me.

"You worked for Carmichael, Pike, and Jeffreys, right? What did you do there?"

Her face pinches as if she tastes something sour. Blowing out a breath and scratching her scarf-covered head, she takes her time answering. Something shifts in her face the exact moment she decides to share.

"I was a senior marketing manager. All the campaigns that put that place on the map were mine. I also brought them into the twenty-first century with social media and apps," she says bitterly.

"What happened?"

The tension and anger coming from her tell me I might not like the answer to my question. However, I've been protective of this woman from the moment I locked gazes with her. I want to know what has caused this change in demeanor.

"I made the mistake of dating a friend of my boss. He thought that meant I'd be open to fucking him. When I refused, things got interesting." She shrugs.

My jaw tightens. I sit up and cross my legs to mirror hers. I can see the hurt and distrust shining in her eyes. I want to erase it.

"I'm not that guy. I'm attracted to you. Very attracted to you, but I want to get to know you.

"I want to hire you. I've been needing someone to take over my social media and give it an overhaul.

"You can use footage from the tour or whatever. You'll have access to us from here and you can feed that to the fans. If you were behind Carmichael, Pike, and Jeffreys before the bullshit pitch they gave me, then I want to see what you have to offer.

"I'll give you an advance. We can set that up first thing in the morning, along with a service contract. It's a win-win for us both. What do you think?"

She stares at me for a long time. Her eyes fill with hope and uncertainty. I wait patiently, not wanting to scare her off.

"How would our sleeping arrangements work?"

"I can sleep up front," I reply.

"In those seats. No, I can't… I wouldn't be okay with that. What if you slept on a palate in here?"

"You're concerned about me." I wink. "I knew we had something between us."

She rolls her eyes before fixing them on me. I want to lean in and capture her lips, but I fight to remain right where I am. Not that the tether I feel forming between us helps.

"You're offering me a job. I'm just making sure you're going to be able to pay up," she says.

I reach to tap the tip of her nose. "You care. It's okay. I respect you more for making me work for it."

"You're not working for anything. If I'm going to work for you, that's all that will be between us."

"You're fired," I say with a straight face.

She drops her shoulders and looks down at the papers surrounding her again. I feel like a jerk instantly. Asshole move, for sure.

I lean in to brush my lips against her cheek. When her eyes lift to mine, I resist the pull to cover her lips. Instead, I brush her cheek with my fingertips.

"It was a joke. I need you here. As long as you're my employee, I'll respect your boundaries. You're just one of the guys," I say reassuringly.

She gives a small smile. It takes my breath away. It's the smallest gesture, but something about it says so much.

"Thank you. I'll take the job," she says.

"Saga," I breathe, pausing to clear my throat. "I still want to get to know you *for my music*. I want to spend time with you *for my music*."

She gives a tiny nod. "Okay. For your music," she says.

Somehow, deep down inside, I know we're lying to ourselves. The look in her eyes, as she agrees, tells me that I'm not the only one feeling this attraction.

Good luck getting out of this in one piece, Bishop.

As I get lost in her gaze, I know I'm totally fucked. I just hired my own destruction. I'm not going to make it out without getting singed.

"Now, tell me more about what you need from me. You know, with your social media."

I grin then reply. "We've all tried to manage it, but we all suck. The places we've hired haven't been any better. We need a better rate of engagement," I explain. "We want to know we're relevant to our fans."

"A lot of places oversell themselves when it comes to social media. If they don't understand your demographic, then it's a hit-or-miss situation."

"See, you already sound like the woman for the job."

I stare into her eyes, wanting to get lost in her and her gaze. Her voice is as enticing to my ear as she is to my eyes. Her presence settles me as well.

"You look tired. I should go back out front," I say.

"No, I'm good. I like talking to you. It's keeping my mind off all my crap."

"Stop worrying. I have a friend taking care of the car. It will meet us back in LA and you'll be able to see your way through those bills. You have a job now." I give her a smile.

"I still don't know why you want to help me. You don't know me."

"I believe that we meet people for a reason, a season, and a lifetime. Each person you come across fits into one of those categories. I tend to treat everyone with care. You never know which one they'll fit under."

The conversation continues and I find myself more and more taken by this woman. This is going to be my greatest challenge, but I'm ready.

CHAPTER THREE

Not Expected

Saga

I wake up sprawled across the bed sideways, but that's not what gets my attention. It's the heat pressed to my back and the warmth fanning my neck. It takes me a moment to register where I am and what's going on.

My anxiety starts to abate when I take in the interior of the tour bus bedroom, only to shoot back up when I realize I'm wrapped in Bishop's arms. It's his heat surrounding me. My clothes are still on. That's a good sign.

The last thing I remember is talking to him all night. After the job offer, we talked about what he needed and directions he'd be open to. He has a great following as it is, but I can see room for improvement on social media.

Those eyes sucked me in repeatedly last night. Bishop proved to be nothing like I expected. He's attentive when you talk to him. Not something I would've expected from a superstar.

Remembering our conversation from last night brings a smile to my face. Now, I can remember lying on my side and yawning while trying to listen to his every word. His voice is hypnotic. I must have fallen asleep at some point.

"Mm… you even smell good first thing in the morning," he groans sleepily against the back of my neck.

I cover my mouth. "You haven't smelled my breath," I chuckle.

He rolls away, releasing me. I try not to acknowledge the bereft feeling that begins to settle in. If I'm honest, lying here with his arm around me was the most secure I've felt in months.

"Want some breakfast? We have bacon, turkey bacon, and Canadian bacon. I make a mean omelet and my waffles are stellar if I say so myself," he says as he sits up.

"I'll have whichever you decide to make."

He chuckles. "I'm having all of that, babe," he says, patting his stomach.

"Oh," I say and knit my brows. "Maybe half of what you make yourself?"

"I've got you," he chuckles again. "I'll use the bathroom outside with the guys. This place is all yours."

"Thank you," I whisper as I watch him stand and stretch.

His shirt lifts, revealing tanned skin. I do my best not to ogle him. That is until he releases his hair and runs his hands through it before fixing it into that bun again.

He does it so fast I can't tell how long it is, but it seems pretty long and thick from what I can tell. I watch his tight ass as he walks out of the room. I shouldn't be checking him out, but it's hard not to. I groan and pull myself up from the bed.

"This is going to be a long trip home," I mutter.

I go through my things to find something comfortable to wear. Once I gather everything I need, I head into the bathroom to freshen up. My sister comes to mind and I think about giving her a call.

I can't help wondering if I should have involved her in what happened six months ago. My sister is an attorney. She used to be a prosecutor.

I know all this mess will piss her off. Although, she now works in PI law. I sigh and shake the thought off. I'll handle this all when I get home.

"Things are turning around. You'll get back on track. Fuck Tom," I mutter to myself.

Stepping into the bathroom, I'm impressed by its size. Then again, with a guy as big as Bishop, I guess this is appropriate to accommodate him. Instead of being nosy, like I initially wanted to, I place my things down and get to my shower.

Okay, okay, I do take his shower gel and shampoo to sniff them. They both make my mouth water as my mind goes to waking surrounded by a mix of both and what I assume is his natural scent.

"Saga, he's your boss now. Pull your shit together and wash your ass. You don't have time for him or any other man," I huff to myself.

I'm surprised by the disappointment that hits me as my thoughts sink in. I had sworn to myself I wouldn't get into another relationship for at least the next two to five years. I'm that done with men.

However, there's something about Bishop. I stop my thoughts in their tracks. No men. Especially not my new boss.

Bishop

She felt so right in my arms. I remember telling myself I'd just close my eyes for a moment once she passed out last night. Next thing I knew, I woke to Saga lying in my arms.

I blow out a breath before balancing the plates in my hand to knock on the bedroom door. I've given her plenty of time to get showered and dressed. Although, my mind has been on her in that shower since I walked out of the room.

"Here we go," I say as I make my way back into the bedroom.

"Thanks," she says, looking at the plate warily as she takes it.

The guys are crowding the front of the bus. Besides, I'm not ready to share her. I want more time like last night. Listening to her talk about all the things she can do for the band's social media had me in a trance.

I could tell she knew what she was talking about. Watching her eyes light up and the wheels turn in her head sucked me right into the excitement with her. It didn't hurt that I got to hear that sexy voice and watch those sexy as fuck lips move.

"No problem."

"I should've asked for a quarter of what you're having," she says as she eyes the plate in her hands.

"Eat what you want. I'll finish the rest," I say.

"Seriously? You'll probably pass out before you finish your own."

"This?" I say, pointing at my plate. "This is just my first plate."

Her mouth pops open. I sit on the bed beside her and start to dig in. She's still staring at me and the portion size on my plate as I chew.

"I've always been a big guy and I've always loved to eat," I say after swallowing my bite of omelet.

"You seem to be pretty fit. I would think being on tour would be like going on a cruise. Everyone always comes back with a few extra pounds," she says.

I grin to myself. She's not wrong. Tours can be hard on the body. I've learned my lesson in the past.

"We tend to stay active. Well, as active as you can while on a bus most of the time," I say, pointing to the pull-up bar over the door. "That comes in handy most days."

She gives a smile while nibbling on a piece of bacon. She's so damn cute while she's eating. Her hair is down again, covering her eye. She's dressed in jeans and a T-shirt.

"So we'll be stopping again soon, right?"

"Yup, good old Detroit. We only have one show there though," I reply after swallowing some more of my food.

"Okay, cool," she says, cutting into the omelet and placing a forkful into her mouth. "*Mmm*, oh wow. This is so good."

I swallow back the dirty images that come to mind with her moaned words. I narrow my eyes at her. She has to know she's turning me on.

Yet, as she ignores me to devour the rest of the food on her plate, I know it has nothing to do with me at all. I grin. She's not like any of the women I've met in my past.

Not once did she try to seduce me last night. She wouldn't have had to do much. If she gave the signal, I was all for it.

"Do you have a boyfriend waiting for you in Cali?" I blurt out as jealousy starts to take root from the possibility that she does.

She makes a sour face and places her plate on the bedside table. I watch as she finishes chewing and swallows the food in her mouth. The look in her eyes says enough without the words.

"No, the guy I was dating lived in Miami. He used to come to New York for our dates. That's a nonissue now," she says when she finally speaks.

"Got it." I nod. "Gorgeous is single."

"And not ready to mingle. Especially not with my potential boss," she says softly.

"A deal is a deal. I had the contract emailed over. We have a printer on the bus. I'll get it printed out once we're done eating," I reassure her.

"Cool."

"Have you ever dated a White guy?"

"Have you ever dated a Black girl?" she shoots back.

I give her a grin as I chew on my waffle. I wipe the sticky feeling from my lip and stick my thumb into my mouth. Saga's gaze follows the motion, causing me to smile more.

"A couple," I reply.

She seems taken aback by my response. I chuckle, finishing the rest of my food, I place the plate down beside hers. I pick up the one she set aside and point at it.

"You done?" I ask.

"You really plan to finish that?"

"Sure do."

"Yeah, I'm finished," she says, shaking her head at me.

"Now, for the answer to my question."

"My ex. He was White." She shrugs. "First time I've dated outside of my race. Not sure if I'll repeat."

"One douchebag shouldn't get to spoil it for all of us," I say.

She tilts her head at me and narrows those pretty eyes. I like her studying me. I want her to see me. I want her to know me.

"You're not going to make this easy, are you?"

"What's that?"

She sighs. "Nothing. Nothing at all."

No, I'm not going to make this easy on her. I know exactly how I plan to win her over. It's how I got the world to love me. I'll sing until she surrenders.

One note at a time, I'm going to make you mine, Saga.

CHAPTER FOUR

Signed

Bishop

"This offer is way too generous. At my old firm this would be twice the amount for a campaign of this size," Saga says with her brows knit as she looks over the contract I've printed and handed to her.

I shrug. "You're traveling with us for the extra social media content. I believe it's a fine salary. Consider any extra a sort of relocation fee since I'm interrupting your return to Cali. Fair enough?"

She looks up at me and stares for a moment. I study her back. I would have given her twice as much for just the consult last night. Her ideas were brilliant.

"It says here that you also plan to furnish me with a new phone and laptop for the position. This is a lot, Bishop."

I frown. "You said they kept your work laptop and you shipped your personal ahead. You can't do the job if you're not equipped." I shrug.

She runs a hand through the front of her hair and nods. "Okay, fine." She sighs then mutters to herself. "This is the best option I have at the moment, so I'm not going to look a gift horse in the mouth."

I wait with bated breath as she picks up the pen and flips through the pages one more time. She bites her lip and leans in as she scribbles her signature on the line.

Releasing the breath I've been holding, I smile. I pick the contract up before she changes her mind and tears it up. There's this giddy feeling in my chest that I haven't felt in a long time.

It's like Christmas morning with my family. Nothing can take the wind out of this moment. I take my phone out and send a text for her advance to be transferred.

Her phone vibrates next to her hand. She looks at it and then snaps her head up to look at me. Her sexy lips are parted.

"What's this?" she gasps.

"Your signing bonus. That will cover that stack of bills. I can't have your mind preoccupied with anything other than your new job. You might miss something," I tease.

"*Bishop*," she drags out.

I wave her off. "We'll be stopping for that laptop and phone soon. Have dinner with me." I hold my hands up quickly as she goes to decline. "It's for the music. I do need to spend time with you to keep the muse flowing."

"Since you put it that way, okay. Thank you, Bishop. I truly appreciate everything you're doing for me. I don't know how I'll ever repay you."

I wink at her. "No thanks needed. You'll repay me with a killer social media campaign and an inspiration for an album worthy of all the hype you build."

She gives me a small smile. I want to lean in and kiss her sweet-looking lips. However, I remind myself that she's my new employee and I need her here to get this album done.

Just like that, the music starts. I get up and grab Lucie so I can sort the song out. I murmur to myself and grab my notebook.

"I'll get out of your way," Saga says softly.

I look up as if just remembering she's there. Not that I could forget her presence. She's fueling the music flowing through me. Her sweet scent fills my head as I strum my guitar.

I roll my tongue in my mouth, wondering if she tastes as good as she smells. She ducks her head as I look at her. I know I'm not keeping the heat out of my gaze.

"I'll let you know when we get to our stop. See you in a bit," I say and nod, returning to the song developing in my head.

Saga

Bishop slips his hand into mine and tugs me closer to his side. My belly drops and fills with a tingling sensation. I chide myself and swallow down all thoughts of him holding me close.

"It's for the music. Having you close keeps it going," he murmurs as I try to pull my hand from his. "I also want to keep you close in case… things can get crazy in the blink of an eye. The hat doesn't always do the job," he murmurs the last part quietly.

I call bullshit, but I stop pulling my hand away from his as we walk through the mall. He looks down at me and winks. There's that sexy, heated look in his eyes again.

I swear I thought I was going to melt under the table when he looked at me earlier while strumming his guitar. I finally allow myself to admit he's a sexy man. He moves with an effortless sex appeal.

However, I'm not going to allow myself to get caught up in those looks. I'm here to do a job and get my life back on track. Once this tour is over, I have a lot to think about.

Falling into this man's bed isn't going to help that process in any way. I'd like to think I'm smarter than that. Yet when he places his palm on the small of my back to lead me into the computer store, I'm not sure I am.

His warm palm sends shivers up my spine. I have to bite down on my lip to keep my composure. It's a simple freaking touch, but my knees are ready to buckle under it.

The hand he's been holding is still tingling from his touch. I shove it in my pocket to ignore the feeling of his loss. How can he have this effect on me in such a short time?

I turn to look at Dwayne, Bishop's security guard. He gives me a warm smile but doesn't look as if he feels this is inappropriate like I do. I try to relax.

We're going to buy me a work laptop. Nothing more. Bishop seems like a protective guy. That has been clear from the moment we met.

"You all right?" Bishop asks as we wait for someone to come and help us.

"Yeah, I'm fine. Just thinking."

"We'll make this quick and get to dinner. Unless you want to stop somewhere else."

"Actually, if we can find someplace where I can pick up a few toiletries, that would be great. If you don't mind."

"No problem. We can go wherever you need."

The way he looks me in my eyes as he says the words places me in a trance. I can't find words for the life of me. I'm usually a lot more composed than this. There's just something about this man.

"Hi, can I help you guys with anything?" one of the sales associates bounces over with a tablet in her hand and says, saving me from embarrassing myself.

"We need a phone and a laptop. Saga here will explain to you all she'll be doing with the equipment. We'll take it from there," Bishop says smoothly.

The young girl gasps, but I'll give her credit for how quickly she recovers. She tugs at the front of her shirt then runs a hand down her ponytail. I shake my head. I guess no one is immune to this man.

"I'm Kerry, I'll be happy to help. Tell me all you need, and I'll get you sorted out," she says as she now stands straighter and with her shoulders back.

Too bad for her, Bishop doesn't seem to be able to keep his eyes off me. I notice his eyes glaze over and smile. The music is at it again.

Not wanting to keep him away from the bus and Lucie for too long, I hurry to tell Kerry what I need. I almost burst into laughter when Kerry rushes over to tell her coworkers who's in the store before she collects our items to bag up.

I know that's what she's done because they all look in our direction as if trying to confirm her suspicion. Bishop places a hand on the small of my back and tugs me into his side. He then leans in and speaks against my temple.

"This is about to get awkward. I'll have Dwayne pay, but we should head out of here," he whispers against my skin.

"Oh, okay," I breathe as I try to ignore the shiver his warm, minty breath sends through me as it fans against my skin.

Bishop says something quickly to Dwayne and we exit the store just as fast. Once out of the store, he pulls out a pair of shades and shoves them on.

"Does that happen a lot?"

"More than I would like. It's been a long time since I've been free to buy a pack of bubble gum for myself."

"Maybe we should forget about my stop. I'm sure I can find time to get those things another time. I wouldn't want you to get mobbed over deodorant."

"There it is again, you're concerned about me. I like it," he croons.

I shake my head. The man signs my checks. Of course I'm concerned. However, wanting to keep that pretty smile intact might have something to do with it as well.

Lord, help me.

CHAPTER FIVE

One of the Guys

Bishop

I saunter to the front of the bus, wondering what all the commotion is about. I have been in the back of the bus working on a song. Saga had gone up front to give me space—I didn't want—and to see if she could bond with the guys and get a feel for them so she could better do her job.

Of course, the guys didn't listen to me. She hasn't been with us more than two full days and they're up to their pranks on the bus again. However, her sweet laughter fills the bus along with the guys' as she sits up front with them.

She falls into Fendi as she wipes tears from her eyes. I watch as she tries to catch her breath. It looks good on her.

It's a far cry from how I found her in that diner. Seeing her like this makes me want to be the cause of her laughter each day.

The sparkle in her brown eyes, that gorgeous smile it's all calling to something deep within.

Saga looks like she belongs here. Fendi is laughing just as hard from beside her as Thrush looks pissed. This is a scene I'm used to on this bus. I guess they decided not to hold back.

"What's going on?" I ask as I take a seat up front in the common area of the bus. We're all over six feet, so we had to get a bus that would accommodate all our heights.

The aisle is wide to give us the legroom we need. The bunks are all extra long for sleeping comfortably. This bus sleeps seven. My master in the back and six bunks in the center of the bus.

Dwayne, Ed, and Martin, Fendi's bodyguard, all ride with the band. Like I said, we're all big guys. However, this bus has never seemed as cramped as it does now with Saga on it.

Not because she's taking up space but because she looks so small around all of us. It makes me more protective of her. She looks so tiny as she sits laughing against Fendi.

I narrow my eyes as they're all laughing too hard to answer me and Thrush looks too angry to bite out a single word. I lift a brow at him, but he shakes his head and storms over to the kitchen sink.

He turns back to me and plops a block of ice on the table before me. I wrinkle my brows as I stare at it. Then, it dawns on me what I'm looking at.

"Bro, they froze your drumsticks," I say and fight not to burst into laughter.

Thrush turns to glare at Saga. "I think she did it. No, I'm sure she did it. These idiots have never been this creative," he snarls.

My mouth falls open and I turn my gaze on Saga. She gives me a sheepish grin and shrugs her little shoulders. I lift a questioning brow at her.

"I didn't want everyone to stop having fun because of me. I figured if I joined in, you couldn't be too hard on them," she says.

"I fucking love her. That shit was genius," Fendi croons.

"You know what? I'm not mad at her. I'm mad at these assholes for telling her just how to fuck with me. Welcome to the family, gorgeous. Payback will be a bitch," Thrush says and winks at her.

My heart warms as I take this as the guys initiating her into the family. The guys are not always so welcoming to newcomers. This means a lot to me because I want her here and I want her to feel safe and welcome.

I hope she knows what she's opened herself up to. These guys can get crazy with the pranks. Sometimes, there's nothing else to do.

Although, I have to admit she just earned hella points with me. I shoot her a wink. She ducks her head shyly. Now, I'm even more intrigued by this girl.

In my book, she just became a fucking rock star. I grin and give her a slow clap. As Thrush sits and starts to chip at the ice with a knife, I can't hold my laughter in any longer.

"Assholes," Thrush mutters under his breath.

Saga

I've just gotten off the phone with Isha and finished changing into my nightclothes. I can still hear the guys up front teasing and taunting each other. With a smile on my face, I shake my head.

I jump as the door opens and Bishop steps inside. I've been jumpy since Thrush promised payback. I think the anticipation of his payback is going to do me in more than the prank itself.

I like the guys. They're a lot of fun and really down to earth. Again, something I wasn't expecting.

They've made me feel like one of them. Not one cringeworthy moment has passed between us. Instead, I feel like I have gained six new big brothers.

I say six because this one right here. Bishop Love. He doesn't look at me like a brother would and I don't get the feeling he ever intends to change that.

As I take him in, I hope the look I'm giving him isn't the same. He's shirtless, in only sweatpants, with his hair pulled up on top of his head. From the cocky look that comes to his face, I get the feeling my hopes are wasted.

"You know you set yourself up with that prank. Say the word and I'll call them off," he says.

I shrug my shoulders. "If I were the new guy, would you call them off?"

He gives me a sexy grin. "No. He'd have to suck it up and take it."

"Cool. I'll handle it."

He chuckles. "Yet you've been jumping out of your skin all evening."

"Like you said. I asked for it. I made my bed; now I'll have to lie in it."

I regret my words the moment they're out of my mouth. Bishop's nostrils flare and his heated gaze drags over my body. I shift from foot to foot and tug my little shorts out of my crotch.

With a single look, this man has made my panties moist. *I am here for a job. This is my boss*, I chant to myself.

He moves to sit on the bed and pats the space beside him. I hesitate for a beat then pad closer and sit next to him. He looks at me and opens his mouth as if he's about to say something, then closes it back as if thinking better of it.

He searches my face with those intense eyes as if he's committing every inch to memory. Then his eyes light up. I'm curious as to what's going on in his head.

"What's your favorite food?"

I'm shocked that this is what he chooses to ask. I take a moment to think. Then a smile comes to my lips.

"Quesadillas. I love a good quesadilla," I reply.

"Only one," he murmurs to himself.

"Huh?" I say in confusion.

"You only have one dimple. I wanted to see if I could make you smile to make sure I was right. You only have one. On the right side," he murmurs.

I tilt my head to the side and study him back. He smells so good. I have to fight not to lean in and inhale deeply.

You know when you find that one scent to place in your space that always welcomes you home? That fragrance that welcomes you in, no matter where you are and teleports you right back to your living room or bedroom or whatever your favorite room in your home is. That's how Bishop smells.

I frown to myself. Maybe it's time I go to bed. My thoughts aren't helping me see this man as I should.

"Um, so good night," I say and force a yawn.

He smiles and nods at me. "Yeah, good night."

And just like that, his eyes take on that look. I smile as this is a reminder of why I'm here. His music.

Nothing will happen between us because I'm only here to do my job, get home, and be a muse for the music. I don't need to think too deeply about any of this.

With those thoughts clear in my head, I climb into bed and under the sheets. I'm Saga Marie Walden, I don't jump into relationships with random men and I don't do casual sex.

CHAPTER SIX

Detroit

Saga

The energy, the pulse of the music through the floor that's flowing up through my body, the sheer excitement pulsing through the screaming crowd—this is insane. I'm so far out of my depths. I'm used to being in a corporate office calling the shots, creating and launching campaigns from my desk.

I never had to think about the details and work that goes into something like a major concert like this. There are so many pieces to it all. Bishop has insisted on having me glued to his hip for the entire day. My new phone is full of footage from throughout the setup and sound check.

I can't wait to get this all up on the band's social media and Bishop's personal profile. I have so many ideas for moving his campaign forward. After the huge signing bonus that hit my bank account, I have a bit of extra motivation.

"Detroit, you've been great. I was hoping I could try a little something new out on you," Bishop says into the mic with that sexy voice of his.

My nipples tighten against my bra as he speaks to the crowd but turns to look at me, waiting in the wings. He winks and turns back to his fans. I lick my lips and lean into his words.

"I've started my new album and I'm thinking of calling it *Love Notes*." A sexy grin comes to his lips as he looks at me again.

He gives me a lazy once-over and my heart nearly lurches from my chest. I move aside as Joey, one of the young roadies, rushes Lucie out to Bishop. Bishop takes a seat on the stool another guy just placed next to him. He takes Lucie and strums a few notes.

"I hope you guys like this first song. I'm quite pleased with it," he says in a husky tone that has my panties suddenly moist.

I mean, look at him. He's already a big man, but as he stands on stage, his presence seems to take over everything. He's larger than life up there.

Even as he looks all sweaty, his hair sticking to his face and his T-shirt clinging to his wet skin. It looks as if someone drenched him with a bucket of water.

He begins to play the intro. It's a soft melody that feels like a caress. I'm captivated before he opens his mouth.

Not like I've been all night as I watched and listened to his set. No, this is different. These notes are calling for my soul. Just as his voice does when he begins to sing and the band joins in.

I've been wanting more. Craving, needing something new
Life is hollow when it's centered around yourself
That's what I told the reflection in the mirror

Looking into the future, trying to draw the answer nearer
Then came you
The answer I didn't know I needed but exactly what I wanted
I want you
In ways I've never wanted anyone else
So help me understand, what is it you want in a man?
Cause I need to be him, I want to be…him—
Is it romance?
We can dance under the stars, I'll bring my guitar
Sing you songs from the heart. Could that be a start?
I promise to do my part—
Do you think you can let me in?
Just tell me where to begin—

I know I said I didn't want to get involved with him if I was working for him. But I'd be lying if I said that I haven't grown intrigued by this man in the last two days. My mind travels back to him humming this exact tune as I was signing my contract. His eyes sparkled with mischief the whole time. Now, I think I get why.

Is this the song I inspired?

I think I might be in trouble. I'm glad I set some ground rules. I won't be letting my guard down during the next four weeks. I'm not willing to pay that price. I can't afford it.

The lyrics only draw me in more as he finishes the song. I remind myself they're just words. He's not singing about me or to me. He doesn't even know me.

"Thank you. Thank you so much," Bishop says as he stands and takes a bow.

My hand holding up my phone is trembling. I've recorded most of the set, but this is so epic and raw. I have to get his permission to post it on his page. The fans will love it.

I can't take my eyes off him as he saunters toward me. His long legs carry him close with a swag few men his height and size can pull off. Not for the first time, I admire his thick thighs and muscled frame.

When I look at Bishop, Vikings come to mind. His hair is loose around his shoulders, stopping midchest. I wonder what those long locks feel like.

He stops before me, leaning to speak in my ear. "That one felt right. I can't wait to see what else you bring me."

Without another word, he moves past me to the people that start to surround him. I turn to look at the man who's trying to scramble my head. Everyone gravitates to him.

Bishop Love is a force all of his own. Talented, charming, and sexy as fuck. All things I have no business ticking off.

"I might be in trouble," I murmur.

CHAPTER SEVEN

Didn't Answer

Saga

I sit on the bed in the tour bus with a smile on my face. I'm so excited by the results I've created already. Since I got out of the shower, I've been refreshing and checking their socials. I can't help smiling with pride.

"They're going crazy over your new song. You guys should definitely log in and comment back to a few fans. They'll love that. Or you guys can give me a few responses so I know each of your tones and your log-ins, of course, and I can comment for each of you," I say excitedly.

I'm loving the engagement. What people often don't get is that while a public figure may seem to have a following, a following willing to interact is the real gold. It's harder to get that to happen than it is to build numbers on a profile. Once you hit a sweet spot, bots will take care of that.

Engagement shows there are more true fans than bots or lookie-loos. I'm very pleased with the results so far. Bishop was totally on board with me posting the song from tonight and I'm so glad we did.

"I'll talk to the guys in the morning," Bishop says tiredly.

I glance up from my computer and can see the exhaustion written all over his face. I was surprised he didn't head out to party with the others. Instead, he came back to the bus with me and changed into a pair of sweats before making us something quick to eat.

He climbs onto the foot of the bed and lies across it. I don't have the heart to ask him to move. He's not bothering me. If I chose to lie down, my feet wouldn't even reach that far.

Besides, the adrenaline from the night is still coursing through me. I don't think I could pass out if I tried. I'm still in awe of everything I've seen and learned about setting up and then performing a live concert.

"You look so tired," I say.

"I'll be fine by morning," he says and turns on his side to face me and reach for my foot.

He pulls my leg from beneath me and palms my foot to begin to massage it. I lean back against the headboard and groan. He hits the ticklish part of my foot and I jump, pulling from his hold.

"Sorry," he chuckles tiredly.

He then reaches for my other foot and repeats the massage on it. I close my eyes and relax. My feet are tired and sore from the day.

"Are you going to answer me?"

"You asked something?" I open my eyes and lift a brow.

I don't believe I dozed off. When I look into his tired eyes he gives me a sly smile. Now I'm really curious.

"The song. Will you answer the questions from the song?"

I bite my lip and blink a few times. My cheeks heat as I think of the lyrics to the song. I've watched the video enough to know them by heart.

"You want to know what I want in a man, right?"

He gives a sleepy nod. At first, I think about not answering. It's not like he needs to know this information. We're not going there.

"For your music, right?"

He snorts and shrugs, a sexy smile on his lips. I know I should go to sleep and avoid answering, but I start to spill the answer as if he's pulling it from my lips.

"What do I want in a man? I could probably tell you more of what I don't want."

"I'm okay with knowing that," he says in a deep husky voice.

I look down at him. Although he's still rubbing my foot, his eyes are closed. I figure he's not going to remember any of this as he's already half-asleep.

I look up at the ceiling and allow the question to truly sink in. What do I want in a man? It's a darn good question.

One I'm not sure I know the answer to. I haven't really taken the time to think about it. I frown, it's something I should be able to answer more readily.

"I want someone who's going to put me first. I don't mean all the time. Like I get that work is important to most. I wouldn't stop him from pursuing his dreams and goals.

"I'm talking about having someone willing to fight for me. When it counts. I shouldn't have to question if I'm important to him.

"Love doesn't equate to sex, but lovemaking is important. I don't want to feel used. I want to be touched and made to feel like I'm there. I matter."

I pause as his hands still. I look back down at him and his eyes are blazing as he looks back at me. I sit up and begin to put my things away so I can take my butt to bed.

That look in his eyes isn't going to do anything for anyone but get us both in trouble. He needs a muse and I need this job. Nope, no more talking. It's time for bed.

Bishop

"Good night, Bishop."

"Good night."

She turns out the light, officially ending our conversation. I climb from the bed and move down to my blankets and pillow on the floor. We need to hit the road, so there's no hotel tonight.

Once the guys get in from partying, we'll be on our way. I'm grateful she turned the light out before she could see how much her words truly affected me. I'm hard as a rock.

Who wouldn't make a woman like her feel like she matters? I would make her feel like the goddess she is. She wouldn't feel used or like she didn't matter. I'd make her see stars and would be sure she felt me.

There would be no question as to how she makes me feel and my need to return the favor. Damn, who the fuck has she been with? If I had a chance to erase her past from her mind…

Let it go, Bishop.

I growl the thought in my head as I reach down to squeeze my hard as fuck cock. If I weren't so tired, I'd go shower and rub one out.

Instead, I lie there, thinking of my face between those thick thighs. Images of her screaming and writhing beneath me dance in my head. Her head thrown back as I kiss her neck and thrust into her.

I groan and roll onto my side. I might need to force my ass up for that shower. Damn, this is going to be a long-ass four weeks.

When thoughts of her sexy body won't allow me to sleep, I do get up for that shower. I stand and look toward the bed where she's curled on her side. She's so fucking adorable.

I force myself to look away and head for that shower, but the music starts and I head for Lucie and the front of the bus instead, murmuring lyrics the whole way.

CHAPTER EIGHT

Content

Bishop

Saga said she wants to make us real and relatable. Which is why she's been hanging around the guys to get footage of them in their most raw moments.

I'd be lying if I said it doesn't make me jealous to see her bonding with them. I know it's irrational. She's doing the job I pay her for. To do that, she needs to interact with the entire band.

Although I have no shame in what I've done to help her get her job done while keeping the guys from getting too close. It's not like this doesn't come from the heart. These kids are important.

"The fans are going to love this," Saga says as she takes pictures of the guys teaching the kids to play their new instruments.

"Hopefully, this will bring more attention to the need for creative arts in the community. The more funding we can get them, the better."

Saga turns to me with a sparkle in her eyes. "Fendi said you guys purchased all the instruments and donated to keep the arts programs open in the schools surrounding this neighborhood."

I shrug, not wanting to brag. I may have set today up to facilitate my needs, but these kids mean a lot to all of us. Not all the band members grew up with deep pockets and stable home lives. We try to give back as much as we can.

"We do what we can. Jag usually finds inner-city programs we can support. We do what's needed from there."

"All while on tour. That's impressive. I mean, with all I've seen you guys put into shows and the travel, this is very commendable," she says.

Turning back toward the kids and the guys, she moves closer to where Bop is teaching a little boy to play a guitar. The smile on the kid's face is infectious. I find myself smiling as well.

"Excuse me, Mr. Bishop," my name is called timidly.

I look down to find another small boy looking up at me. He has messy brown hair and piercing gray eyes. There's a small, nervous smile on his face.

I squat to get eye level with him as his eyes grow wide. I give him a smile and whistle when I see the sweet, brand-new guitar in his hands. I point to the instrument.

"You know how to play that thing?"

He bobs his head eagerly. "Yeah, a little, but I want to learn to get better so I can play like you and sing lead one day," he says shyly.

"Is that right? Well, come on. Show me what you've got," I say and stand to lead him over to some chairs.

I help him up into one of the chairs and sit in the one next to him. Quietly, I watch with a smile as he settles his instrument in his lap. The thing is almost as big as he is.

I'm taken by surprise when he begins to sing one of my earlier ballads. The kid has a sweet voice. His playing isn't half-bad either.

"Hey, buddy, that's not bad at all. You mind if I show you something?"

His eyes light up. "No. I mean, yes. Sure, Mr. Bishop," he says excitedly.

I pluck him up from his chair and set him on my lap to better help him with the guitar. I show him a few chords and then we play them and sing my song again.

The kid is a fast learner. I don't miss that we're drawing a crowd. Kids and staff members alike surround us. However, we keep playing and I keep showing him the right progressions for the song.

My heart swells and I have to admit to myself I may have done this to put distance between Saga and the guys, but these events have become highlights of these tours for me. Then I look up and lock eyes with Saga.

The way her head is tilted as she studies me with her lip trapped between her teeth reminds me how much I want to sing my way into her heart. When she first joined us, I considered this could be a one-sided attraction. Now, as I look into her eyes and see the lust there, I know it's not.

I shoot her a wink and smile. The way she shakes her head makes me wonder what she's trying to clear away. Thoughts of how she wants me or thoughts of why she shouldn't.

"Evan, your mom is here. Why don't you thank Mr. Bishop and go pack up your things," one of the staff members says.

Evan's shoulders sag before he slides from my lap. He turns to look up at me. That's when I notice his lazy left eyelid.

He gives me a big smile and rushes forward to hug my neck. I'm taken a bit by surprise. I didn't think the little guy was strong enough for such a tight grip.

"Thank you, Mr. Bishop. I'll never forget this. You made my day," he whispers in my ear.

"You're welcome, kid. You keep practicing. One of these days, I'll see you on the big stage."

"I sure do hope so."

He pulls away and waves goodbye before running off toward his mom. I wrinkle my brows as I take in the mousy-looking woman. I narrow my eyes as I take the two in.

My gut tells me not to let them leave without doing one more thing for Evan. I wave Dwayne over and stand to whisper in his ear. He nods and takes off without questioning my words.

"You were so great with him," Saga says as she makes her way to my side.

"He seems like a good kid and has a ton of talent already," I reply.

Saga

"Get the fuck outa here," one of the guys calls out and they all begin to laugh.

I look up and smile at their antics. Shaking my head, I focus back on my laptop in front of me. I'm sitting outside the bus as the guys have started a bonfire.

Ed is manning the grill and there are coolers of drinks for everyone. They deserve this time, just kicking back. That was good work today. The looks on those kids' faces were priceless.

I got some great pictures and videos. I've uploaded some to each of the guys' accounts, as well as the band's main account. The fans love the realness of seeing the guys give back and engage with the community.

"Brace yourselves, ladies," I murmur as I hit publish on a video of Bishop singing and teaching that little boy to play the guitar.

My heart has swelled from seeing it firsthand and through the footage I've been going through. The moment was so sweet and made Bishop seem larger than life and so down to earth at the same time. I had to clench my thighs as Bishop looked up at me and we locked gazes.

I've been trying to forget that look since it happened. I shake my head before I get carried away and drown in my lust-filled thoughts again.

"Want a beer?" Fendi asks as he comes over and holds one out to me.

If this were Thrush, I'd be wary. He still hasn't gotten his revenge for that prank. If I didn't know better, I'd think Bishop did call him off.

"Sure," I say and close my laptop.

I can't help smiling as I think of the little girl who clung to Fendi's leg after he taught her to play her first guitar today. She was one of many he taught but by far the most smitten and grateful. Now, in this parking lot, these guys look nothing like the gentle giants I watched with those kids. They had genuine patience and kindness.

Fendi hands the beer over and nods his head before taking a seat at the table the guys pulled from the bus and set up with chairs. I take a sip of the beer as I narrow my eyes and watch Bishop.

He's throwing a frisbee around with Thrush and Dwayne. Their deep chuckles and cheers fill the night air. They're all so relaxed. None of the high energy from performing and none of the persona they show when fans are around.

This is just them. Ordinary guys. Bishop Love is just a kind man. A rock star but so much more.

I've learned so much about this man since we've met. He's not at all what I expected. None of the guys are, but Bishop stands out in his own right.

"This is great. You were right. The fans are going crazy over this stuff," Fendi says.

"You guys did a really good thing and all of you looked as if you wanted to be there. That will go a long way. Fans can see through the bull if looking close enough."

"Yeah, I guess you're right. Although we love events like this one. The kids are cute and it's fun giving them a skill that could change their lives."

"Do you know what the deal was with the crying mom and the little boy? I didn't record any of that, but I saw it."

Fendi looks at me. A sad look comes over his face and his eyes go distant for a beat. He clears his throat then takes a sip of his beer and clears his throat again.

"He did for that kid something I wish someone would have done for me," he finally replies.

"What was that?" I ask cautiously.

"You should ask Bishop."

Just then, Bishop saunters over and places a plate in front of me and one in front of himself. I dig into the burger because it's been a long day and I'm actually starving. I hadn't planned to pry, but as we eat Fendi throws me under the bus.

"She wants to know what was going on with the kid and the mom," he says, causing me to snap my head up, wide-eyed.

"Oh, um, yeah. I was just curious. You don't have to tell me anything," I rush to say.

Bishop gives me a smile and wipes his mouth with his napkin. I drop my gaze to my plate as my cheeks heat. I don't want to come off as nosy. It was clear that was a private moment.

"Evan and his mom needed some help. They were abused by Evan's dad. I'd say it's lucky for them the bastard dropped dead, but now cash is tight. They were on their way to losing their home.

"I helped out to make sure they have food and a roof over their heads. His mom will have employment before the end of the week." He shrugs like it's no big deal.

"You did that for them?"

"Yeah, the kid doesn't deserve that. He's had enough shit in his life, and he still managed to smile. Something felt off and I asked Dwayne to see what he could find out. Then I did what I could to help."

"And you didn't bother to tell me so I could get it on film?"

"Not everything needs to be shared. Everyone wants to make everything content. We need to remember when to close doors. That family needed help, not a front-page story about their heartbreak and struggles."

"Wow," I breathe.

This man just keeps blowing me away. Just when I think I have him figured out, I learn something new.

"Bishop, bro. We were in the middle of a game. Get your ass back out here," Thrush groans.

Bishop scoffs down the rest of his burger and hot dogs, then shoots me a wink. I'm left speechless, watching after him. He just became sexy on an all-new level.

I clench my thighs and chant to myself how nothing can happen. He is my boss. A very nice guy, but my boss.

"He likes you."

I turn to Fendi and stare at him for a moment. What did he just see? I hope I'm keeping my thoughts and feelings hidden.

"I think he's cool too," I say and look down at the table.

"But he *likes you*, likes you. You should know that's not—"

"Yo, Fendi, come on. We need another. You're up," Bishop calls, waving him over.

"You're good for him. That's all I'm saying," Fendi says as he stands and raps his knuckles on the table.

I sit bewildered. Does everyone think Bishop and I have something going on between us? I frown to myself, wondering what Fendi was going to say before he was interrupted.

Do your job and make it home, Saga. That's all you have to do. Do your job, make it home, and stay away from Bishop Love.

CHAPTER NINE

Perfection

Bishop

"Good times ahead," I say the lyrics and frown.

I hate it. This song isn't saying what I need it to. I feel like I'm forcing it.

Sucking my lip into my mouth, I try to think of something else. The scent of Saga's perfume floats to me on the wind. I close my eyes and inhale.

"You're doing an amazing job, by the way," I say as I look up from my guitar. "That video you posted of me playing the new song went viral and got the label's attention. They're losing their shit over the response. They want me to keep playing new stuff on the tour."

Saga looks up from her laptop and gives me that gorgeous smile. Her hair is blowing in the wind. We've been sitting out by the water while I attempt to write a new song.

This little stop has benches and restrooms with a beautiful waterfront view. The sun is out and the air is crisp. However, nothing compares to her beauty and the bright smile she gives me.

"That's good to hear," she says.

"Why don't you just start your own thing? You know, get a few more contracts. You're smart," I say as I think about her situation.

"Still need clients and clients come with connections. Blackballed, remember?" she says and frowns.

"Piece of shit," I mutter to myself.

"You can say that again," she says, turning back to her laptop.

I go back to musing and strumming my guitar. Saga stands and stretches, drawing my attention. She lifts her arms above her head, causing her shirt to rise and reveal a patch of brown skin and her cute belly button. The leggings she has on are hugging her thick thighs.

The music is forgotten as I lick my lips and start to think about the sexy body beneath her clothes. Damn, I still want her. I know what we agreed to, but I'm growing more attracted to her by the day.

"Do you work out?"

"Not as much as I used to. Had to give up my gym membership," she replies and shrugs. "Why? Are you calling me fat?"

Her eyes are narrowed, but her lips are twitching up in the corners. I want to reach out and tug her into my lap. There's nothing fat about her.

"I love a woman with curves. You have the perfect amount of everything," I say.

As soon as the words are out of my mouth, inspiration hits. I scrap the song I'd been trying to force out and start a new one. The melody comes right to me.

Saga

There's that look again. His muse is back. I smile as I watch him with his head bent over his guitar. A piece of hair has fallen from his bun and rests on his face.

He looks gorgeous. The way he wraps his arms around his guitar so lovingly makes me remember what those strong arms feel like. They were comforting and warm, like his presence. A girl could get lost resting in arms like those.

My phone rings, breaking my musing. Not wanting to disturb Bishop, I grab it and start to walk off a bit. I twist my lips in indecision when I see it's my dad.

I sigh. I'm not ready to tell him what's been going on. He'll lose his shit. First, he'll chide me for not telling him. Then he'll storm in to fix it.

I'm grown, but my father has this tendency to want to run my life when he thinks something can be done better his way. I respect my dad and value his opinion, but he can't fight my battles for me all my life.

He's going to be so disappointed.

I blow out a breath and take the call. If I don't, he'll get suspicious. The last thing I need is for him to start prying into my life.

"Hey, Daddy," I sing into the phone.

"Sweet pea, how's that big city treating my baby?" he says.

My stomach twists. I hate lying to him. I had planned to tell him to his face. I figured he'd be so happy to see me, it would soften the blow of my failure.

"You act as if I don't come from a big city," I chuckle, dodging his question.

"Speaking of which, we'd love to see you. I'm hoping we get a visit this year," he replies.

"I think I can make that happen."

I know I can make that happen. It will be a longer visit than he might be anticipating. Mom, on the other hand, will be happy to have someone to fuss over.

"It looks like your brother will be getting engaged. We'll be expecting you at the engagement party."

"That's amazing," I say excitedly.

"Yes, it is. I'm still waiting on you and your sister to settle down with nice young men. I'm not getting any younger. I'd like to walk you down the aisle while my knees are still good," he says pointedly.

"Not everyone can be as lucky as you and Mom," I say.

"Your mother and I may have fallen in love at first sight, but it took work to stay together. I have so many fine young doctors and other great candidates for you to meet. Take some time off and come home. I'll introduce you to a few," he says.

I roll my eyes. *Candidates.* Like this is some kind of campaign and not my love life.

"I'm taking a break from dating for now," I reply, turning to look at Bishop.

Just as I look at him, he reaches up to comb the wayward piece of hair out of his face. He sucks his lip into his mouth as he jots something down. Absentmindedly, he reaches for the chain around his neck and pulls it between his lips.

He does that often. Not for the first time, I wonder about the guitar pick he wears around his neck like a charm. Bishop seems to be so deep and intentional about everything he does. I can't help but feel like there's a story there.

Dating isn't on my radar, but I'm looking at the one man who has made me question that decision. As if sensing my eyes on him, he lifts his head. Those sharp eyes lock on me and the chain falls from his plump lips. I suck in a breath.

Daddy sighs on the other end of the phone. "I want someone to love you as much as I do. Someone who will give you the world as you deserve," he takes a pause.

After a beat, he continues. "Ah, but you're my strong one. You always do things your way. I just don't want to see life pass you by. I want to see you with a family of your own."

I know my father means well. My heart aches, knowing I'm hiding something from him. I almost blurt out the truth, but I hold my tongue.

Instead, I say, "I'll be just fine, Daddy."

"Call your mother. She's been worrying about you for some reason. Put her mind at ease. You know how she gets."

My heart starts to pound. My mother has an uncanny sixth sense. I've been avoiding her as much as I can.

"I will. Listen, I have some work I need to finish up. I'll talk to you soon," I say.

"I love you, sweet pea. Don't work too hard," he replies.

"Love you too, Daddy."

I hang up and look out over the water. My brother is a surgeon and my sister has started her own law firm. They fit the Walden family picture perfectly.

Hearing that Legend plans to propose to his high school sweetheart only causes me to seriously look at how my life has derailed from where I thought it was headed.

"What are you doing with your life, Saga?" I blow out.

Lost in thought, I stare into space. A year ago, my life was perfect. I had my condo. A new car. My accounts were more than healthy. I had even looked at a few houses in the suburbs.

I wrap my arms around my middle as I try to figure out where I went wrong. I'm so lost in my thoughts I don't hear Bishop as he walks over to me. He startles me as he places a hand on the small of my back and leans to speak in my ear.

"You okay?"

I jump and turn to look up at him. I cover my chest with my hand, trying to calm my racing heart. Mirth dances in his eyes as he watches me.

I glare at him but lose the scowl as he allows his laugh to escape and reaches to brush my bangs from my face. He's too handsome and alluring to get angry with. That smile and laugh are infectious.

"Asshole," I laugh as my racing heart begins to calm. "Yeah, I'm okay. Just talked to my dad."

He nods in understanding. I don't know how, but something in his gaze tells me he totally understands how I feel. Which is crazy because I haven't said a word about the conversation or my feelings about it.

"Want to talk about it?" he offers.

I think about that. Do I want to talk to this man, practically a stranger, about my life and my fears? I haven't even told Isha how I really feel.

"You don't need to finish your song?"

He waves me off. "I can get back to that. You look like you could use a listening ear. You never know; you might spark something."

"Oh, in that case. Never mind, I don't want my personal thoughts and feelings becoming a song."

He reaches for my hand and pulls me to him. He searches my face with his mesmerizing eyes. Slowly, he pulls my arms around his waist, then wraps his arms around mine. He begins to hum and sway us.

"I would never put your personal feelings in a song. Now, mine, those are fair game, but you… you are free to share anything with me.

"Let me be your vault. Throw me your secrets and your thoughts. I'll lock them away and hold them for you.

"If you have any that I can help you sort through, I'm at your service there too. Talk to me, Saga. Let me in. You know you want to." He gives a teasing wink with his last words.

I smile because he's right. I do. However, this feels way too intimate and borderline inappropriate for employer and employee, but I want the friendship he's dangling before me.

"I have an idea."

"Do you? What's that?"

"Did you see there's a TV hidden in our room?"

"On the bus?" I ask in surprise.

"Yeah, how about we go back inside? I'll make some popcorn and we can pick something to binge-watch. If you decide you want to talk, I'll be all ears. If not, at least you can get your mind off your thoughts."

I search his face as I think his words over. I still don't know why this guy has decided to be so nice to me. I mean, all the guys in the band and on the crew have shown me nothing but kindness, but Bishop has gone that extra mile to be the friend I didn't know I needed.

"I like the way that sounds. I'm game."

"Cool, let's make this happen, gorgeous. Are you an extra butter girl?"

"I love extra butter in my popcorn," I say with a smile.

"I knew you were after my heart," he says with a sexy grin.

CHAPTER TEN

Chicago

Saga

I'm breathless as I stand off stage. Once again, he's sharing a new song, and it's… perfection. That's what he named it, and rightly so.

> *Heaven must be missing an angel*
> *Everything from your button nose to your cute little toes*
> *It's perfection—*

The crowd goes insane as he sings the last note. I'm rooted to the spot. I can't believe he wrote an entire song describing me.

"Thank you, Chicago, you've been good to me," he croons to the crowd.

"You know there's a reason he hasn't written in four years."

I startle as the voice breaks me from my trance. I look at Jag standing beside me. I get the feeling he doesn't like me very much. He's the one crew member who's always cold to me.

"I'm sure it's not so easy to pour your feelings out to others. That has to take time," I reply.

"It's more complicated than that. Bishop is more complicated than that. Whatever you do, don't get involved with him. Let him write the songs, but don't fuck with his head," he says, narrowing his eyes at me.

"Excuse me?" I say, turning fully toward him with my hands on my hips.

"Last thing he needs is to fall for another muse. I need him to finish this album. Don't fuck with his focus," he snaps.

"First, you better watch who you're talking to. You don't know me. I've never been rude to you or made it seem like I'm here for anything other than to do my damn job and get back home. I don't care who you are; show me some fucking respect," I growl back at him.

He snorts. "They all fall into his bed. You're no different."

"What the fu—," I start, but the word never gets to leave my mouth.

Heat seeps into my back as a hard body presses to it. I fight with everything I am not to sink into the feeling. I know it's Bishop. I can smell his cologne and sweat.

"We have a problem here?" he says smoothly.

"Nope, Saga and I were just having a little conversation, is all," Jag says with a sly smile. "Isn't that right?"

I don't say a word. I just signed my contract. I'm not going to let this asshole ruin a good thing for me. Same asshole, different face. I'm used to guys like him.

"Here, make yourself useful," Bishop says, handing Jag his guitar.

He then places an arm around my shoulders and tugs me into his side. He's hot and sweaty, but I don't pull away. Without another word, he turns and leads us to his dressing room.

We step inside and he closes the door behind us, firmly shutting everyone else out. A clear sign that he's not interested in guests tonight. Well, with the exception of me.

"Make yourself comfortable. I'm going to take a shower," he says, moving toward the bathroom while pulling his shirt off.

His back is droolworthy. The way his muscles play beneath his tanned skin has my mouth watering. He has a tattoo on his back.

It's of music notes rising out of the flames like a ribbon reaching for his left shoulder. It looks 3D and so realistic. I bite my lip and turn away to take a seat on the couch.

I get lost in looking through the footage I have on my phone. I find myself replaying the "Perfection" song again. It's the little details about me that take the song to the next level.

The beauty mark under my left ear, the fact that I have a dimple on the right but not the left side of my face. His description of my eye color and the little mark on my right sclera—again, his attention to detail shows through. Yet, it's not just the details.

It's the fact that he's calling it all perfection. Something he wants to cherish as his own. I can't get the feeling in the lyrics out of my head.

"Did you like it?"

I look up from my phone to find Bishop with a towel wrapped around his waist. His hair is damp, hanging down his back. I nearly swallow my tongue.

His torso is chiseled more than I ever would have thought. The *V* reaching out of the towel is deliciously sexy. So is the little trail of hair that disappears into the towel.

"Um… yes," I say huskily. I swallow and clear my throat. "It was beautiful."

His lips turn up in the corners, his eyes sparkling. "Like what you see, Saga?" he says in a dangerously sexy voice.

"I… you. You're in great shape. I think your fans would love to see you like this," I stammer out.

If possible, his smile turns even more wicked. Pushing a hand into his damp hair, he gives me a sin-filled, sensual look and strikes a pose.

"Go ahead. Let's give them something to talk about," he says, his voice dropping low.

"Seriously?"

"Why not?" he says and licks his lips.

I'm only stunned for a moment before I lift my phone and start to snap pictures. The mirror at his back provides the perfect backdrop, allowing me to get his back and front. In one swift move, he releases the towel, clutching it tightly in front of his most intimate place.

My lips part and I draw in a deep breath. My finger shakes as I go to click a few more shots. I lower the phone and stare into those blue eyes.

"Those last ones are only for you," he says with a wink, pulling his towel back around his waist.

I look away without responding. I keep myself busy loading the pics and videos to his page. His Instagram account goes nuts as soon as I load the pics of him in his towel.

His laugh rings out, causing me to look up at him sitting in the chair before the vanity. He's spinning back and forth, carefree, with his phone in his hands. I force myself not to look up his towel, but damn, I want to.

"I guess sex does sell. Look at this. My phone is going crazy," he chuckles.

"You have to be used to this by now," I say.

"Not the way you would think," he replies and shrugs. "It's been a long time since I've been… normal. I think that's why I like having you around. You still don't fall all over me. I'm just Bishop to you. Not Bishop Love."

I think on his words for a bit. That must be hard. Not having people take you for more than an onstage persona. I've seen the way people become awestruck when he's around.

"I think I'm enjoying getting to know the man behind it all. You seem like a pretty decent guy to me," I say.

"Saga, the things I haven't shown you yet," he says with a sexy grin.

"Unfortunately, since the tour and my contract are up in three weeks, there's a lot I won't be seeing," I toss back.

He gives me a curious look but doesn't say anything. A knock sounds on the door before I can ask about it. He stands, grabs a pair of jeans and tugs them on under his towel. The knock sounds again as he tosses the towel around his neck and moves to the door.

"We're headed out to the hotel. Are you ready?" Jag's voice carries into the room.

"Yeah, I'm on my way. Don't worry about me. Saga and I are going to grab something to eat first," Bishop replies.

"You don't want to grab something with the guys?"

"No, I feel the next song coming. I think we should hang alone for a bit," Bishop says, not hiding the irritation in his voice.

"Yeah, all right. The label called, by the way. They're loving the new stuff. You're booked to lay it all down when we reach home," Jag says.

"I figured. See you later, man," Bishop says and closes the door.

I snort to myself. Jag's an asshole. I make a note to steer clear of him for the rest of the tour.

"Babe, you ready? I want to get something to eat and hit the sack," Bishop says as he pulls on a shirt.

I stand and nod my head. He holds out his hand for mine. I should ignore it and just walk out the door, but against my better judgment, I take it.

The moment I do, my belly drops and warmth races up my arm. His eyes search mine before he gives me a cute smile. It's not one of his cocky smiles. It's entirely different.

"What?" I ask.

"Nothing, gorgeous. Just thinking," he says, squeezing my hand in his.

Bishop

"I'm so fucking full," I say, pulling Saga into my arms as we stand in the elevator.

I bury my face in her neck and groan. I'm a big guy. I usually eat a lot. I was starving after the concert, but I may have overdone it on the surf and turf.

If I'm honest, it was all of the water I drank. Every time I looked across the table with something to say, my mouth would go dry, and then I'd gulp some water down. This is what this woman has reduced me to.

"I've seen you eat way more," she giggles. "You're like a bottomless pit."

"You're really going to talk about me like that?" I breathe and tickle her side.

"Bishop, no," she gasps and tries to wiggle out of my hold.

"I love your laugh," I say as she turns to face me and tips her head back to look up at me.

Being with Saga is so fucking easy. I crave her presence even when she's near. Holding her, even if only for a moment is like a soothing balm to my soul. Something I've been telling myself for the last four years I don't need.

Two years of fucking to numb the pain, two years of celibacy. None of it has worked the way having Saga with me has. I want to hold on to this feeling for as long as I can.

"So, my room is next door to yours?" she asks, ignoring my compliment.

"Technically, yes," I say and wince.

She narrows her eyes. "What does that mean?"

"We're in a suite together," I say and hold up my hands. "It's a two-bedroom suite. You have your bed; I have mine."

"And we're here for two more nights?" she says cautiously.

"Yeah, two more concerts. Babe, I just want you close. Your vibe drives me," I say.

The elevator dings on our floor. Instead of saying anything else, she turns and steps off. I watch her hips sway as she moves forward. She pauses and looks back over her shoulder.

I give her a wolfish grin before following after her. She shakes her head and turns back to head to our room. What I would give to spend the night making her my dessert.

I frown when I think of her body language earlier while Jag talked to her backstage. I'll be having a talk with him. I don't need him prying into my life.

"Have a good night," she calls over her shoulder as she heads to the bedroom with her bag sitting outside of it.

"Good night, gorgeous. Dream of me," I call after her.

"In your dreams," she scoffs.

And just like that, I have my next song. My full stomach is forgotten. I rush to grab Lucie and close my bedroom door. For the rest of the night, I get lost in a new tune to send to the boys by morning.

CHAPTER ELEVEN

Sweet Dreams

Bishop

My eyes are closed as I croon this one out. It's personal. I'm letting go of my past.

> *In my dreams—you and I are just right for each other*
> *You were made for me and I was made for you*
> *In my dreams—you lie on my pillow and whisper that you love me*
> *I used to think the world was over and I was lost in it*
> *I'd been broken and tossed away before you*
> *Now I'm open… open to love, open to find my way home*
> *Tell me I'm not alone. Tell me you're feeling this too*
> *I can't bear to be hurt again*
> *Not like back then*
> *I'm trusting you with all that I am*

In this dream, it feels right, even if it's one night
I'm so happy I found you
In my dreams—you and I are just right for each other.
You were made for me and I was made for you.
In my dreams—you lie on my pillow and whisper that you
love me

When I open my eyes, I don't look at the crowd. I look over to the wing of the stage, where I know pretty brown eyes are waiting. Our eyes lock and I say so much as I stare back at her. She lowers her lashes, breaking the connection.

"All right, Chicago," I say into the mic as I turn back to the crowd. "How was that one?"

The crowd goes insane and starts to repeat the chorus of the song. That old love that I used to have for this shit bubbles up in my chest. It feels good.

"Love you guys," I call and get up to leave the stage.

I'm headed straight for Saga. I want to have dinner with her again tonight. There's still so much I want to learn about her.

"Bishop," Jag says as he steps into my path. "I have some people here you need to meet with."

"Later," I say, moving around him.

"It can't wait for later. The label wants you to sit down with them tonight. We already have reservations," he says to my back.

"Fuck," I murmur. "Give me twenty."

"Yeah, all right. Oh, it's only dinner for five," he says. "We don't need this going to social media."

I look over my shoulder and glare at Jag. "You all right?"

"Yeah, I'm fine. I'm keeping my eyes on the goal here," he says.

"Careful, shit can change fast around here," I warn and turn without waiting for a response.

We'll be having that talk tonight. I don't know what the fuck his problem is. We've known each other for a long time. Jag, of all people, knows it takes nothing for me to cut someone off if I don't feel they're in my corner.

"Hey," I say to Saga, reaching to brush her hair out of her face.

"Hey," she whispers.

I wave Dwayne, who's the head of my security, and my cousin over. I'm not happy about this, but the label has been in talks with new sponsors for the next tour. It's my job to charm the big pockets.

"What's up, Bishop?" Dwayne says as he approaches.

"Take Saga back to the hotel. Make sure she gets into the suite safely," I say.

"I can get back on my own. Shouldn't he be with you?"

"I'll be fine," I say. "Order room service. Kick back and relax. I'll see you when I get in."

I can see the questions she won't ask in her eyes. I move closer, placing a hand on her hip. I love that she comes to me willingly.

"I have to meet up with some people the label sent out. As soon as dinner is over, I'll be on my way to you," I lean into her ear to say.

"You don't owe m—"

"Didn't say I do. I just want you to know where I'll be. I'll see you in a bit, beautiful," I say, cutting her off.

Reluctantly, I release her and turn for my dressing room. With each step I take away from her, I start to feel like I can't breathe and agitation starts to rise. This better not take all night.

Saga

I have no right to be jealous. I have no claim on Bishop whatsoever. Yet, when he asked Dwayne to get me back to the room, the first thing I thought was that he was ditching me to hook up with one of the many groupies who were always around.

It's foolish how I've allowed myself to get sucked into his lyrics. They're songs, entertainment. It's what he does. I keep telling myself not to fall for him.

Don't be stupid, Saga.

That's the millionth time I've told myself that. It would be a colossal mistake to fall for Bishop. I know nothing about him and he's… he's a rock star.

That alone should make him off-limits. Still, I've never seen him behave the way I thought a rock star would. He ignores the women, I've never seen him drunk or high. He's just a really down-to-earth guy.

"Babe," he calls through the suite.

I bite my lip and think about pretending to be sleeping. The more time I spend around him, the more I think about making stupid decisions concerning him, like falling for him.

I look at the clock. He's back early. If he did lie about the meeting, that wasn't much of a hookup. I chide myself for my thoughts.

"Coming," I call back.

I stand and look down at the shorts and tank top I have on. I reach up and touch the scarf on my head. I start to take it off and change my clothes, but I stop in my tracks. The last thing I need to do is impress him.

He's my boss. That's it. Make your money and get home.

"Hey," I say when I walk into the common area and find him slumped on the couch with his head back.

"Come here," he says when I go to sit in one of the accent chairs. He pats the seat beside him. "I won't bite. Come here."

Hesitantly, I move to sit down next to him. He reaches for my legs and pulls them into his lap. I should pull away, but the tired look on his face and the warmth of his hands on my thighs stop me.

Looking at me through tired eyes, he says. "Talk to me, gorgeous."

"About?"

"Whatever you want, as long as I get to hear your voice."

I think, not knowing what to say. I've had a ton of questions for him. That song tonight said so much, but I'm not sure if I should pry.

He gives a chuckle. "Let me help you out. Are you an only child?"

"No, I have a sister and a brother. Both younger than me," I reply. "What about you?"

"Three brothers," he says. "Third oldest."

"How old are you?"

"Thirty-two," he says with a crooked smile.

"Oh… wait. Really?"

He doesn't look older than twenty-something. I thought I had him by a few years. The stubble that has grown on his face may place him closer to thirty tonight, but still. I'm in shock.

"I'll be thirty-three a few months after the tour. You don't look your age either," he says with a grin.

I go to ask him how he knows my age, but I think about the job and the contract. I'm sure he did a background check before hiring me. People tell me all the time that I don't look thirty-one at all.

"Where are you from?" I ask.

"My dad's Italian and Dutch. My mom is Scandinavian. They both grew up and met in Wisconsin. Dad struck it rich after his hippie days were over and they moved to LA," he replies. "You?"

"Born and raised in Cali. Calabasas was all I knew until I turned twenty and ran off to New York," I say.

He gives a low whistle. "Those are some deep pockets there."

"My father's father was wealthy. That was passed down, but Daddy worked his way through medical school, becoming a renowned surgeon." I shrug.

He reaches for my hand and starts to play with my fingers. Butterflies start to take off in my belly and I find myself holding my breath. He keeps his eyes on my long-overdue-for-a-manicure hand.

"Why New York?"

"Do you have any idea how suffocating it can be to live under parents who think you should be perfect. I needed to put distance between us. New York was the next best place in my head.

"You know what they say. If you can make it there, you can make it anywhere." I snort. "Well, I guess I failed that one."

He brings my fingers to his lips and kisses the tips. My heart flutters. Heat spreads throughout my body.

"I don't think you failed at all. Your path just changed. You don't know what life has for you now.

"I see it this way. Sometimes you have to cross to a new lane to get to the destination that was truly meant for you," he says.

"Bishop Love, the great philosopher." I chuckle.

"I've seen and done some shit. I like to think I've learned from some of it," he says.

"Including having your heart broken?"

He lifts his gaze to mine. Those blue eyes feel like they're trying to penetrate me. I dare to hold his gaze as I wait for his answer.

"You caught that?" he says softly.

"Yeah."

"I think I always knew we were wrong for each other. I love what I do. I've never been drunk off the fame. Bev… she wanted it all. The fame, the life, and everything else.

"I did everything I could to keep her happy. In the end… nothing was enough. I wasn't enough," he says as he looks down at our linked hands on my thigh.

"She's probably kicking herself now," I say.

"As much as a dead person can," he says angrily.

"Oh my God. I'm so sorry. I didn't—"

"Don't worry about it. It was a few months after I found her cheating on me. She overdosed on the guy's tour bus," he says bitterly.

The room falls silent. I don't know what to say to that. I want to pull him in my arms and comfort him. Now, a lot makes sense.

"I hope you don't blame yourself," I say softly.

"For two and a half years. I sure did. Took me a long time to see there was nothing I could do. But at first, I couldn't help wondering if things would have been different if I had been enough."

"See, that's the thing. Is it that we're not enough? I thought my boyfriend would be the one to have my back. You know, when I lost my job and my life turned upside down. Evan turned his back on me for his friend.

"We were only dating for a few months, but I thought things were heading somewhere," I scoff. "I questioned not being enough in the beginning. Then I got over it. It's his loss, just like it was hers."

"Any man who let you go is a fool. It was his job to protect you and take care of you," he says with so much passion in his words. "He fucked up. Now someone worthy can take his place."

I inhale a shuddered breath. Suddenly, the air in the room feels so thick. He holds my gaze as he reaches up and removes the chain from around his neck.

"I think it's time I let this go. It was a gift from her. A lucky charm, if you will.

"I don't think it's brought me any luck. It never did, if I'm being honest. The pick… she gave it to me for my first tour. So much went wrong, but we were able to laugh most of it off.

"I placed it on this chain as a reminder of those laughs. For so long, I've wanted to find my way back to those laughs. Now it just feels like a weight around my neck, tying me to the worst times in my life."

"Why take it off now?" I ask as he gets quiet, with a thoughtful look on his face.

"The past is the past. If you don't heal from it, you don't move forward. At least not functionally.

"Four years, I haven't written anything in four years. Not a single desire to. When I wrote that song I sang tonight, I felt the need to let go.

"Then I took a look at what was stopping me. I started to peel back the layers and I found out a few things about myself. I can't find or have what I want if I allow the past to cling to me.

"Wearing this around my neck is holding on to all that anger, pain, and confusion. I don't want that," he says, his eyes locking with mine with a pleading look.

This might be getting too heavy. I pull my legs from his lap. His eyes follow their retreat.

"It's late. I'm going to get some rest. Big day tomorrow, I'll be getting a few interviews in with the band. You guys were great tonight, by the way," I say as I stand.

"Did you like the song?"

"Yeah, it's going to be a great album," I say.

He stares at me for a moment as silence fills the room. I shift on my feet, searching for something to say. His eyes roll over me from head to toe. The heat that ignites in his gaze has warning bells going off in my head.

"Good night, babe," he says, his voice coming out in a raw rasp. "See you in the morning."

"Good night," I say and rush off to my room.

Saga

I groan at the sound of my name being called. I'm not ready to get up. What time is it?

I roll onto my back and pry one eye open. Bishop is standing over me with a smile on his lips. I look him over and groan.

How does he look so sexy this early in the morning?

"What time is it?" I cover my mouth and say.

"Eight. Come for a run with me," he replies.

Groaning again, I roll back over and snuggle into the bed. "What?" I say into the pillow.

"Come run with me," he repeats. "You said you had to give up your gym membership. We can run together."

"Get out."

"Come on, baby. I need to blow off some steam," he says.

I hear the hint of frustration in his voice, which makes me turn back over. I note the tension lines on his face. His eyes are pleading with me.

"What's wrong?"

He blows out a breath and sits on the edge of the bed, then leans back until he's lying across my legs. He turns his head to look at me.

"The label's giving me shit. They love the new songs, but they want fewer ballads and more of the raw shit I'm known for," he huffs.

"You mean more of the sexy stuff?"

"Yeah," he says.

I swallow. "So… you're not feeling the sexy stuff?"

His eyes drop to my breasts, then bounce back up to my eyes. That heat from last night returns. Damn, this man is fine as fuck. I'm wet from just a freaking look.

He licks his lips. "I'm feeling it. I just wanted to do something different this time around."

"Um… I'll be ready in twenty," I say.

"You know what? I'm sorry. Go back to sleep. I want to get some music down," he says with that look in his eyes.

I don't argue. For one, I want to go back to sleep. Secondly, I know that look. He'll be at it until he has another song complete. I can't wait to hear what he comes up with.

Bishop

She doesn't even have a clue how fucking sexy she is. First thing in the morning, no makeup, her head wrapped in that scarf, her voice heavy from sleep—she's still sexy as fuck. I wanted to peel the sheets back and crawl in bed with her.

"Every time you let me in you," I groan the lyrics out.

If the label wants raw and gritty, I'm going to give it to them. I have so many images of Saga writhing beneath me in my head. Those thick thighs wrapped around me.

I want her so bad I can taste her on my tongue. I lick my lips and jot down a few more lyrics. I smile as I think of the look on her face after I sing this one.

I'm more concerned with her reaction than what the label will think. I want to watch her breasts heave and her eyes glaze over. Maybe I'll invite her out on stage for this one.

"Fuck."

I grab my cock and shift in my seat. I'm torturing myself. Maybe I should've made sure her contract ended at the end of the tour.

I don't know how she missed that it doesn't. I should've told her when she mentioned it, but I couldn't seem to force the words out. The end of that contract means I can go after what I want.

"Knock, knock." I look up to find Jag standing in my bedroom doorway.

"Here with more bad news?" I grumble.

"Come on, man. Don't shoot the messenger."

"Whatever, do you mind? I'm working," I say.

"Sure, sure. I just wanted to make sure we're cool. I heard you last night. I don't want this chick to come between us," he says.

I stop strumming my guitar and put it down. When I stand, I'm towering over Jag. He's five-seven to my six-three. I glare down at him.

"You didn't hear me. If you did, you wouldn't be here calling her a chick and talking shit. Jag, you're skating a very thin line," I seethe.

"Why this girl? You plowed through dozens of them after Bev. I see you falling for her. What happens after she fucks with your head? Dude, the label isn't going to be forgiving again," he barks back.

"Girl? She's a grown-ass woman. We're not in high school anymore. Grow the fuck up."

"Me, grow up? You wouldn't write a fucking song for four years. I've been busting my ass, dancing through hoops for the label so they didn't cut your ass—"

"Some fucking dance, you've kept me on tour, living like a zombie. But whatever it takes to keep the money coming, right?" I snarl.

"It was what was best. You were falling apart. Acting like nothing happened. I can't see you like that again," he says.

"Then back the fuck off," I growl.

He lifts his hands and takes a step back. I rub my forehead and turn back for my guitar. I sit and ignore his presence. I'm over this conversation.

"Just be careful," he says.

"Get the fuck out," I snarl.

"Fine, I'll see you later."

CHAPTER THIRTEEN

Chicago Heat

Saga

Something has been up with Bishop. When I got out of the shower yesterday, I heard the door to the suite slam shut. I wasn't sure if Bishop was coming in or leaving.

Not too long after, angry music started to come from his room. He didn't show his face until later in the evening and his mood was off. Not the free and fun-loving guy I've been getting to know. He was more brooding and moodier.

"This is our last night in your lovely city, folks," Bishop says to the crowd.

The rest of the band plans to go celebrate at a club after the show. I was invited, but Bishop seemed pissed. I'm not sure what's going on with him, so I've been steering clear.

"I'm not going to leave you hanging though. Chicago has been eye-opening and I have a song that I want to share from the coming album before I go," he continues.

He starts to play the melody and it's hot, heavy, and a little angry, but it's sexy too. The band joins in and my heart starts to slam. It's amazing how he and the guys are in sync whenever he gives them a new song to learn. The band has great chemistry.

I'm too grown for anyone to tell me who to love
If I want to taste your honey, that's exactly what I'll do
You're the only one that can tell me I can't be inside of you
I've fucked around and brought others pleasure
But they will never be you—
The next time I set the sheets on fire, it'll be to chase your
desire
I'll teach you I was made for you
Come here, baby, let that chocolate melt in my mouth
This face was made for riding, and the only rider is you—
You feel this just like I do; we ain't got nothing to prove
Fuck the world; I want you for my girl
I'm dying to grind into you
Bend over and spread your legs
I'm not ashamed to beg
Did you hear what I said
Come here, baby. I want you in my bed

If I think I'm stunned by the sultry verse spilling from his lips, I'm reeling when he starts to groan the chorus. I'm hot and wet from his pleas for something hot and dirty. Something I shouldn't want to give him, but at this moment, I damn sure want to.

My chest heaves as I pant. I'm dripping wet as his voice fills the stadium, making promises of ecstasy. He's making it clear he's talking to me.

> *This Saga will continue*
> *Every time you let me in you*
> *Drip, drip, baby, make me soaking wet*
> *Imma eat you up until you drip down my neck*
> *Drip, drip, gorgeous, make me soaking wet*
> *You've made me your slave; now come and collect*
> *This Saga has just begun*
> *This ride is yours; come have some fun*

My name falling off his lips is like sex itself. I lean into his words, yearning to hear them closer. Like, in my ear, while he makes good on his promises of pleasure.

Those blue eyes are locked on me as his voice drips sex. I'm winded from the thought of riding him to this exact song. I can't imagine what the other women in the audience feel.

The raw rasp of his voice, as he croons, has me trembling and panting. I lick my lips and shift on my heels. Bishop's eyes drop to my hips and he smiles. Shaking his head, he turns back to the audience.

I don't even hear the rest of the song. I'm too busy, lost in thoughts of letting him make me call his name. I lift my hand to fan my face but think better of it and smooth it over the back of my hair.

I snap back to reality when I realize I'm supposed to be recording this. I stop the recording on my phone and shove it in my pocket. My gaze lifts just in time to find Bishop standing in front of me.

"Did you like it?" he asks as he stares down at me.

"It was… Yeah, I liked it," I reply.

He dips his head and kisses my cheek. I look up into his eyes when he pulls away. My cheek tingles with the sizzle he leaves behind.

"Thanks, Saga."

"For?"

"Giving me something to sing about," he replies and moves past me.

Well, damn.

I'll be needing to get a change of panties. I don't know what just happened, but I know I need to reinforce the wall between me and my boss. This has messy written all over it.

"Don't fuck up this job, Saga," I whisper to myself.

Bishop

I don't know if I'm more pissed at Jag or with myself. I let him get in my head. I've been distant with Saga because of his words. That song I played tonight came from a place of anger and desire.

"You all right, Bishop?" Dwayne asks.

"Yeah, I'm good," I say, sipping at the same beer I've been nursing since we arrived.

I had to walk away from Saga earlier. Those tight blue jeans and heels have been fucking up my head all night. I want to peel them off and bury my face in that fat pussy.

From the look in her eyes, if I pushed now, she'd let me. Yet, I'm trying not to go there. I'm going to keep my word. As long as she works for me, I'll keep reeling it in.

You idiot, why'd you make such a stupid promise?

I haven't a clue, but I'm regretting it as I watch her hips sway on the dance floor. I don't usually come out to these after-parties. The guys do, but I normally carry my tired body to the bus or hotel and pass out.

When my drummer, Thrush, asked Saga to join the rest of the band and she said yes, I knew I'd be going along. Now, I wish I'd gone to the hotel. I want this woman so bad, my bones ache.

"Fuck this," I mutter as I push from my seat and head out to the dance floor.

I give the guy dancing behind Saga a death glare. He backs away as I stop to tower over him and Saga. I give him a nod, reassuring his ass he made the right move.

I plant my hands on Saga's hips and she opens her eyes to look up at me. She parts her lips and widens her eyes, but her body comes to me without protest.

With our eyes locked on each other's, I start to sway us to the rhythm of the beat. Saga moves with me, moving her hands to my waist. I bite my lip and let my eyes fall to her full breasts. The *V* of her T-shirt gives me a view that I admire.

"Why aren't you chasing down your next conquest for the night?" she says with a saucy smile on her lips.

"When have you seen me chase down a conquest?"

"Good point," she says and nods her pretty head. "Why is that? Don't you have women falling all over you?"

"Are you jealous?" I tease.

"No. Curious."

"I've been celibate for two years. I'm not interested in conquests," I reply.

Her pretty eyes round in surprise, softening into a look of awe and intrigue. She bites her lip and looks up at me through her lashes. I can see the question in her eyes and I answer it with my own.

Oh, hell yeah, I'd break my celibacy for you.

"Interesting," she breathes, licking her lips.

"You're killing me," I lean to whisper in her ear. "If you were mine, Saga. I'd worship every inch of you. You're gorgeous."

She shivers in my hold, causing me to grin against her ear. I want to flick my tongue out to taste her, but I hold back. She has to feel this. The pull is so strong.

I feel like I'm going to be consumed by this connection from the inside out. She slips her hand into the hair at my nape. I turn my face to look into her eyes.

Her eyes are glazed over, but it's from more than the alcohol she's been drinking tonight. I see the lust. It would only take an inch. An inch is all I need to have my first taste.

"What are we doing?" she says, breaking through the battle in my head.

"Dancing," I reply, placing a little distance between our faces.

I shove a leg between her thighs, still moving to the music. She groans and places her head against my chest. I lower my hands to just above the curve of her ass.

"Bishop," she moans my name as I rock our bodies together.

Fuck, I'm so hard, I'm about to bust through my pants. As if that's not enough, she turns, placing her back to my front. I growl when she presses her ass into me.

I have a tight grip on her hips as she grinds against me. Her head falls back and her spine arches. I can't help but think about thrusting into her from behind.

I pump my hips forward and she lifts onto her toes. I love that I tower over her as she bends to my body. I have to have at least a foot on her. It's the sexiest shit to me.

I want to wrap around her and protect her. I want to pleasure her small body with mine. I want to know how we fit together when we're soaking my fucking sheets.

"Shit," I bite out. Shoving my hand in the front of her hair like I've wanted to do since first seeing her, I tug her head back. My lips go to her ear. "I want to fuck you until you can't breathe. I want to feel you come all over me."

"Bishop," she gasps.

"Fuck, baby," I groan. "Say my name again."

"Bishop."

I go to take her lips, but she startles, jumping from my hold. I frown, releasing her hair. She digs in her pocket and pulls out her phone.

Shit! Isha.

This is the first time I regret my insurance plan for Saga. Her friend couldn't have called at a worse time. Saga puts the phone to her ear and starts to stumble through the crowd. I follow, wanting to keep an eye on her.

"Hey, Isha," she slurs once we're outside the club.

I purse my lips and look around us at the people milling about. There's still a line of people trying to get into the club. We really shouldn't have come out here without my security, but I'm not taking my eyes off her.

I move closer, shielding her with my body. I turn my back to the waiting line of hopeful partygoers as I keep hidden from view as well.

"No, we're at a club," she says. "Yeah, I had a few."

I grin at the little giggles she releases. Saga looks up at me through her lashes. She bites her bottom lip.

"He's fine. He's been writing songs about me," she says.

My smile widens. I cup the side of her face and tug at the lip she has trapped between her teeth. When it pops free, I stare at the plump flesh, licking my own lips.

God, I want her.

I go to dip my head to steal a kiss, not caring that she's on the phone. Her eyes flutter closed. However, just before our lips connect, cameras flash.

"Bishop Love," someone squeals.

In an instant, everything turns to chaos. A crowd starts to rush us. I pull Saga into my chest and start for the alley nearby.

She stumbles in her heels. I lift her in my arms and coax her legs around me. I never miss a step as I carry us away from the mob running after us.

Saga buries her face into my neck as she clings to me. One of the bouncers from the club is standing by the side door smoking. He narrows his eyes as he sees us coming. Recognition colors his face and he pulls the door open wide.

"Hurry," he barks.

I push harder and dart inside. I hear more than see the door slam shut behind us. I look over my shoulder to see we're alone.

Turning, I back Saga against a wall and sag into her. Pressing my forehead to the wall beside her head, I inhale deeply. It's as I catch my breath that I start to register the heat of her pussy against my waist.

I lift my head and look into her eyes. Heat flickers back at me. My cock twitches, demanding to get at her. My eyes fall on her lips.

With her eyes on mine, she unwraps her legs and slides down my front. I don't give her much room, causing her body to press close to mine. She can't hide the lust that comes to the surface.

"Oww," she whimpers when she lands on her feet.

She tips to the right, but I grasp her in my hold. Her face contorts in pain. I look down at her ankle to see it's already swelling.

"Damn," I say in annoyance with myself and the situation. "Put your weight on me."

I press a kiss to the wrinkle on her forehead. I can see she's in pain. Pulling my phone from my pocket, I dial Dwayne. He's probably pissed as fuck that I darted off without him.

"I'm trying to get through this crowd," Dwayne snarls into the phone.

"Go back to the front of the club. I'll carry her out that way," I bite out.

"Carry her? What's going on?"

"Saga hurt her ankle. I need to get her to a hospital."

"I don't have insurance," she whimpers.

I purse my lips at her but ignore her protest. I bark out a few more instructions before Ed and Jared arrive in the hall we're standing in.

"She all right?" Ed asks.

"She hurt her ankle. Let's get out of here. We need to go through the front," I say.

Ed, my second-in-command of my security team, nods. I lift Saga in my arms, pulling a yelp from her lips. I kiss her temple and murmur soothing words as I carry her through the parting crowd Ed and Jared lead us through.

"This is embarrassing," she huffs into my neck. "Only me."

"I'll make it up to you, promise," I reply.

"This wasn't your fault."

I tighten my lips. It was, but I don't want to argue about it. If I weren't sniffing around her like a horny teenager, this wouldn't have happened.

Pull your shit together, man.

CHAPTER FOURTEEN

I'm Here

Saga

Dwayne ushers us into the SUV and closes the door behind us before he jumps into the front passenger seat. Bishop sits with me in the back, pulling my legs into his lap, then takes my shoe from my foot. As we settle in, the adrenaline and alcohol begin to wear off.

Tears spring to my eyes and I suck my lip into my mouth, allowing a whimper to slip. My ankle is throbbing like nobody's business. I don't realize the tears start to spill over until Bishop reaches to cup my face in his hands as he swipes them away.

I release my lower lip and purse them against the pain instead. Bishop gets this look in his eyes and I feel terrible. This isn't his fault. I drop my eyes to my lap.

"Look at me," he murmurs, causing me to snap my gaze back to his. "What can I do? We'll get you to a hospital as soon as we can, but tell me how to get your mind off the pain."

"Bishop, I don't have insurance. You can take me back to the bus. I'll put some ice on it. It's not broken. I don't think."

He grunts and snorts. "You don't think. Saga, I'm taking you to the hospital and I'm taking care of the bill. We're going to make sure it's not broken."

I release a heavy sigh as my lips begin to tremble. I'm in so much pain. It's increasing by the second. Bishop's eyes drop to my lips as he looks longingly at them.

I'm almost tempted to lean in and kiss him. However, I know that's only the alcohol in my system talking. At least, that's what I tell myself.

Instead of kissing me, like his eyes say he wants to, he places his forehead to mine as if trying to give me some of his strength. I ball my fists into his shirt, taking all he's trying to give. I know I shouldn't, I should pull away and move back across the seat.

I have so many conflicting feelings going on inside me. I don't know if it's the songs, the alcohol, the dancing or a combination of it all, but I feel this intense connection to him right now.

"Bishop," I call, breaking into the moment.

Bishop

I close my eyes for a moment, knowing I'm probably crossing a line. However, I can't help but want this to be a thing for us. I want to have the freedom to comfort her at any time, any place, without thinking about it.

I want her to be mine. Before I lose myself and take her lips, I pull away and look into her tear-filled eyes. She brushes her thumb against my cheek and gives me a sweet, trembling smile.

"Yeah, baby?"

She closes her eyes and releases a long breath. When she opens her eyes again, I can see the war happening within them.

She's not immune to this. I know she has to feel this connection as much as I do. She's just fighting it a lot harder than I am.

"Thank you," she whispers.

"For what?"

"All you've done and are doing for me."

"I want to take care of you. I'm here whenever you need me."

"Will you talk to me to get my mind off the pain? Your voice always soothes me," she says softly.

I want to tell her I have other ways to get her mind off the pain. If not for my driver and security, that would be my preferred method of distraction. However, I shake those thoughts off.

"What do you want to talk about?"

"Tell me something about you."

I pause to think. At first, I have no idea what to say. As I think it over, Saga's big brown eyes search my face.

I smile as something comes to mind. This is the perfect topic. I want Saga to begin to see a future with me. I want us to be together.

"I want to be a father. I'm pretty stoked to be one, actually."

"Really?" she says with wide eyes.

"Yeah. Why do you sound so surprised?"

"I don't know. Not that I don't think you would be a good father, but what makes you want to be one?"

"My dad and my uncle. When I was younger, I noticed how much they enjoyed it. No matter what, they made time for their boys.

"I remember the smile they had for us. If I was at Dwayne's house, my uncle would come home and scoop him up with this huge smile on his face. Same with my dad when he came home.

"They were busy men, but they always gave their boys attention. Not all of my band members had supporting fathers coming into this. My father supported me every step of the way.

"Even when he looked sad about me leaving home, he supported me. My uncle was a big support too. He talked Dwayne into coming on to be my head of security," I explain.

"Wait, I can't even blame this one on the pain. Dwayne is your cousin? Why didn't I catch on to that?"

"I guess it slipped my mind to point it out. Yeah, we're first cousins. His dad and mine are brothers. Dwayne is two years older than me, but we've always been close."

"Oh my God, I can totally see it now." She lowers her gaze. "So you want little boys of your own?"

"I'd be happy either way. Boys. Girls. I want healthy children of my own to love, protect, and cherish. I remember my father being there for me during some of the toughest times in my life, and to this day, that means a hell of a lot to me.

"I want to be that for my children," I say and smile.

Saga looks at me and her eyes soften. The energy between us seems to increase. The need to kiss her is so intense.

"Your future wife and children will be lucky to have you."

"Nope, I'll be the lucky one," I say and pull her against my chest.

I tuck her head beneath my chin and hold on to her tightly. I don't want to let her go. This feels like exactly where she belongs.

"Saga?"

"Um?"

I open my mouth to tell her I want to be hers, but close my mouth again as I think better of it. She snuggles in closer to me. I can't help kissing the top of her head.

Before I know it, I hear her tiny snores as she passes out. With a smile on my face, I allow her to sleep until we get to the hospital and I carry her inside.

CHAPTER FIFTEEN

Should Be Mine

Saga

I can't believe I got drunk and twisted my ankle. It's just a sprain, but I haven't been able to put weight on it. Which is why Bishop has been waiting on me hand and foot.

He insists on carrying me around like some small doll when I'm anything but. It's been a week since that last show in Chicago and I'm still embarrassed about it.

Not to mention, I can't get his words out of my head from that night. I learned a lot about Bishop that evening. He willingly showed me he's just a man. A man with the desire to live a life with a woman he loves and a family he cherishes.

I'll be honest; the knowledge is sexy all by itself. Then there is the man himself. I don't know how, but Bishop has grown more attractive.

"Hey, gorgeous. You hungry?" Bishop asks as he stands in the doorway with his arms above his head.

For a moment, all I can do is stare. I heard him, but he looks so good I'm having a hard time thinking. His hair is up, but strands are hanging loose in his face. Those muscled arms are an attention grabber all on their own.

"I'm all grilled cheesed out," I say, patting my belly.

"We're stopping for Chinese, smart-ass," he says with that sexy grin of his.

"In that case, I want beef lo Mein. Oh, and two egg rolls," I say and lean to reach for my bag.

He moves into the room, snatching my purse out of my reach. I frown up at him. He holds the bag behind his back and glares at me.

"It's my treat, baby. I'm not going to let you insult me by offering your money," he says.

"You've been treating me since we met. I have a job now, you know," I huff.

He puts the bag down before climbing over my body to lie beside me. Turning onto his side, he props his head on his hand, looking up at me. I look away, not wanting to get lost in his gaze.

"A job that you're amazing at," he says. "Sponsorship offers have been coming in. Our social media accounts are performing three times better than they were. The label has taken notice."

"That's great. I wish I could find a way to get the focus off us and those pictures." I sigh.

Those pictures are where most of my embarrassment has come from. The look on my face as Bishop leaned in to kiss me. My goofy ass stood there all dreamy-eyed and lost. He could've been selling me paint for my soul. From the look on my face, I would've bought the whole gallon.

Let's not even talk about the ones of Bishop carrying me while running. I look like a bewildered rag doll. Isha won't shut up about any of it. I'm sorry Bishop promised her a daily call.

"You're worrying too much about those. Who cares what they think?"

"I never even thought about my reflection in the pictures of you in your towel. Like, who sat there and magnified the damn picture to point out I was the one taking it?" I say incredulously.

"You would be surprised," he chuckles.

He has taken all of this a lot better than I have. I was in shock when the pictures from his dressing room we'd posted—only cropped and emphasized to show that I was the one taking it in the background—were reposted. Rumors of Bishop having a relationship with his marketing consultant have been all over the news and entertainment rags.

Each time I try to spin it, they've been turning it right back around. It doesn't help that they now have pictures of him carrying me around in Nashville and South Carolina. We've been inadvertently fueling the flame.

"How's the ankle?" he asks, but from the look on his face, I can tell he's thinking something else.

"It's better."

"Hopefully you'll be back on your feet for Atlanta."

"I hope so. I need to find a place to clean my clothes while we're there."

"I'll send them out with my things. Joey will take care of it," he replies.

"I can wash my own clothes," I say.

"Maybe you can, but you won't," he says, tapping the tip of my nose.

He reaches for his phone, his fingers flying across the screen. I take the time to watch his profile. He's such a handsome man. With a few days stubble on his face, it only gives him more sex appeal.

"Okay, all set," he says, resting back on his side, head in his palm. "What are you up to today, gorgeous?"

"I thought I'd go for a long stroll in the park," I tease.

He groans. "I know this has to be driving you crazy. Being on this bus can be bad enough. Being here with a bum leg, that must suck," he says and gives the most adorable pout I've ever seen.

The way his eyes sparkle draws me in. I tear my gaze away and busy myself with my phone. He shifts his body until his head rests on my thighs and he's looking up at me.

"What are you doing?"

He doesn't reply right away. That look of contemplation is in his eyes again. He reaches for my phone and takes it from my hand.

"Why does it bother you so much that they think we're together?" he finally says.

"I… I didn't say it bothers me. I just… I didn't think you wanted these rumors out and I… I want to keep my professional reputation," I stammer out.

"So why not just go with it? Why fight against this? You're the inspiration behind an album that's highly anticipated. I'm making your job easy," he says.

"What?"

He sits up and cups my face. "The fans will go crazy if they know my girlfriend is on tour with me and I'm writing an album for her," he says.

"I'm not your girlfriend," I breathe.

A crease forms in the center of his forehead. His eyes search mine. I don't register that I'm holding my breath until he speaks.

"That's the other thing I'm trying to figure out. Why aren't you?"

"Why aren't I what?"

"Mine. You should be mine," he says, closer to my lips.

I don't know who leaned into who. I just know we are a hairbreadth away from each other. It would be so easy to close the tiny distance and make the connection.

"Bishop, I told you how my whole life was just ruined by men. I need—"

"You need to understand that I'm not them. As your boss, I wouldn't fuck with your lively hood just to be a dick. As your man, I'll protect you from everything and anything I can. So, I'm going to ask you again, gorgeous. Why aren't you mine?"

"We shouldn't—"

I don't get to finish my sentence. He captures my lips and fries my brain cells. Bishop doesn't just kiss me; he consumes me. The hunger in his kiss has my toes curling. I whimper and wrap my arms around his neck.

"Fuck, you taste better than I dreamed," he growls, shoving his tongue deeper into my mouth.

It's not a sloppy teen invasion. Bishop uses his tongue like a well-trained artist, skilled and precise. He plucks me up from the bed, bringing me to straddle his lap.

His hands go to the hem of my shirt to lift it, but a knock sounds at the door. It's like a bucket of ice water. I jump away, scrambling out of his lap.

"Foods here," Joey calls through the door.

"Shit," Bishop says, drawing a hand down his face. "I see that look. We're not done, babe. Not by a long shot."

"Let's go eat. It will give us time to clear our heads," I say.

"Nothing to clear over here. I know what I want," he says with heat in his eyes. "This is inescapable, Saga, but I'll give you time to think."

Before I can say a word, he leans in and plants one more kiss on my lips for good measure. I'm dazed when he pulls away. The sexy grin on his face says it all.

I'm so fucked.

Bishop

I should've known that one kiss wouldn't be enough. I wanted a taste to hold me over and I wanted to show her how good we would be together. I think we both learned a little more than I expected.

Now I stand leaning against the bus, lost in thought, wondering how one woman can turn my world upside down. I'm gone for her. Everything about her makes me want to know more. Have more.

"What's up with you and Saga?" Dwayne chuckles as he blows out smoke from his cigarette.

We've stopped to let everyone get off the bus and stretch for a bit. We're almost to Atlanta. Saga refused to let me carry her over to the bench she's now perched on. I had to bite my tongue the entire time I watched her limp over to it.

"Complicated," I grunt.

"Isn't it always?"

"I understand where she's coming from, but that doesn't change how I feel about her," I say.

"I'm glad to see you interested in someone again. I mean, I know you guys aren't together, but I can see the potential. You know?" he says.

"I didn't say we're not together. She just needs to realize we are. I'm not backing down. I'm just giving her room to process."

He chuckles and shakes his head at me. "Still the same old Bishop."

"She's different. I like the way she thinks and she… she just brings me this peace I haven't had in a long time. If ever. I need that more than I thought."

"Yeah, I know what you're talking about," he says. "I got shit to handle when I get back home."

I turn to look at my cousin. Dwayne and I grew up together. There's nothing I wouldn't do for him and it's the same with him for me.

"You can go home if you need," I say.

"Nah, I'm putting that shit off as long as I can. It's not going to be pretty," he snorts.

"You know that I'm here for whatever you need. Just let me know."

"I think you should go talk to her," he says, nodding toward Saga and ignoring my offer.

"Yeah, you're right."

I push off the bus and start for the other side of the rest stop. Saga looks up just as I get about two feet away. She looks at me warily as I take a seat beside her.

Reaching for her leg, I pull it into my lap. I start to rub her ankle as I watch her face. She gives me a small smile as she sighs.

"Thanks," she says.

"Anytime. I wish you would've let me bring you over here."

"I have to start getting around on my own sometime," she replies.

"Yeah, but you weren't doing the best job of it. Don't be stubborn."

"Ah, no one told you? That's my middle name," she teases.

"I can see that," I say and grin. "So, do you want to talk?"

"About?"

I blow out a breath. "We both know what I want to talk about."

"You know, if we're going to date, you're going to have to be a little more direct with me. I'm not a mind reader," she says.

"Saga, I want to… wait. If we're going to date?"

"I don't think I stammered, Bishop," she says with a sexy smile.

Grasping the back of her neck, I lean in and take her lips. She's only hesitant for a few seconds before she opens for me and returns the kiss. I groan when she twirls her tongue around mine.

"I'm falling hard for you," I say against her lips. "I'm honest and I'll always tell you how I feel and you need to know now that I'm falling so fucking hard for you."

"I might be in the same boat," she says breathlessly.

"Might?"

"Yeah, might. Rule number one, never show a dude all your cards. His actions have to back his words. You have to earn my feelings," she says.

"Babe, you haven't said a thing. I'll earn them all right."

"You're trouble."

"The best kind."

CHAPTER SIXTEEN

Turn Things Up

Saga

"You need help with anything?" he asks as he enters the room.

He's shirtless, with his jeans riding low on his hips. I have to keep myself from drooling. We've finally arrived in Atlanta and have settled into our suite. I can't wait to sit in the bathtub and relax.

That was my plan before Bishop walked in here, distracting me from a single clear thought. I sit on the edge of the bed, staring at him, trying to process his question. He gives me a sexy smile and leans over me to kiss me.

Absolutely not helping the situation. His lips are so soft but firm. I love the way he dominates a kiss with no apologies or questions. He kisses me as if he knows I belong to him and always will.

"What did you say?" I breathe when he breaks the kiss.

He chuckles and kisses my forehead. "Do you need anything in here? I ordered room service so you don't have to try to walk around anywhere."

"Oh, no. I was just going to take a bath," I say.

"I sent Joey for a few things. I'll run that bath for you after we eat. He should be back by then," he says.

"You have a one-track mind. I don't know how you can eat so much," I laugh.

"I'm a lot of man. I need the energy," he says and winks. He scoops me up in his arms and starts for the living room of the suite.

Sitting on the couch, he places me in his lap. He lifts a hand to brush my hair out of my face. I turn to nuzzle his palm.

He groans. "I'm trying my best to take things slow. You keep doing shit like that, slow is going to go out of the window."

"I'll keep that in mind," I say with a saucy smile.

He shakes his head. "You're something else. We get a few days off before and after the next two shows. I know you need to take a day or two for your ankle, but maybe we can go on a few dates after we wrap."

The hopeful look in his blue eyes pulls me in. I lean in and kiss his lips, not able to help myself. Reaching for the tie holding his hair up, I release it and watch his locks spill down around his shoulders.

"I'm down for whatever," I say. "I'm in good company. I'm not complaining."

"I love how easy being with you is. You're like the quiet to my storm. I feel like I need to thank you for that… lay the world at your feet and worship every moment I get to hold you in my arms," he says while staring into my eyes.

My breath whooshes from my lips. The man has a way with words. I feel my heart giving itself away without so much as a bit of my permission.

"I have nothing for that," I chuckle. I cup his handsome face. "I hope you turn out to be everything I think you are."

"I'll be anything you want me to be," he says before leaning in and capturing my lips.

He drops his hands to my waist and grasps a tight hold. I whimper into his mouth as he deepens the kiss, then run my hands down his bare chest, savoring the warmth and smoothness of his skin.

Just when he pushes up my T-shirt to touch my bare skin, there's a knock at the door. He growls in frustration before placing me gently on the couch and going to answer the door. I palm my face and exhale.

When he returns, a girl with a cart follows him in. She moves the plates to the table and places two chocolate shakes beside them. I can't help the smile that comes to my lips as I remember meeting Bishop in the diner for the first time.

I look to him and he shoots me a knowing smile. Warmth spreads through my belly. This connection between us is only growing. I feel like he can read my thoughts.

When the girl lifts the lids, the aromas that take over the room are mouthwatering. I know right away the massive burger is for him. My stomach growls when I take in the quesadilla and fries on the other plate.

"You remembered."

He taps his forehead. "I record everything you say."

With a smile, I turn my attention back to the room service girl setting the table. I see her trying not to stare at Bishop as he stands there shirtless. I cover my mouth as I laugh behind my hand.

I can't blame her. I'm almost positive she knows who he is. I half expect her to ask for an autograph or picture. Bishop pulls out a tip and hands it over. She beams and turns bright red.

"Th… thank y… you, Mr. Love," she stammers out, confirming my suspicion.

She rushes from the room, looking back over her shoulder with a goofy smile on her face. Bishop doesn't even seem to notice. He turns for me, plucking me from the couch to carry me to the table on the other side of the room.

"You know you can stop carrying me around everywhere," I say.

"Where's the fun in that?" he says, kissing my temple. He sets me down and snatches one of my fries. I pop his thigh before he can dance out of the way.

"Hey," I pout. "You have your own."

"Tastes better off your plate," he says, licking his lips. He moves to sit across from me, lifting a fry from his own plate. He places it in front of my lips. I take it into my mouth. "See how much better that tastes knowing it was mine?"

I chew on the fry and shake my head at him as I smile. I start on my own fries and realize he might just be right. His fry was much better.

We eat in silence for a little bit as he devours the burger in front of him. I love watching him eat. It makes him seem… normal. Not at all like the rock star sex god he portrays to the rest of the world.

"Do you think you'll have the album done by the time we reach LA?" I ask, trying to find something to fill the silence with.

"Yeah, I'll have it done," he says with a twinkle in his eyes. "I have a few more tunes I want to perfect and I'll be ready to record the whole thing when we get back."

"That's great, right?"

"For the label, of course. It's been bittersweet for me," he replies.

"Bittersweet?"

"This one has been personal for me. I've been sharing it with the world, but I would rather have just shared it with the person I wrote it for first," he says as his eyes lock on mine.

I feel my cheeks heat. "I've been enjoying getting to hear you play them in concert with the band. It's... the songs come to life for me. You and the guys are so amazing. I love experiencing them live."

"You do know that this will always be our lives. You've been upset about the pictures. That's going to be our life, babe. They will always be a part of us. Always peeking into our world," he says.

The worry I see in his eyes is something new. Again, making him human, real on some new level. I take a moment to think over his words.

He's bringing up a valid point. He's Bishop Love. People want to be him, they want a part of him, and they want to be with him.

"You say all that as if we're going to be together for a long time," I say and bite my lip.

He pauses with a fry halfway to his mouth. He drops the fry and places his elbows on the table, leaning in. The worry I saw just moments ago vanishes.

"I don't know what you thought being mine meant, but let me clear that up for you. You're mine until the end of time, Saga. I was yours the moment you walked into that diner.

"You've owned a piece of me since I looked into those eyes, gorgeous. When I commit, I commit. I want it all. Your good, your bad, and your ugly," he says, with that heat in his gaze.

I'm smiling so hard my cheeks hurt. I lean in and snatch one of his fries to pop into my mouth. He chuckles and winks.

"In that case, bring it on. I'm ready if you are. Let's give them something to talk about," I say, repeating words he once said to me.

"I hope you mean that, baby, 'cause they're gonna talk," he says, that worry returning.

"I don't give up easily when I want something. I think we'll be just fine."

"We have a lot in common already. I never give up on what I want," he says. His voice drops and his words come out huskily.

"We shall see."

Bishop

It took everything in me not to strip down and climb into that tub with Saga. If I'm not mistaken, I saw disappointment in her eyes when I had to take a call right after helping her into the bath.

I haven't spoken to my mother in so long I decided against ignoring her call. Now, I wish I had. Knowing that I'll be returning home soon, she wants to throw me a party, which is code for setting me up with someone.

"Mom, I'm fine with the party. I'm just warning you that I'm not interested in whoever you have lined up to throw at me," I say into the phone.

"Who says I'm going to throw someone at you?"

"Okay, you're talking to Bishop, not Knight or Prince," I scoff.

"Would it hurt for you to find a nice girl to settle down with?" she asks in irritation.

"Who says I haven't?"

"Do you mean the girl in the pictures?"

I'm not sure I like her tone. My guard goes up right away. I'm well aware that Saga's gorgeous brown skin will be an issue for some. I could give two fucks and anyone who tries to make it an issue to my face will have a problem.

"Is it a problem if I say yes?" I reply.

"What do you know about her? Do you know who she is? Do you know who her family is? Do you—"

"What does any of that matter?" I snap.

"Bishop, you watch your tone with me. I'm still your mother. I'm not asking those questions to be a bitch," she tosses back.

"Then why?"

"Because I *do* know her family. This is such a small world. I can't believe you two have never met before this. Bishop…

"I don't get the impression from Doctor Walden that he'd be okay with his daughter dating a musician. You have a battle on your hands to have this one in your life," she says.

"A battle I'm willing to take on."

"So you are involved. She's beautiful and very intelligent. Her father's pride and joy. I can't tell you the number of dinners

I've been to and heard him dote on her relentlessly," my mother says.

"She's all of that and more. She's the one," I blurt out.

"Oh, honey. Dr. Walden is a good friend of your dad's, but I've always gotten the feeling that he wants his children to marry… Black. I… I don't want to see you hurt," she says cautiously. "What if she doesn't want to go against her father's wishes? You're my son—"

"Mom," I call, cutting her off. "Saga is a grown woman. She makes her own choices. I think she can handle her father."

"I should invite her parents to the party. Maybe that will ease the situation."

"There's no situation, Mom," I say and blow out a breath.

"Oh, Bishop," she sighs. "You will learn one day that I'm always right. I'll invite them."

I throw my head back. Why do I bother? She's going to do whatever she wants. She's been driving my dad crazy for years.

"I love you, Mom. I'll see you when I get back," I say before she drives me crazy.

"I'm happy for you, Bishop. The music you've been writing for her is beautiful," my mother says, catching me off guard. "I love you, son."

The call ends and I'm left sitting with my mouth open. I guess I do underestimate that woman. I smile and run a hand through my hair.

"She totally busted me," I chuckle.

"Hey."

I look up to see Saga standing in the doorway in a black silk robe. I jump up to lift her off her feet. My room is clear on the other side of the suite.

"You should've called for me," I say as I lift her into my arms.

"I told you I'm capable of walking on my own," she says as she wraps her arms around my neck.

I sit on the edge of the bed with her in my lap. Her robe gapes open, stealing my attention. Her breasts come into view, sending blood rushing to my cock.

Reaching for the tie of her robe, I tug it free as I hold her gaze. I peel the silky fabric open, revealing her naked body beneath. Her nipples are like pieces of chocolate candy, begging me to suck them into my mouth.

"You came all this way on your own, did you need something?" I breathe.

She squirms in my lap, lust filling her eyes. The way she looks at me, I know I'm not making it through this night without being inside her. My want for her has me starved.

"I was hoping you could give me a massage. Um… my ankle," she says as her gaze drops to my lips.

I palm her left breast and start to stroke her hardened peak. "Is that all you need?"

She shakes her head. "No, I need you."

"Come here," I whisper, leaning in to kiss her full lips.

I grab a handful of the back of her robe and pull it from her body. Once her arms are free, she reaches to push her fingers into my hair while she grinds into my lap. I groan.

I start to kiss my way down her soft neck. She smells so fucking good. The weight of her breast still in my palm has me impossibly hard.

In a swift move, I shift her onto the bed and hover over her body. Dipping my head, I cover her nipple with my mouth. She arches her back off the mattress, calling my name out.

"Easy," I chuckle against her mound.

When I place my hand between her legs, I find her dripping wet and ready for me. I circle her nub a few times before slipping two fingers into her tight pussy. I work her with my mouth and hand as she writhes beneath me.

I love that she has sensitive nipples. The more I suck, the wetter she gets. I don't know what I want more. To keep sucking her breasts or to move down and taste her juicy pussy.

She begins to quake with her first orgasm, making my decision for me. I want to drink up every drop.

"Oh my God," she whimpers.

"I haven't even gotten started, baby," I say as I kiss my way down her torso.

I taste every inch of skin on my way down. I don't want to miss a single inch of flesh. I plan to worship the fuck out of this body all night.

I pull my hand from her soaked core and push her thighs back, opening her up to me. Moving in for my first taste, I roll my eyes in the back of my head. She tastes so damn good.

"Bishop," she gasps as I dive in to eat her up like my last meal.

I was born to eat pussy. Now I know I was born to eat hers. Nobody, and I mean nobody, eats pussy like I do. I make it an art. It's like writing an epic song every time I'm between a pair of legs.

"Holy shit," Saga screams.

I grin and keep going. I lick, suck, lick, and dive in for more. She tries to back away, but I grasp a tight hold of her thighs, pinning her in place. She moves her hands from the sheets to my hair.

"I'm coming," she cries. "Oh, God, I'm coming. Please."

This time, I want her to come all over my cock. I reach to unfasten my jeans and shove them down my hips. Palming my length, I cover her body with mine and line up with her entrance.

Looking into those brown eyes, I start to sink into her. Her lips part and she lifts her entire upper body off the bed when I'm seated to the hilt. When she hits the mattress with a bounce, releasing a breathless gasp, I groan and start to grind my hips.

I pin her to the bed with my cock. I'm so deep inside her I don't want to pull out. She screams as I pulse inside her and she spasms around me. Her second orgasm tears through her.

"Shit, that's it. Soak my cock with that fat pussy. I can't wait to eat you again," I groan out.

"Baby, I'm going to come again," she moans. "Fuck, you're not even moving. Your dick is so fucking big."

I lean in and peck her lips. "You want me to move?" I say in a tight rasp.

"Please, I want to feel you," she pleads.

I start to pump my hips, moving in and out. I tighten my fingers on her hips and shift my right leg beneath her ass as I increase my pace.

"Ah, is that what you need?" I groan. "Fuck, you're about to come again. Shit, I love how your body responds to me. This pussy knows this cock belongs to her."

"I've never come this much in my life," she pants.

"We still have all night."

They're going to have to pry me out of this pussy. I'm going to be in here all night long. I've never felt this good in my life and I don't want it to end.

"Fuck," she screams out.

"I love a screamer," I breathe in her ear. "Let's see if I can snatch your voice and your soul."

Saga

Did he just say he's going to snatch my voice and my soul? Oh, God. I wasn't ready for this. Where did this man come from?

I claw my nails down his back as he hammers into me. I don't think it can get any better until he reaches between us and presses the heel of his palm to my clit. The pressure on my nub and the feel of his hand sends my brain into overload.

With the angle he's thrusting at and the weight of his hand, he sends me to another place. When he turns his hand and uses his fingers to massage my clit, I'm totally done for.

"Bishop, oh, fuck," I scream. "What the fuck."

"You're so wet," he pants. "You're squirting all over me."

He doesn't say that in disgust. It's as if he's relishing the fact that he has gotten me to. He pulls out, giving me false hope of a reprieve.

I'm flipped on all fours faster than I can take my next breath. He reaches for one of the pillows and tucks it under my belly. My ass is in the air like an offering to him.

He wastes no time taking that offering. His face is buried in my core, working that sinful mouth. Damn, this man can eat some pussy.

"I can't," I whimper as I feel myself building again.

He doesn't back off. Instead, he responds with a greedy groan and his fingers pushing inside me. My legs tremble beneath me.

He thrusts back into me right as I hit the pentacle of bliss. I see stars. This man has rendered all other men useless. I don't ever want another man touching my body.

"That's my girl," he croons as I explode again.

He tips my head back and takes my mouth in a kiss that has my thoughts making no sense whatsoever. In the span of seconds, I've promised him babies, my trust fund, and a new Lamborghini. Insane, I tell you.

I don't have a damn trust fund. My father said he wasn't going to ruin us and make three entitled brats. I don't have the money to buy Bishop a Honda much less a damn Lambo.

"Yes, yes," I cry out as he works right through my release.

I feel his hot seed shoot into me, but he doesn't stop thrusting. I wait for him to soften, but it doesn't happen. He keeps going.

I once told Isha she was a damn liar when she told me about a guy she was sleeping with who would come and could still go. I guess I owe her an apology. I have seen the light.

"How's your ankle, baby?"

"Oh my God. My ankle? It's my kitty you should be worried about," I pant.

He chuckles and kisses my neck. He reaches for my clit, tapping it as he pounds into me. My eyes roll back. I scream and gush around him.

Yup, he can have my babies. Or am I supposed to have his? Damn, someone is snoring loud as fuck.

Bishop

She's passed out on me again. This time, I'll let her sleep. It's been a long night.

Running a hand through my sweaty hair, I smile down at her. She's so fucking gorgeous. I can hardly stand to keep my hands off her.

Not to mention, I had two years of fucking to make up for. Boy, was Saga worth the wait. Her tight, wet pussy quenched every thirst I had.

My head starts to buzz with music. My fingers itch to strum my guitar. I look at Saga, torn between lying here with her and getting this song out of my head.

"Da-da-dah," I sing. I tug at my hair. "Fuck."

I slip from the bed and grab my guitar. Not bothering with throwing on any clothes, I sit on the couch in the living room and start to play. It starts to come together. I grab the pen and paper on the table and start to jot down the words.

I have two verses and half a hook when Saga appears in her black robe. I smile at her as she stops before me. Reaching out, I wrap an arm around her waist.

"Did I wake you?" I murmur into her belly.

I close my eyes, savoring the fact that she smells of us. If I didn't think she was sore, I'd peel this robe from her body again to have her once more.

"No," she says, moving to sit beside me. "Will you play for me?"

I lean to peck her lips. "Whenever you want," I reply. "What do you want to hear?"

"Is that a new song you were just playing?" she asks.

"Yeah, it's not ready though."

She gives me a blinding smile, placing her head on my shoulder while looking up at me dreamily. I don't know what I did to earn that look, but I want to put it there as often as I can. I kiss the tip of her nose.

"Play me your favorite song," she says.

"That I can do."

I start to play the notes to Aerosmith's "I Don't Want to Miss a Thing." She beams as bright as the sun when I start to sing the lyrics. This song says exactly how I felt when I watched her sleep.

"Your voice is so amazing," she says.

I kiss her, forcing myself not to linger. Just as I go to pull away, I nip her full bottom lip and give a little tug. Desire fills her eyes.

I turn away before I forget my restraint. She starts to massage my back and I'm in heaven. This is the perfect moment.

There's this deep connection between us I can't explain. It's something I can feel in my bones. Like a part of my life that's always been there, but now it's waking up to her presence. A fire that's been dormant, waiting for her to appear.

"Play me something that will totally surprise me. A favorite that no one would think you would love," she says excitedly.

"I know just the song," I say and smile.

Moving my guitar to the side, I move back on the couch and tug her into my lap. Once I have her settled, I reach for my guitar again and start to play while she's cradled in my arms. I kiss the top of her head before I start to sing.

The lyrics from "Sway," by Michael Bublé, begin to pour from my lips. Saga turns to look up at me. I wink at her surprised expression.

She beams back at me before she turns and snuggles into my chest. I start a gentle sway as I sing to her. When I get to the chorus, she reaches into her robe's pocket and pulls her phone out.

I look on curiously as I continue to sing. The song starts to play through her phone. I stop playing and place my guitar down.

"You didn't like my singing?" I say with mirth in my voice.

"I love your singing, but I want to dance with you," she says and stands.

She grabs my hands, tugging me to stand. I lift up, still naked and wrap my arms around her waist. She places her hands on my shoulders as we sway to the song.

I start to sing the lyrics, bringing a huge smile to her face. I move my leg between hers and start to sway a little more. Her smile falters a bit.

"Shit, your ankle," I say.

"It's fine."

I purse my lips at her. Dipping, I lift her around my waist by her ass. She moves her arms around my neck and our eyes lock.

Saga places her forehead to mine as I sing some more. Her heat pressed against me becomes distracting as I dance around the room. Not able to hold back any longer, I connect our lips.

We get lost in the music and our moans. This connection between us feels like it's weighing down the room. I've never felt this in sync with anyone. It's more than the physical.

Although her silk-covered breasts pressed to my bare chest, have my skin humming and my heart knocking. I'm hard and pulsing by the time the song starts to replay. I grab a handful of her hair as I devour her mouth.

"Make love to me," she pleads.

"Are you sure? Babe, we've been at it for hours. Aren't you sore?"

"I'm fine, please," she says against my neck as she starts a trail of kisses.

"You keep saying you're fine," I groan.

"Because I am," she whispers. "I want you to make love to me. Will you do that for me, Bishop?"

I look her in the eyes. "Yeah, baby, I will."

I release her robe and push it from her shoulders. She whimpers as I tilt my head and move in to suck on her neck. Reaching between us, I guide my cock to her heat. Then I guide her onto my shaft with a tight hold on her ass.

We both groan as I enter her. Her warmth sucks me right in. It's like nothing I've felt before.

I move my lips to hers, needing to invade every opening of her body. I shove my tongue into her waiting mouth. She moans and dances her tongue with mine.

I release her ass long enough to place my fingers in her mouth, coaxing her to suck on the digits. As I continue to sway us to the music, she pulses around my length.

"That's it. Suck harder for me. Get them nice and wet," I groan out.

Once she has my fingers soaked, I move my hands back to her ass to hold her tight as I bounce her on my shaft. Her tight pussy sucks me in and out, making a sweet music of its own.

"Oh God, Bishop," she pants as she looks me in the eyes.

I slip a finger into her forbidden hole and she whimpers, throwing her head back. Her pussy begins to flutter around me. She opens her mouth in a silent scream as she begins to drip all over me.

"I can't get enough of you," I growl into her neck before sucking the flesh between my lips.

I groan and shift my arms beneath her thighs as I bend my knees and bounce her at a more steady rhythm, using my forearms to balance her. My eyes roll in my head as she screams my name hoarsely while locking her fingers in my hair as she tugs.

I feel her warm pussy tightening and know she's going to come. I growl and bounce her harder. I'm panting as I rock into her.

"Saga," I groan.

I lick from the base of her throat up to her chin, then take her sexy lips. As she squeezes the life out of my cock, I know I'll never want anyone the way I want her. I'm inside of her and still crave her so much my chest aches.

"You're amazing," I breathe in her ear.

She whimpers incoherently in response. Her body is shaking in my hold. She convulses right off my length as if she's trying to get away.

With a smile on my lips, I take her right back into the bedroom. It's only right that I soothe her pussy with my tongue after plowing through her so thoroughly. I kiss her long, slow, and passionately as I hold her body to mine.

"You're mine, Saga. I can't let you go," I whisper into her shoulder as she tucks her face into my neck and sighs.

Saga

"It's my favorite spot in LA. We have to go when we get back," he rumbles against my temple.

I snicker. "That tickles."

"What, when I talk next to your skin like this?" he says, causing me to squirm in the bathwater as I laugh harder.

"Your laugh is like music. I love it."

"Your voice does something to me. I like that," I say.

I intentionally avoid the word love. I'm not ready to acknowledge the fact that I'm falling fast and hard for this man wrapped around me.

"How are you feeling?"

"Better."

"Good," he says, placing his mouth by my ear as he starts to hum, "Sway."

He might have been right about that last time. I'm so sore, but the way he danced with me around his waist while singing to me was so sexy. I had to have him.

This bath will have to do for now. I'm in heaven with Bishop humming in my ear and his big arms around me. I should be sleeping, but I can't seem to find it in me to pass out.

"I don't want to stay trapped in here all day. Let's go sightseeing," I say into the silence.

"No," he says.

"Why not?" I look at him and pout.

"Saga," he blows out. "Your ankle. You shouldn't have been dancing on it. We're not going to take off running around Atlanta."

"It's just a little tender. I'll be fine," I say. Reaching to cup his face, I plea. "*Please.*"

"No," he shakes his head, that gorgeous smile on his lips.

"When the shows are over, we'll take the city by storm. Your ankle should be healed by then. Not a moment sooner. I saw you wincing," he replies.

"It's the first time you haven't carried me everywhere. Of course, it will be a little sensitive."

"You just made my point. It hurts. We're staying in," he says firmly.

"I don't like you," I say, poking my lip out.

"That's a shame because I l—"

His words are cut off by the ringing of my phone. Bishop reaches his long arm out of the tub to pluck it up off the top of my robe. When he hands it over, I see it's my dad calling.

I go to ignore the call, but my gut tells me to answer it. I chew on my lip as I answer. I feel like a teenage girl all over again. I used to hide my boyfriends from my dad, knowing he wouldn't like the type of guys I was so drawn to.

"Hey, Daddy," I answer the line.

"Where are you, Saga?"

The hard edge in his tone tells me he already knows the answer to this question or at least has some clue. My stomach turns in knots. I wonder how much he knows.

"Atlanta," I reply.

"With this… the singer in the news?"

I'm such an idiot. How didn't I think about the fact that pictures of Bishop and I have been splashed all over papers and news channels everywhere? I was so busy trying to curb the story and do my job that I didn't think of its real impact or reach.

"Yeah, that's my boss," I reply.

"What happened at Carmichael, Pike, and Jeffreys?"

"I was fired, Dad. It's a long story. One I wanted to tell you in person," I say.

"How long was I supposed to wait for that to happen?"

"I was actually on my way to tell you when I found my new job," I say, trying to sound chipper.

The silence that greets me is not good. I know my father. I may be a grown woman, but in my father's eyes, I will always be his little girl.

He can smell the bullshit a mile away. He knows I'm avoiding or leaving something out. When I hear my mother in the background, I shudder. This is going downhill fast.

"Saga Marie, why on earth are you running around with that singer looking all dreamy-eyed and lost? What is this about your job? What's going on?" my mother says into the phone.

"It's a long story, Mom. I'll be there in another week or so to explain it all," I say.

"Are you dating that boy?" she pushes.

"Yes, I'm dating that man. It's new. The reports were premature in starting their rumors, but yes, that's my boyfriend," I say and sigh.

Bishop squeezes his arms around me and kisses my neck before burying his face there. I can't help the smile that comes to my lips.

"What happened to taking a break from dating?" My father's voice comes through the line.

"Bishop happened. I wasn't looking to get into a relationship, especially not with my boss. We sort of just… happened," I reply.

"We have a lot to talk about, Saga. There are plenty of young men I have in mind to introduce you to when you get back home. Get this out of your system now. We'll discuss it further in person," my father snaps and the line goes dead.

I sigh and drop the phone back on the floor. I have a million thoughts going through my head. I should have known this would be a problem.

"Dating a white guy is going to be a problem?" Bishop says, causing my shoulders to tense even more.

I note that his body has tensed up as well. I'm quite sure he was able to decipher the nature of the call. However, I pray he didn't hear my father's words.

"It's not that. It's… can we not talk about this? We were having such a good time. I'll deal with my father. He and my mom will have to realize I'm a grown woman, which will have to start with me acting like one.

"I can't believe I was going to run back home. Just… just let me deal with my family. This is still new. We can wait to add all of that drama to the mix. For now, let's see how this all works out."

He's silent for a moment. I look into his eyes and see a war going on. Giving a tight nod, he pecks my lips.

"I know what it's like to have meddling parents. Just know that I'm committed to you. To us," he says.

"Got it," I say and kiss him back. "Now, about going out."

"No," he says simply, shutting me down.

"Fine."

CHAPTER EIGHTEEN

Locked Away

Saga

I don't know what I expected for this little break in between shows. However, Bishop has proven to be very attentive as a boyfriend. I've never been more pampered by a guy I've dated in my life.

The part that I love, while Bishop has the money to pay for me to go down to the hotel spa or to have someone come into the suite to provide the service, he has opted to be my service provider.

He's given me a massage with oils and fed me chocolate-covered strawberries. He has run me a bath with bath salts and placed candles and scented oil diffusers around the room. The man even played the finished songs from the album, just for me, while I soaked in the tub.

It all sounds so different in the intimate space. I've heard every word so much differently. I can't believe it will all change again once recorded in the studio. I can't wait.

If he were anyone else, Isha would say he's cheap and that's why he didn't pay someone to do any of the pampering. However, I know that's not the case. Bishop genuinely wants to pamper me himself. He spent a ton of money on products to do this himself, not knowing what to get, so he bought everything.

He was adorable when he returned with his haul. Seeing his face is how I know it's not about the money. Bishop genuinely wants to make sure I'm happy.

Like now, he has that same huge, goofy smile on his face as he returns to the bedroom with a huge bag in his hand. When he gets to the bed I'm sitting on, wrapped only in my robe with a pair of panties on, he turns the bag over and dumps it.

My mouth falls open as bottles of nail polish hit the mattress. There has to be a bottle in every shade. Did he buy every color in stock? I cover my mouth and laugh.

"Pick a color," he croons.

"Bishop, seriously?"

"I want to paint your cute little toes. Yes, seriously."

I tap my finger against my lip as if thinking of which color to pick. My gaze lands on a bottle of black, sparkly polish. Not my style, but I'm drawn to it.

I shift on the bed to reach for it, plucking it up from the pile, I hold it up to Bishop as I sit on my knees. He wraps his hand around the polish and my hand, but before pulling away, he leans in and pecks my lips.

However, that doesn't seem to be enough. Instead of pulling away, he cups the back of my head and deepens the kiss. I moan into his mouth and wrap my arms around his neck.

I give a whimper when he pulls away. I was sort of hoping he'd take things a little further. Who am I kidding? I wanted him to take things a lot further.

Unfortunately for my pulsing kitty, he takes a seat on the bed and pulls me close before tugging my legs from beneath me and into his lap. I tilt my head to the side as I watch him shake the bottle of polish and pat it against his palm.

"What do you plan to do with all the rest?" I say, glancing at all the other bottles.

He shrugs. "I'll probably ship them home for date nights when I have you at my place."

"Oh, so there will be date nights?" I say teasingly.

"Date nights, sleepovers, vacations, fly outs, you name it," he says with a sexy wink.

"Fly outs?"

"Yeah, I'll have shows around the world. If you're not already there for some reason, I'll fly you out to spend time with me."

I love the way he says it so simply. As if I should already know this. Since we made things official, he's been doing that a lot—speaking in absolutes.

Almost like it's forever implied that I'll be a part of his life. I'm sort of digging the possessiveness, but it's more than that. It's a sense of comfort that we feel with each other.

I can't help but smile as he bends his head over my toes and paints them. Loose strands of hair surround his face. He's surprisingly gentle with his large, warm hands.

My mind goes to visions of him doing this for his little girls. The way he spoke of being a father, I know he would. I can see them smiling at their father happily while Bishop paints their toes and sings them whatever song he comes up with for them.

I'm completely through as those little girls begin to form in my head as little versions of me. Right on cue, he begins to hum while he paints. It doesn't sound like one of the songs I've heard already, telling me he's getting a new song in his head.

He blows on my toes and lifts his gaze to mine. I smile and wiggle my little piggies. Bishop lifts my foot and kisses my big toe.

"How did I do?"

"You're good at this."

He shoots me a wink and at first, I believe he's going to make me ask how he's so good at this. I even think of not asking, not sure I want the answer. However, when he speaks up, I learn something new about Bishop.

"In high school, I was fascinated by nail polish. I wasn't confident enough at first to wear it on my hands. So, for a while, I painted my toes.

"Only my family and people who I was comfortable around in my home knew when they saw me barefoot around the house and by the pool.

"Eventually, I got over it and did my hands too. I got good at painting them myself," he explains.

"And here I thought you were going to tell me about an ex or something."

I smirk and look at him through my lashes. He gives me a heated stare, allowing his eyes to roll over my body. I bite my lip, waiting for his next move.

"I like you jealous. It looks sexy on you."

"You think so?"

He snorts. "Very. I thought I told you about looking at me like that," he rumbles.

"I don't think I heard you," I say innocently.

His sparkling blue eyes take me in heatedly. Then he pounces. I squeal and fall back against the bed beneath him. He nips at my neck as he snakes his hand between my legs.

He pushes my panties aside as he kisses my neck. A growl comes from his lips as he finds my folds weeping for him. I gasp as he pushes his fingers into me and bites down on my neck.

"Bishop," I whimper.

"I'm going to fuck you so hard you'll be singing my name like a prayer," he breathes into my ear, causing me to gush for him.

Just to be snarky, I begin to sing his name to the tune of "Ave Maria." He bursts into laughter and kisses the side of my face, not stopping his ministrations. I moan as his long fingers move in and out of me.

"You're crazy, you know that?" he chuckles against my lips.

"What's life without a little fun?" I purr.

"I'll show you some fun."

Bishop

I crawl down her body, nuzzling her robe open with my face and planting kisses against her smooth skin. Her tight, wet pussy takes my fingers with ease as her juices soak my digits.

I lick my lips, ready to taste her already. It killed me to massage her supple body without taking her earlier. It wasn't about me. I wanted to give her pleasure.

To be honest, I hadn't planned on fucking her this soon. It's that sexy-ass look she gives me. I don't know how to resist it. Not to mention, I've wanted to suck on her lips and spend hours doing so since waking up this morning.

"Bishop," she moans as I settle on my belly like a sniper.

She smells so good. Pulling my fingers from her body, I stick them into my mouth. It's a fight not to hum against her flavor bursting on my tongue, so I don't bother to try.

"Mm, baby. You taste like you were made for me."

She looks down her body with a smile on her lips. The desire dancing in her eyes makes the music start to play in my head, but I'm not about to leave her here to get it out. Instead, I dive into her sweet pussy.

Saga begins to writhe beneath me and call my name. I smile into her heat and hum the tone in my head as I eat her up. Slipping my fingers into her tight kitty—as she calls it—I strum her inner walls like I'm playing my guitar.

When I look up, I find her squeezing her breasts. It's such a beautiful sight; I think I'm going to poke through the mattress just from watching her. I was already hard. But I know I need to be inside of her soon, if not right now.

"Bishop," she screams as she comes.

With a satisfied grin, I crawl back up her body and take her lips, her juices dripping down my chin and all. Saga kisses me back feverishly. We're both hungry for each other.

I only break the kiss to peel her panties down her legs, tossing them over my shoulder once I get them off. She sits up and tugs at my T-shirt, but I take over and tug it over my head for her. She shrugs out of her robe while I release my belt and open my jeans.

"Babe, please, I need you already," she breathes.

My pants forgotten, I reach for her throat and hover over her lips. Flicking out my tongue, I lick her plush mouth, then nip at her lower lip, tugging it. She moans and reaches to pull me to her.

"How bad do you need me?" I say against her lips.

"So bad I can't breathe."

I take her lips in a bruising kiss, shoving my tongue into her mouth. My pants still around my hips, I shove into her waiting wet folds. We groan into each other's mouths as I thrust into her. Her walls squeeze tightly around me, making it impossible not to groan and embarrass myself.

"So fucking good," I breathe into the kiss. "How have I lived without knowing this feeling?"

"God, how am I surprised by how big you are every time? I love the reminder each time you enter me for the first stroke."

She slips her hands beneath my jeans to palm my ass. As she claws at my cheeks, I begin to thrust in and out. I pound into her while balancing on my toes and kissing her hard.

It doesn't take long for me to realize I'm not going to get to the rest of the things I have planned for our date. This is where I want to be for the rest of the day and most of the night.

I'm addicted to this pussy and totally in love with Saga. This is it for me. I'd give my life for this woman.

Bishop

"I wish I could have been there," Saga says.

Her laughter rings out through the room as I tell her old stories of the band and past tours. I love her laugh. Man, I love everything about her. I've come so close to telling her all night.

Yesterday was awesome. Our date turned out better than I thought. Today has been just as great as we got to know each other more.

I close my eyes and bask in her warmth as I sit on the floor between her legs. She's sitting behind me on the couch in our suite. Saga has her hands in my hair, massaging my scalp as we talk.

This is heaven. It feels so good. I can't help longing to have this in my life permanently.

"That so reminds me of something me and my brother and sister would do," she says through her laughter.

"Tell me something," I murmur.

"What's up?"

"What are your siblings' names?"

"Don't laugh."

I look up at her and stare at the mirth in her eyes. I already know their names can't be as eccentric as mine and my brothers. She has nothing to worry about and I tell her as much.

"Trust me, with names like Lord, Prince, Bishop, and Knight Moran, I have no room to judge."

She bursts into more laughter. "You can't be serious. That's your brothers' names?"

"Yup," I say, popping the *P* as a smile comes to my lips. "Come on. You just laughed at us. You have to tell me now."

"Legend and Reminisce."

"Saga, Legend, and Reminisce." I shake my head. "Our folks were all getting high back then."

"Indeed they were."

We both laugh together and crack a few more jokes about our names before diving into stories of our childhood. I believe we lose track of time as we get lost in each other's words and the comforting vibes surrounding us.

"Your family sounds so loving. I can see why you want to be a father."

There's a change in her voice that piques my interest. I sit up and pull my hair back up on top of my head. I turn to look at Saga and she has a pout on her lips as if she wasn't done playing in it.

I stand and stretch, then take a seat beside her. Wrapping an arm around her shoulder, I tug her into my side. I've missed her lips, so I take them in a quick kiss.

"My family has its quirks, but we love each other. Your family sounds loving from your stories. Why the change in your tone?" I prod.

She sighs. "I love my family. They're great. They mean the world to me. It's just… You know what, never mind. It's nothing."

"You know you can talk to me. What you say remains between us. I want you to learn to share with me. I want to be a listening ear."

She blows out a breath. "I love my family. It's just. Since I was little, I've felt this need to be perfect. I had to excel at everything to get my father's approval. I just hate disappointing him.

"I don't even remember what made me this way. It's been ingrained in me for so long I don't remember a time when I didn't feel the need to be perfect.

"Sometimes I feel like I'm missing out on life because I'm playing by the rules to keep from being a disappointment. This is probably the furthest I've colored outside the box in my life," she says.

"What do you mean?"

"The job, dating my boss. Throwing caution to the wind. This is so not like me," she says in all but a whisper.

If I weren't paying such close attention, I might not have heard it. I think her words over. Then, I think of Saga when we first met. Her words click into place as I remember that version of her.

"Maybe you met me right when you needed to shake things up."

She looks up at me with a smile. I swear, in this moment, as she looks back at me, I can see love in her eyes. I kiss her to convey the words neither of us has spoken.

I can taste those very words on her lips. I break the kiss and glance over at Lucie longingly. It's a battle to sit here as the music burns in my head. I'm torn between wanting to spend time with Saga and needing to get this song out.

I'm saved by the ringing of her phone. Saga gives me a knowing look as she kisses the corner of my lips and stands with her phone to head into the bedroom.

She gets me and that's more than I could ever ask for. With a smile, I race to grab Lucie and start on a new song. It spills from me faster than I can get it down on paper.

Saga

I move into the bedroom and close the door behind me as I answer the call from my sister. I climb onto the bed and lie across it. Instantly, Bishop's cologne fills my lungs from the sheets and a smile comes to my lips.

"Hey, Reminisce. Your ears must be ringing. I was just talking about you," I sing into the phone.

"Hey, you. What's up?"

"Nothing. I'm taking some time to chill while on a little break."

"Girl, cut the crap. What's going on with you? What's with all the stuff you had shipped to my place without any explanation?

"Then Mommy and Daddy had these looks on their faces every time I brought your name up at dinner. Those looks are usually reserved for me. What fresh pile of shit have you put your foot in?"

I sigh and roll my neck to release the sudden tension that's building. I should have known when I saw her number that this was coming. However, I saw the look in Bishop's eyes and decided to take the call so he could have time to write the song I saw dancing in his head.

"I… it's sort of embarrassing. I was fired and blackballed. I had been heading home when my car broke down. Luckily, I ran into Bishop Love and he offered me a job and a ride back to Cali.

"I'm now a part of his crew and I'm on his tour. Not what a Walden girl should do, so yeah, the parents are mad at me right now."

"First, don't think we're not coming back to the blackballing and firing business. Second, I heard about the pictures and meant to call you sooner, I've just been busy with work."

I'm not surprised. Reminisce isn't one to follow the gossip rags. She probably has no idea who Bishop is in the first place.

"You didn't need to waste your time. We weren't seeing each other when those pictures came out and the rumors started."

"Ah, now we're getting to it. You're seeing this guy? No wonder they looked like their heads were going to explode."

"Saga, don't worry about them folks. You have done everything they've expected of you and then some for as long as I can remember. This is your life. Live it," my sister says firmly.

I wish I could be more like my younger sister. She has carved her own path since day one. That's expected of her. I don't have that luxury.

"Rem, I want to throw caution to the wind. He makes me happy. I haven't felt this way in… ever.

"The truth is, when I'm with him, I don't feel smothered. I feel free to breathe and take life by the horns. I don't think Mommy and Daddy would understand how I feel, so I've pushed it to the back of my mind.

"I don't want to deal with it, so I'm ignoring it. I'll cross that bridge when I get there. For now, I just want to be happy," I say.

"You know me. I'm all for your happiness. I say, do you.

"I really want to see those pictures now. Ugh, if not for this huge case, I'd be all in your business. Alas, I'm going to mind the business that pays me. I have to go, sis. I love you."

I laugh. I know my sister. She'll forget about those pictures before we hang up. She's going to mind her business.

"I love you too."

CHAPTER TWENTY

Atlanta

Bishop

I've written two songs during the last few days. One of which I'm not ready to share with the world. I don't know if that one will make the album at all.

But this one. This one, I want Saga to hear. I want the world to hear it. Spending the last two days locked away in a hotel with her has been amazing and life-affirming.

I know what I want and I know who I want it with. I've found what I've been missing all this time. Well, before the end with Bev.

"Atlanta, Atlanta, Atlanta, you've been so good to me. I have something extra special I want to sing for you tonight. Are you ready?" I call out to the crowd.

While they go wild, I turn to look at Saga waiting in the wings. She's perched on a stool I insisted she sit on during the concert. She tilts her head and gives me that beautiful smile.

"I'm going to play this one on my own tonight. I haven't shared it with the guys just yet. It's a bit near and dear to my heart," I say as the crowd dies down.

I start with the first few cords and pause. The crowd goes crazy. My heart's pounding.

I wipe my sweaty palm on my jeans. I didn't think I'd be this nervous to play this one. Reaching for my water, I take a sip and swallow down my nerves.

Here goes nothing.

Saga

He looks so nervous. I've never seen him like this on stage. I lean forward in my seat, holding my breath.

He fixes Lucie and starts to play again. The crowd here is so loud. They're going crazy before he opens his mouth. I'm pulled in by his very first words.

I have something I need to tell you
Hush… give me a second to get this out
When I say this, I want you to really hear me
It's crazy; I've said the words a million times before
They've just never meant the same as they do when I say them
to you
Come dance with me as I sway you to the music
Say the words with me; I see them in your eyes
This comes from my heart
Here goes…

> *I'm in love with you*
> *I love you so much I don't know what to do*
> *There's so much other shit I could say, but at the end of the*
> *day—*
> *the fact is… I love you—*
> *Now everybody knows…*
> *I'm in love with you*
> *I love you so much I don't know what to do*
> *Everyone has something to say, but at the end of the day—*
> *the fact is… I love you—*

His eyes are locked on me as he sings the words. I'm stunned. I don't know what to do or say. It's not like he's in front of me to say anything, but I'm still speechless.

He gives me a look as if to ask me if I understand the words. I give him a nod and his face lights up with the brightest smile ever. In this moment, I know I'm in love with him too.

"I don't think you know how big that right there is." I turn at the sound of Dwayne's voice.

For such a big guy, he moves with such silence. Or it could be that I was so absorbed in the music and Bishop's words that I didn't hear him walk up. I give him a warm smile.

"It's a beautiful song," I choke out.

"That it is, but it's much bigger than a song. He doesn't give those words up too freely these days. You mean a hell of a lot to him," he says.

"He means a lot to me too," I say in almost a whisper as I look back out on stage.

I love you, Bishop mouths and shoots me one of those winks.

I blow him a kiss as I try not to cry like an idiot. My mind goes back to a few days ago. I think he was going to tell me those same words then.

"Did you get that on video?" this time it's Jag's bitter voice that asks the question.

"Joey is recording tonight. Bishop didn't want her up on her ankle," Dwayne answers for me.

"Yeah, but what's she supposed to be doing? We're not paying her to sit around and be a groupie," Jag says.

I hop down off my stool to give him a piece of my mind, but Dwayne is already in his face, growling like a big grizzly. Dwayne is as tall as Bishop and, shockingly, a bit wider. *I* stumble back and he's not even in my face.

"What the fuck did you just say?" Dwayne seethes at Jag. "You just heard him declare how he fucking feels about her and you dare to disrespect her?"

"It's a song—"

"Shut the fuck up. Even if he wasn't singing about her, if I ever catch you talking out the side of your mouth to her again, I'm going to break my foot off in your ass. She's family. Has been since she stepped on that fucking bus," Dwayne snarls.

Just as he finishes digging into Jag, I feel heat at my back and a hand splays my belly. I turn my face up to see Bishop glaring in Jag and Dwayne's direction. His jaw is set tight and his eyes are blazing.

"We have a problem here?" Bishop barks.

"Nope, I've got this," Dwayne says with a wolfish smile as he pats Jag's cheek. "The little guy just got lost again. He's good now. I set him straight."

"Fuck you," Jag snaps, turning to storm off like a toddler.

"Don't mind him. He's just pissed he can't get pussy without Bishop," Dwayne turns to say to me.

I cover my mouth as a laugh bursts free. Bishop cups my chin, turning my face up. He captures my lips with a mind-numbing kiss. I'm breathless when he releases me to whisper in my ear.

"I love you."

Biting my lip, I look up at him. He narrows his eyes at me. I get ready to say it back, but the usual crowd starts to descend.

"Bishop Love," a few women squeal.

He places a hand on my back and starts to guide me to the dressing room. We're at the door when Jag appears again. I can feel the tension between him and Bishop right away.

"Irving is here. Skip the shower. He's coming to talk to you," Jag says.

"Yeah, all right," Bishop says, opening the door to lead me inside.

"Alone, Bishop. This is business," Jag says tightly.

"Who the fuck do you think you're talking to?" Bishop explodes.

"Hey, hey," I say, reaching for his face when he won't turn to me.

He looks down at me. His expression is hard and unyielding. I stroke his cheek, lifting on my toes to kiss his lips.

"I'll go see what the guys are up to. I can get some photos and stuff. It's fine," I say.

He turns to look over his shoulder, waving Dwayne closer. "Make sure she gets to the guys without a problem. Don't leave her side," he says.

Turning back to me, he tugs me closer by the waist and kisses me hard. I try my best not to whimper into his mouth. I fail in the end as he cups my ass and squeezes.

"I'm coming to take you home as soon as I'm done," he says huskily.

"Okay." I nod.

"Get your ass inside. I got shit to say before Irving shows up," he snarls at Jag.

So much for me defusing the situation.

Bishop

"We love what you've been doing. The songs are amazing. We're hoping for a big bang at the end of the tour. We think it will really get the fans revved up for the release of the new album," Irving says excitedly.

"I'll do what I can," I say dryly.

I'm still pissed as fuck with Jag. If I hadn't known him most of my life, I would fire him. He's taking our friendship too far. I'll only bend so much.

"Do you think you'll be able to get this all laid down in time for the new release date?" Irving asks.

"What new date?"

"I haven't gotten around to telling him about that," Jag says nervously.

"This is hot. We want to stay on top of the buzz. You have three weeks to record when you get back. We'll be releasing the album three weeks after that. We already started to prepare the rollout," Irving replies.

I pull a hand down my face and scratch my forehead. It's not impossible, but it's going to be a fucking challenge. I'll be overworking my boys, just coming off a tour.

"Do I have a choice?"

"That's my guy. I knew you would get it done," he says as if I just promised I would make it.

"Yeah, are we done here? I need a shower. I'm exhausted."

"This is some good stuff. I'll be in Vegas. I can't wait to see what you come up with," Irving says. "We'll keep the very last song for the album release. Make that one a hit for us."

"You got it," I snort and get up to go into the shower.

That last song will be my best yet. It's my last. I'm tired of this. My mind goes to Saga. I'm ready for something new in my life. It's time for a major change.

I want to start a family.

Payback

Saga

Dwayne knocks on the guys' shared dressing room door before turning the knob and poking his head in. I stand waiting in the hall while going through the footage Joey took for me on my work phone.

I can't help the smile on my face. I wasn't expecting Bishop to tell the world he's in love with me through his new song, but I loved that song. Joey had a much better angle than I ever got.

I text the video of Bishop singing the new song to my personal phone, wanting to listen to it again later. Dwayne backs out of the guys' dressing room with a high-back barstool for me. Placing the barstool beside me, he nods for me to sit.

I roll my eyes but take a seat. I know Bishop would blow a gasket if he found me standing and waiting. Dwayne posts up in front of the door and crosses his big arms over his chest.

"They're getting dressed. We can head in in a minute. You need anything?" he says to me once I'm settled.

"No, I'm fine," I say, turning my attention back to my phone.

Joey did good. I continue to go through the footage to see what I can post next. I usually post something different to each member's profile and Bishop's newest song to the band's profile. A few minutes go by then the dressing room doors open again.

"We're decent. You guys can come in," Thrush croons.

Dwayne gestures for me to enter, stepping aside for me to walk in before him. I slide off the stool and start for the entrance, not looking up from my phone to walk the short distance. I don't even think twice, not until the guys burst into laughter.

I stumble back with a stunned and confused look on my face. I blink a few times, trying to comprehend what just happened. Thrush stands doubled over in laughter.

"I told you payback would be a bitch," he laughs out hysterically.

My mouth falls open as I look into the room. My lashes are stuck to the tape I walked right into. These assholes placed tape across the threshold for me to walk into, keeping me from entering the room.

I look at Dwayne and glare. He purses his lips and holds his hands up. His face is red from trying not to laugh.

"That shit was priceless," Fendi cracks up.

I place my hands on my hips and cock my left one to the side. I roll my jaw and scoff. Suddenly, I don't know if I want to kick Thrush's ass or laugh.

"Well played. You better sleep with one eye open." I seethe.

Bop comes to peel the tape down. I move forward to snatch my lashes off. I had wanted to look extra special tonight, so I wore them.

"You guys are trying to get murdered. Bishop is going to be the one to get revenge. I don't envy you," Dwayne chuckles as we step inside.

"I just want him to know I had nothing to do with it," Bop says.

"That was just mean," I say and take the seat Bop offers me.

I sit gingerly, not trusting any of them. I had thought Thrush had given up on getting me back after I hurt my ankle. Boy, was I wrong. I'll admit, that was a good one.

"You guys are insane. After that song, you dare to harm her? I knew you all were crazy," Dwayne says.

"Don't act like you didn't help me. He comes for me; he's coming for you," Thrush says as he moves to take a seat.

"Nope, we're not going to tell him. We're even. No need to drag him into it. We're having fun," I say.

"This is why we like you," Fendi croons. "What brings you here? I thought for sure Bishop was going to lock you up in his dressing room."

"Irv is here to see Bishop," Dwayne murmurs before I can reply.

"Oh," the others say in unison and wince.

"Anyway, I've burned off everything I ate today. Someone get me a menu," Bop says.

"You guys mind if I record?"

"Go on. I think the fans would love to see me roost these two after a show," Fendi croons.

"You roost me. That would be the day," Bop grumbles under his breath.

I begin recording and spend the next hour laughing so hard my belly hurts by the time Bishop comes knocking to take me away. I leave knowing our bond has grown deeper and I have four new friends for life.

They even got Dwayne to throw in a few jabs. He's funnier than I would have thought. Like Bop, Dwayne doesn't seem to speak much.

I guess it's the job. Or it could be I took one for the team. That prank broke down the rest of the walls everyone had held up.

Bishop

"I was going to tell you," Jag says as he follows me out of my dressing room after Irving leaves.

"When, after I drop dead from exhaustion?"

"Right, because you're not already a zombie," he bites out.

I stop in my tracks and whirl on him. Glaring down at him, I try not to explode right here in this hallway. I work my jaw and wait for the people walking by to move out of hearing distance.

"I may have been a fucking zombie, but as my friend, I thought you had my back to keep me from getting fucked in the ass. You and I both know I've been on the verge of burnout and the guys aren't too far behind. Fendi and Thrush have both been in wrist braces over the last year.

"Now we're to get this album done in three weeks. Are you fucking kidding me? How long have you known?"

"A few days," he murmurs. "I didn't say anything because I was trying to buy more time. I do have your back, Bishop. I always have your back."

"Right," I scoff and turn.

He goes to follow me. His footsteps grating on my nerves. I stop and glare over my shoulder.

"Go find something to do. I'm tired of looking at you. Every time you open your mouth lately, I want to punch you in it."

"I'm only doing my job, man."

"Stop talking," I bark.

I don't even bother to watch him disappear. I turn and head for the guys' dressing room. I'm still fuming when I go to knock. Saga's laughter rings out through the closed door.

Dwayne opens the door and reveals Saga sitting on the couch, holding her stomach and wiping away tears. Instantly, my anger begins to fade. Hearing her laughter is like a soothing balm to my soul.

I don't know what I did before her. Jag was right. I was a zombie. That's the problem though, I don't want to just move through life anymore.

I want to live. I deserve to enjoy my life. Something needs to change.

"Baby, you ready?" I say when Saga locks gazes with me.

"Aw, come on, Bis. Come join us for a bit. Saga was having fun with us," Fendi says.

"Not tonight." I shake my head.

Bop places a hand on Fendi's arm when he goes to protest. I'm grateful to him because I really don't want to tell them what happened with Irving yet. They should get to breathe easy for a little longer.

I snort to myself. Was that what Jag was thinking when he didn't tell me? I almost blurt the news out as I have the thought.

However, their chuckles as they wave goodbye to Saga make me keep silent. They're all happy. I want it that way.

Saga and Dwayne exit the room. I place a hand on Saga's back as Dwayne leads the way out. Ed appears to tail us, along with the rest of the guys.

"Are you hungry?" I lean to say into Saga's ear.

"I know you are, so I'll have whatever you get," she says with a smile.

I drop a kiss on her lips. I don't bother to tell her that for the first time, I might be too tired to eat. I'll get us something anyway. It's been hours since I fed her.

A few fans linger as we step into the parking lot. My SUV is already waiting. I smile exhaustedly and sign a few autographs on the way. Quickly, I usher Saga inside.

I couldn't be happier to climb into this SUV to head back to the hotel. I don't want to hear my name. I don't want to sign another autograph.

My head is pounding. I release my hair, hoping to release some of the tension with it. Something needs to give.

All I want is to go back to the room and sleep for a week. Too bad I don't have that luxury. Three weeks, I'm supposed to record an entire album in three weeks.

Where do they get off pushing us like this? I'm going to throttle Jag. He's supposed to keep them from doing this to us.

Making this happen in three weeks is going to be hell on my voice. I lean my head back on the headset, already exhausted from thinking about it. Saga moves closer and cups my jaw.

I open my eyes and turn to look at her. She's like an angel. Suddenly, I feel like I can do anything as long as she's around me.

"You look so tired," she says, staring into my eyes.

"I feel tired."

She runs her thumb over my knitted brows. I cup her face and brush my thumb across her lips. We're silent for a moment.

"Are you okay? What's going on?"

I smile. "You're concerned about me. Always concerned about me."

"*Bishop*," she warns.

I sigh. "I'm fine. Just a lot on my plate, baby."

"You want to talk about it?"

I tug her to me to take her lips. The last thing I want to do is talk. I'm tired of talking. I need to forget about all this shit for now.

I deepen the kiss and drink from her sexy mouth until she pulls away breathlessly. I stare at her, allowing my gaze to run across her face. Something is different from earlier.

I just can't put my finger on it. Then it hits my tired brain. I frown.

"Baby, what happened to your lashes?" I ask as I notice the false ones she wore earlier are gone.

She bites her lip and laughs. I lift a questioning brow. This should be good.

Saga never has a hair out of place. Her makeup and hair are always flawless. I just can't see her tearing her lashes off before we get back to the room.

"They were a casualty of war." She snickers.

I furrow my brows, my tired brain not having the power to follow what she's talking about. I shake my head and pull her back into me for another kiss.

This is all I need. My love for her is carrying me through. I'm growing tired of how things are going, but Saga is my light in a dark place. I crave her more than anything.

I break the kiss and murmur against her lips. "I love you."

CHAPTER TWENTY-TWO

Celebrity Dating

Saga

Anticipation builds in my belly as I ride in the Porsche seated beside Bishop. He reaches across the console to lace his fingers with mine as he smoothly maneuvers the car on the road.

Dwayne and the other security members ride in an SUV behind us. Today, as we climbed into the vehicle for our date, I realized I'm dating a celebrity. I don't know what I expected when I became Bishop's girlfriend.

However, going on dates with security in tow wasn't a part of it. This date has even started off well beyond my expectations. He rented this sleek, sexy car for one and he looks amazing driving it.

He said he felt like driving himself and it would give us alone time without his team surrounding us. I have to admit, it is more intimate. As if reading my thoughts, he gives my hand a gentle squeeze.

"Are you all right?" he murmurs against my hand as he brings it to his lips.

"I'm amazing. I'll be even better once you tell me where we're going."

He glances over at me for a brief moment and winks. "It's a surprise. It won't be much larger."

Now, my curiosity is ready to burst through me. We're riding through country-looking roads. I don't know Georgia well, but I don't believe we're in Atlanta anymore.

I glance at the GPS, trying to see if I can find a clue as to where we're going. The address looks to be a residential one. If I hadn't come to trust this man so much, this is the point where I'd start to panic.

Although, I do trust him. Bishop makes me feel safe. He has been so sweet and attentive since we started dating and way before that if I'm being honest.

So instead of freaking out and shouting for him to stop the car, I sit back in my seat and relax. My mind drifts off to the last week.

I feel like I know Bishop so much better. Our dates in the hotel suite and the last two concerts have given me a greater glimpse of who he really is. This connection between us has grown stronger and I can't say I regret my decision to get on that bus.

It doesn't take long for him to get to a gated property where he turns in. We're allowed in through the gates and both cars pass through. I sit in shock as we pull up in front of a French château-style home. It's simply breathtaking.

"I hope you don't mind. When I started to plan our date, I thought about the club and how things went so wrong. I didn't want to take that risk again. Your ankle has just healed and…"

He releases a deep breath. "I wanted us to be able to have this moment without worrying about my fans or paparazzi. I rented the house and staff, including a chef, for the evening. I promise this will be as fun and romantic as going out to a restaurant and movie theater."

His cheeks turn pink and it's so endearing. I mean, who rents out a house just for a date? He has brought in a private chef and staff to serve us for the evening. Is he kidding me?

"Bishop, this is amazing and so thoughtful. I don't care that it's not some restaurant or sticky movie theater either. This is exciting. Come on," I say excitedly.

Leaning in, I kiss his cheek. He smiles and steps from the car to round it and open my door. I take the hand he's offering and step out of the vehicle. The house is even more breathtaking now that I'm outside the car.

Dwayne and the others take the bags Bishop brought along into the house. We don't follow them inside right away. Instead, Bishop keeps me in his arms, staring into my eyes while holding me in a trance.

Tightening his hold on me, he dips his head and takes my lips in a passionate kiss. I cling to him with my arms wrapped around his neck. He deepens the kiss as he begins to sway me in his arms.

"All clear and I have the signed NDAs," Dwayne announces, breaking into the moment.

I shake my head to clear it and allow Bishop to lead me into the house. His palm feels so warm against my back, bringing so much comfort with the simple touch.

Once we step over the threshold, it all really begins to sink in. I'm dating a real live celebrity. The hired staff are lined up to greet us and from the way they're gawking at Bishop with stars in their eyes, I can't deny who he is or the depth of what that means.

I mean, he couldn't take me to dinner and a movie like a normal boyfriend would. Don't get me wrong, I'm not complaining at all. It's just… wow, I'm dating a rock star.

Will things always be this way? I think I fall in love with him even more as I see all the effort he's put into this to make it seem as normal as possible.

We enter what seems to be the dining room. However, there isn't a formal dining table. Instead, a smaller table covered with a tablecloth is set for two. The candlelight coming from the table sets the ambience for what I'm sure is to be a romantic night.

Bishop pulls my chair for me to take a seat. I sit gingerly and then gasp as I take in the menu lying on top of the place setting. My hands shake and tears prick the backs of my eyes.

How could he ever think this wouldn't go over better than dinner and a movie out there with the world peering in on us? I brush my fingers across the menu. It's printed on iridescent-blue cardstock. Le Saga is embossed at the center top.

I grin and look up at Bishop. He's watching me take it all in from across the table with a smile on his lips. If I didn't love this man before, I know I love him now.

"Le Saga?" I choke out.

"I needed to come up with a name for our little château restaurant," he says, lifting a hand to gesture around us.

Little my left butt cheek. If I thought this place was breathtaking from the outside. I'm stunned by what I've seen so far on the inside.

"Do you do anything small?" I tease.

"No. And certainly not when it comes to you. You deserve nothing but the best."

My cheeks heat and I drop my gaze back to the menu before me. To my astonishment there are multiple choices for our main course, appetizers, and dessert. As I look over the menu one of the young men from the staff comes over to fill our wineglasses and then takes our orders.

"I'll start with the truffle chips and then I'll have the bourbon soak steak and Cajun seasoned veggies and potatoes," I say, my mouth watering from just the sound of the meal.

"I'll have the same but as the surf and turf," Bishops says.

"Would you like the shrimp or the lobster, sir?"

"Give me the lobster tail and garlic-buttered shrimp."

"Yes, sir. Anything else?"

"No. That will be all for now."

The guy takes off for the kitchen. I find it exciting that we can see this chef from here. Our waiter hands over our order and the chef gets to work on making our meal.

I turn back to Bishop with a huge smile on my face. He's watching me closely with a smile of his own. I can't remember the last time I felt this giddy on a date.

Bishop lifts his glass of wine to his lips and takes a sip. He then places it back down, not taking his eyes off me once. The intensity in his gaze almost causes me to squirm in my seat.

"Where were you planning to live when you returned to Cali?"

I sigh. "I have no idea. I was going to move back into my old bedroom at my parents' if they would have me. Staying with Legend is out, but Reminisce is an option. Her place is where I shipped all my things."

"What about staying with me? No pressure. Just know it's an option."

I'm a little caught off guard. I never thought about moving in with him. Things are still so new. I don't think my parents will have a problem with me staying with them until I find a place, but staying with Bishop might be a huge problem.

"Can I think about it," I murmur.

"Of course. Like I said, it's just an offer. I have plenty of space and I'd love to have you with me, but it's nothing we need to decide at this moment."

"Thank you for always being concerned and offering your help."

He waves me off. "That reminds me. Your car arrived at my place this morning. It will be in my garage until we return."

"Well, look at that. I already have something there."

He grins. "If I have it my way, your things will fill my closet and you will call my space your home."

"Boy, you never waste time." I tilt my head at him. "What if I'm the psycho here and I worked my way onto your bus to stalk you and worm my way into your life?"

"Yelp, I'm a goner because I've fallen hook, line, and sinker."

"Seriously, you should be more careful," I chide now that I think of the situation.

Not that I'm some crazy person trying to harm him, but what if I were? Bishop had every right and reason to be as cautious as I had been. In hindsight, he should have been.

"Ah, there's that concern for me again. Baby, you don't have to worry about me ever ending up in a situation like this again. While I might help someone out, I wouldn't do anything that would cause you to question me.

"Since you're stuck with me, no one will get the chance to be in your shoes to try to harm me," he says with conviction.

"Your truffle chips and dip," the waiter says as he places our appetizers in front of us.

They look and smell delicious. Of course, despite having his own, Bishop reaches over and snags up one of my chips and dips it before popping it into his mouth. I smile and shake my head but return the gesture.

The flavors burst in my mouth. My eyes widen and I hum as I cover my mouth and chew. Bishop nods his head and digs into his own food.

"This is divine. Wow, I wasn't expecting that," I moan.

"I know," Bishop says as his gaze drops to my lips.

I try my best not to get lost in his heated gaze. With my eyes on my plate, I finish the delicious food just before the chef and waiter come over with our main course.

My mouth waters the moment they walk over and place the plates in front of us. Everything looks cooked to perfection. The plating is a work of art as well.

"Mr. Love, Miss Walden, I hope you enjoy your meal. It's been an honor to cook for you both," the chef says.

"Thank you," I say.

"Thanks, Chef Kennedy. You outdid yourself. Thank you for doing this on such short notice."

"My pleasure. Anytime."

With that, the chef turns and heads back into the kitchen. I dig into my food and it's pure heaven. The steak melts in my mouth and the flavors are to die for. Bishop groans and nods his head.

"Awesome, right?"

"Chef's kiss. I would say the best thing I've eaten since we've been in Georgia, but that's a lie because I've had your pussy. Nothing can compare to that," he croons.

I nearly choke on the food I'm chewing. I glance around to ensure no one is close enough to hear what he just said. He only looks back at me as he chews with a smug look on his face.

"I have no shame when it comes to you. Why are you looking all embarrassed and cute?"

"Why am I surprised? I've listened to some of your old music. Your mouth is filthy."

He licks his lips. "You haven't seen how filthy it can get. Later," he says and winks.

I shake my head as I watch him eat. I note something as I watch him. Bishop has changed. He has this peacefulness about him that wasn't there before. It looks good on him.

We share the perfect piece of chocolate cake with caramel drizzle for dessert. I can honestly say this was a five-star meal. I wasn't surprised when Bishop said Chef Kennedy is a two-time Michelin star winner. I wanted to lick all the plates after the food was gone.

"That food was so good," I sing as we finish the tour Bishop takes me on of the house.

Apparently, he took the video tour before booking for the night. I should have known he was up to something. Bishop only writes his songs on paper in his notebook. He had his laptop in his lap most of the evening while strumming his guitar here and there like he was working on a song.

I know now that was to keep me from paying attention to the fact that he was planning this date. Again, Bishop has shown how much he pays attention to detail. This date is everything.

"Want to pick your snacks for the movie? I got that one you wanted to see shipped in," Bishop says as we end the tour in the movie theater.

"Wait, the one I showed you the trailer to the other night? That's not supposed to be out for another three weeks."

He shrugs. "You wanted to see it. I made it happen."

I'm gushing with excitement. Although I wave off the snacks. I couldn't eat another thing. Bishop, on the other hand, doesn't even bat a lash as he grabs the snacks offered to us by the staff. He has a full-size popcorn and some candy. The man can pack it away.

My mind goes to how he burns off all that food and my body heats. I guess he does need the fuel. The man is insatiable.

I'm a bit surprised when he doesn't pounce during the movie. He does tug me in for a hot kiss once but breaks it and places a kiss on my forehead. I think I catch a sugar rush from the sweetness of his tongue in my mouth afterward.

I'm going to keep it real. The movie wasn't all I thought it would be. It was okay, nothing like the trailer hyped. I'm sort of happy when it comes to an end.

"Welp, you want to watch another? There's that hot tub, or we could walk the grounds. The place is ours until the morning. We can do whatever you like," Bishop says as the credits roll at the end of the movie.

"That wasn't as great as I thought it would be. We don't have to watch another. I think I would rather stay here and chill for a bit."

Bishop looks around. "You know, this is one of the most comfortable theater rooms I've ever been in."

"I was thinking the same thing. It's more than the seats. The entire ambience is warm and calming. Perfect for a family to gather and watch a movie together."

Bishop gets this look in his eyes as if thinking my words over and envisioning his own family in the space. The more I see him like this, the more I'm able to imagine him as a father. More specifically, the father of my children.

"You know, those were good times. Hanging with my brothers and Dwayne. I loved hanging in the movie room or around the pool out back," he muses.

"You don't have those things in your home?"

"I do, but I didn't put as much thought into them. My focus was the studio. Now that I think of it. I didn't put much thought into any of the rest of the house. I'm hardly home."

"That makes sense, but something tells me you gave more attention to detail than you're giving yourself credit for."

He shrugs. "You might be right. God knows I can't remember what the place looks like. I can't even remember the last time I was home for long enough to look around the place."

"You guys tour a lot, don't you?"

Bishop groans. "Hell yeah. Too much."

I reach to cup his cheek. "You sound so tired. Is it possible for you guys to take a break before the next tour?"

He snorts. "We're going to hit the ground running for this new album. Slowing down isn't in the cards. I'll rest up when I can."

"Are you sure you have time to date?"

He leans in, cupping the back of my head. Taking my lips, he kisses me tenderly. Then he speaks against my lips.

"I will always make time for you. Not doing so isn't an option. You're keeping me sane in all of this," he says and takes my lips again.

We continue to talk and bask in each other's company. Time seems to float by. The staff disappeared some time ago. Glancing at the time, I figure they all must have gone home. Suddenly, Bishop falls silent and his gaze drops to my lips.

I lean into him as if being pulled in by a magnet. He cups the side of my face and kisses me passionately. He groans into the kiss and deepens it.

When we pull apart, he looks me deep in the eyes. His blues sparkling. I reach to finger the strain of hair that's come loose from his man bun.

"This was a really nice date," I say.

"Yeah, I had a nice time too. Sorry we couldn't go to the movies and a real restaurant. I selfishly wanted to keep you to myself."

"This was perfect and I don't think I'm ready to share you either."

"Come here," he croons, pulling me from my seat into his lap.

I settle into his lap and within his warm embrace, thinking things are about to get hot and heavy. However, Bishop only hugs me close while asking me more questions about myself.

His voice is so comforting and each time he presses a kiss to my temple, I'm lulled into a greater sense of comfort and safety. This man is everything.

Bishop

Saga has fallen asleep in my arms. As much as I would love to be inside her sexy body, I'm content with holding her just like this. I wasn't sure how this date would go over.

My biggest thought was about her safety. She's finally walking on that ankle without wincing or hobbling as if it's too much to put weight on it. I didn't want a repeat of what happened at the club.

From the look on her face when we arrived, I figured I got this one right. I enjoyed our time. This was way more intimate and less stressful.

I look down at her sleeping face. I know deep down inside I won't be able to shield her forever, but I'm hoping to keep her in this bubble for as long as I can.

"I need you to trust me. Don't give up on me," I whisper and kiss her forehead.

I send up a prayer, hoping she'll withstand all that is my life. I need her to be strong enough for this because I can't lose her. She's my light leading to the way out.

And just like that, the music starts. Another song is coming. I pull my phone to text Dwayne and check to see if he brought Lucie into the house.

Dwayne: *She's in your room with the luggage.*
Me: *Thanks.*

I get up, trying not to wake Saga in my arms. Carrying her upstairs, I place her in the bed, take off her shoes, and pull the covers up over her. Then I kiss her lips and turn to get my guitar and songbook.

CHAPTER TWENTY-THREE

Together

Saga

"What's going on in that head?" I ask as I look up into his face.

He brushes a hand through my hair as I rest my head on his chest. It's our first night in Vegas. The entire crew pushed through the thirty-hour drive nonstop.

I never knew riding on a bus could be so tiring and fun at the same time. The rest of the band has grown on me. The only person I don't get along with is Jag. Thankfully, he flew into Vegas ahead of us.

"I know the song I'll sing at the last concert here. I just haven't figured out how I'll end the album altogether," he says.

"What direction do you want to take it?"

"I don't know. The others were inspired by things you said, how I felt, I'm not sure how to tie all that up just yet," he says thoughtfully.

"It will come to you. You have a bit of time. A lot can happen in four weeks."

"I can't believe we'll finally be home next week."

"Your birthday is coming, isn't it?"

"You remembered," he chuckles.

Rolling me onto my back, he hovers over me and stares down into my face. His eyes search mine as the gears turn in his head. I reach to caress his cheek. He shaved as soon as we got into our suite. His face is nice and smooth.

"What?" I ask, smiling at him.

"I don't ever want to wake up without you," he says. "That's my birthday wish."

"You're not supposed to tell anyone your wish," I say.

He pecks me on the lips. "I tell my best friend everything."

My heart squeezes. He says some of the sweetest shit. I feel like we've been together for years, not days. The last three weeks have flown by so fast.

"I don't want this to end," I say before I can trap the words in.

"It doesn't have to. I won't let it," he says before kissing me.

The kiss deepens and I moan, wrapping my arms around his neck. He moves his lips to my jaw, working his way to my ear. I push my fingers into his silky hair that's knotted on top of his head.

"I love you," he breathes into my ear.

He looks down at me expectantly. I've yet to get the chance to tell him the words. We seem to always get interrupted before I can. Yet, this feels like the perfect moment.

"I love you too," I say.

He crushes my lips with his as soon as the words are out. He snakes his hands beneath my tank top, dragging his fingers up my sides. I wrap my legs around his waist as I start to grind into him.

I need him and I want him more than ever. Before Bishop, I hadn't had sex in a few years. I've always been cautious of how close I allowed the guys I dated. They had to be worthy and deserving.

Bishop has become that and so much more. I lift my arms over my head as he pulls my shirt up and off me. I sit up so he can unfasten my bra. He peels the fabric away and stares at me in awe.

"You're so fucking beautiful," he says. "It was torture not making love to you on the bus."

I cover my face and laugh. He refused to touch me on the bus because I'm a screamer. Although he slept beside me, holding me once we did go to bed.

"I'm all yours now," I say, throwing my arms in the air and jiggling my breasts at him.

He grunts and dips his head to take my hardened peak into his mouth. I moan and clutch the sheets at my sides. His greedy mouth sucks so hard my back bows off the bed.

"You're mine forever," he says as he releases one breast to go for the other.

Reaching between us, he unfastens my jeans. He tears his mouth away long enough to peel my pants down my legs. I release the death grip my limbs have around his waist so he can get the fabric off.

As I lie beneath him in my panties, he looks down at me, still fully clothed. I want to see him bare. That sexy body should never be covered up.

"Take off your clothes," I say as I look at him through my lashes.

"I will," he says as he looks at me through hooded lids.

He moves down my body to capture the waistband of my panties with his teeth. I shiver as the breath from his nostrils fans my hip. His lip grazes my skin as he tugs the garment from my body, causing goose bumps in his wake.

Tossing the panties aside with his mouth. He dives back in until he's face to face with my core. Still, he doesn't go in for a touch the way I hope for him to.

"Look how wet you are for me," he breathes against my weeping lips instead.

"I need you," I pant.

He runs a thumb through my folds. "I can see that."

"Bishop," I beg.

"Hold on, baby. There's no need to rush. I want to savor this. Everyone always wants to rush through the greatest pleasures in life. The anticipation, the time it takes to build the fire, that's as important as getting to the finish line," he murmurs.

I'm ready to explode already. When he starts to circle my clit with his thumb while singing up against it, I start to convulse. Not for the first time; it plays in my head that he owns my body.

No one else can do the simple things he does to drive me insane. He could tell me to pull his finger and I'm sure it would make me come.

"Yes," I moan when he finally starts to lap at my center with his tongue.

"*Mmm,*" he hums as he settles in for his special brand of torture.

Twenty minutes. He's down there wringing me out for twenty minutes. I know because I keep looking at the clock on the bedside table in astonishment.

His face is soaked when he finally lifts to pull his shirt over his head. The bulge in his pants looks like it might burst through any minute. However, he takes his time unfastening his jeans and peeling them down his legs.

I'm useless as I try to catch my breath. I can only stare at him with a goofy smile on my lips. My mouth waters when his thick, long length comes into view.

Hands down best dick I've ever had. I'd like a lifetime supply, please.

He grins as he strokes himself and watches me. I lift a lazy brow at him as he thumbs away the cum that drips from the tip. Lifting up on my elbows, I grasp his wrist and bring his finger to my mouth.

"Saga," he moans as I suck his finger dry.

His mouth is on mine the moment I release his thumb. He lines up with my entrance, running his tip up and down my folds but not slipping inside where I need him most.

When he breaks the kiss to look into my eyes, I see something different there. Something deeper than any of the other looks he has ever given me. It's an acceptance of sorts, but something more is there… determination… possession.

I can't pin it down to one thing. I just know that his gaze is full of emotions that threaten to consume me and my own feelings for him. He slips into my body and stills.

Pulsing inside me, he never breaks the connection of our eyes. Right here, right now, I know this is the only man meant for me. Forget my past. He is all I need to know or want.

"I love you," we say in unison.

He breaks into a breathtaking smile. I couldn't tell you how the hell I got here. The last seven months are suddenly a blur, but I know I'm right where I need to be.

CHAPTER TWENTY-FOUR

Bishop

"Saga," I call through the suite. "Come on, baby. We need to go."

My heart is in my throat. I know things between us have been moving fast, but instead of pumping the breaks, I've decided to move forward full steam ahead. It feels right.

"I'm coming," she says as she appears from the bedroom.

My mouth runs dry and my cock hardens instantly. She looks drop-dead gorgeous. Her red dress stops midthigh, showing off her thick, shapely legs. She has on a pair of those sexy-as-fuck red bottoms.

I sent her to the spa this morning and she came back glowing with her hair done to perfection. I'm damn proud to call the woman standing before me mine. All that chocolate belongs to me.

"What? Is it too much?" she says, looking down at her dress.

I cross the room to close the distance. With my hand cupped behind her neck, I capture her lips and kiss her like it's the last time I ever will. She locks her fingers into my T-shirt, holding me close.

"Fuck, I want you," I say against her now swollen lips.

"I thought you had to get to sound check early," she chuckles.

"I do," I grumble. "I can't wait to get you out of this dress later."

"Let's go, Mr. Love. I don't want your fans trying to jump me because I kept you from giving them the perfect concert," she says as she gives me that gorgeous smile.

With my purpose renewed in my head, I lace my fingers with hers and lead her out of the hotel suite. I'll have plenty of time to worship her sexy body and all its curves. First, I need to make it through the next few hours.

Make it count, Bishop.

Saga

Something is totally up with Bishop. He's not acting like himself and this isn't how the sound checks usually go. The band is all here, Bishop is center stage, but he has me up here on stage as well.

"Stop fidgeting. You're gorgeous," he chuckles, leaning in to kiss my cheek.

I'm so self-conscious sitting in this chair on stage. There's no crowd beyond us, but I can't help thinking that he might decide to do this again later when there is. I shove my nerves down and give him a smile.

"What are you up to?" I laugh. "Should I record this?"

"No. You just sit there and listen," he says.

I nod and fold my hands in my lap. Bishop and the band start to play and I'm enthralled by the sound that moves through me. Closing my eyes, I sway in my seat.

The brush of Bishop's lips has me opening my eyes again. I'm met with those intense blues and arrested by the love I see in them. His words only reveal the story I see in his depths.

> *If I'm wrong, take the key and lock me up*
> *I'll surrender my life to have you as my wife*
> *So many ways to say I love you*
> *Te amo, baby, Je t'aime*
> *No matter how I say it, it's you and me*
> *I don't think there's any other way for us to be*
> *I'm a man lost without you*
> *I've written these love letters, every single one about you*

I'm holding my breath as the music changes and the chorus comes in. I know what's coming, but my brain misfires as I hear the words spill from his lips. I can't believe my ears.

> *Hear me, baby*
> *I know this might be crazy*
> *But will you marry me tonight—?*
> *I know this might sound crazy*
> *But I need you, baby*
> *Will you marry me tonight—?*

I have huge, fat tears streaming down my cheeks as he sings from his heart. I can hear it in every word. My knee is bouncing. It's all I can do to keep my shit together just a little.

I'm nothing without you
I've thanked God a million times since the day I found you
Didn't know I could fall this hard
Only you could reach this heart that's been scarred
How can a man know life if he's missing his wife?
Completion starts where we begin
You're my lover and my friend—
You're the flame my soul has been looking for—

I sniffle and swipe my tears. He stops playing to wipe away the rest with his big hands. He kisses me softly before singing the chorus again.

Hear me, baby
I know this might be crazy
But will you marry me tonight—?
I know this might sound crazy
But I need you, baby
Will you marry me tonight—?

"Yes," I choke out. "Yes."

He kisses me so hard our teeth knock together. I laugh—squealing when he lifts me from the chair onto his waist. He holds me so tight I think I stop breathing.

"I love you so fucking much. Fuck, I thought I was going to shit my pants," he chuckles.

I laugh so hard I snort. "You're insane."

"About you. We're in Vegas. Will you marry me after the show?" he whispers.

I let the question sink in. My father and mother will probably lose their shit, but this is my life. I'm thirty-one. I don't need permission to marry the man I'm madly in love with.

"Yes," I say, placing my forehead to his.

He kisses me again, this time walking off the stage, heading for his dressing room. He doesn't stop for anyone or anything, kicking the door closed once we're inside. This should be interesting.

Bishop

She said yes. I can't believe she said yes. I've been between her legs, making her say it over and over again since.

I had to shove her panties into her mouth to keep her from screaming the walls down. I've never been this insatiable, but I've never been in love like this before either.

"Come for me one more time," I say into her ear.

I can feel her tightening around me. I pull her panties from her mouth and shove my tongue inside. I want her to taste herself on my lips.

She screams as I pinch her clit and send her right over. I swallow her cries like the delicious meal they are. My heart swells as it hits me square in the chest that I'll get to do this for the rest of my life.

"I'm a mess," she pants.

"Mm," I murmur, kissing her sweaty temple. "You're still sexy as fuck to me."

"I look like I've been screwing in the front man's dressing room," she says with a lazy smile.

"You have been fucking in the front man's dressing room," I chuckle and kiss the tip of her nose. "Don't worry about it. Come shower with me. I'll get one of the guys in here to fix you up."

She gives me a side glance. I laugh and kiss her lips. I'll always take care of her.

"Benny has flat ironed my hair a few times. Have you seen this shit when it's down? Trust me, you'll be good as new," I reassure her.

New concern fills her eyes. My heart squeezes. If she comes to her senses and tells me to fuck off. I'm going to be crushed. I'll understand, but it will crush me.

"Babe," she says as she searches my eyes. "Are you sure about this? Don't you want to have a prenup drawn up or something? This isn't the greatest idea for someone with your type of money."

I cage her face in with my arms as I kiss her. This is why I love her so much. She says those words like a concerned friend, not the girl I'm planning to marry.

"Everything I have is yours. This is right. We're right. I know it with everything I am," I say.

"Yeah, but—"

"No buts. We're getting married before you realize I'm a bottomless pit who sits around playing video games when I'm not recording or on tour," I tease.

"Whatever will I do?" she rolls her eyes and laughs.

"Love me, baby. That's all I ask."

CHAPTER TWENTY-FIVE

Try Bliss

Saga

He didn't sing our song for the crowd tonight. I was sort of grateful for that. I want to cherish that song for as long as I can before I have to share it with the world.

"Mrs. Moran," he croons in my ear as he wraps his arms around me from behind.

Turning my head to look up at him, I can't help the face-splitting smile I give him. We've been married for an hour. I thought I'd freak out by now, but it feels so right to hear him call me Mrs. Moran.

"Yes, husband?" I whisper.

"You have no idea how much I love hearing that shit," he says against my lips.

I can smell the alcohol he's been drinking. This is the most I've ever seen him drink. I guess he's celebrating. Although we've kept it to ourselves for now.

As far as the guys know, Bishop just sang me a song earlier. No one knows that we acted on the lyrics in it. I mean, that would be crazy, right?

"You two could go get a room," Fendi says.

"You guys begged us to come out," Bishop shoots back.

"We're starting to regret that," Thrush says with a smile that takes out the sting of his words.

"I'll give you all a break," I chuckle. "I'm going to the little girl's room."

I go to pull out of Bishop's arms, but he starts after me. I turn to face him, placing a hand on his chest. He looks at me with a crease between his brows.

"I can go to the bathroom on my own. I'll be right back," I say, lifting on my toes to kiss him.

He doesn't look too happy about it, but he allows me to go on my own. I think the alcohol may have played a little part in that. He may need to slow down a bit.

I feel like my bladder is about to burst as I stand in line to take my turn. I run my hand through my hair and smile. Benny did good. Bouncing in place, I roll my eyes at the chatter about the band.

"Did you see Bishop Love?" one woman gushes as she and her friend finish up and start out of the bathroom.

"*Yes*. Oh my God. I want to push that girl out of the damn way. She's been clinging to him all night," her friend says.

"The night is still young," the other one says with an annoying giggle.

I roll my eyes again. Looking down at the ring on my finger, I smile. I don't think any of the guys have noticed yet. It's just a simple band. Bishop made a big deal about us getting proper rings when we return to Cali. I'm happy as is.

I finally get to the front of the line and relieve myself. I feel like I've been away from Bishop for hours as I exit the bathroom. I get halfway to the tables our group has been hanging around when I see the girls from the bathroom now in our section.

The one in the tight pink dress is all up in Bishop's face. My anger starts to rise as I freeze in place and watch this unfold. Bishop has a smile on his lips. It's the smile he gives all his fans, but it still pisses me off.

"What did I tell you?" Jag says at my side. "Nothing special. There will always be the next one."

"What's your problem?" I growl at him.

"I've worked too hard holding him together to see him throw it all away again on another random piece of ass," he snarls back at me.

"Fuck you," I seethe, turning back just in time to see that heifer in the pink dress lean in to put her lips on my husband.

Bishop shoots his hand out to palm her face, mushing her back. His smile falls, replaced by a look of disgust. He stands, swaying a little as he waves Dwayne over to escort the girl away.

His expression says he's pissed as he starts to look around wildly. When his eyes land on me watching him, the blood drains from his face. He starts to stumble toward me.

"I guess he's not done with me," I toss over my shoulder, giving Jag the finger. I make sure it's my hand with my wedding band on it.

I rush to Bishop to keep him from drunkenly pushing his way through the small crowd between us. He cups my cheek, his gaze bouncing around my face.

"Let's get out of here," I say. "We have a honeymoon to start."

He kisses me before nodding his head and tugging me toward Ed. Soon, we're tucked away in our car, heading to the hotel for our first night as husband and wife. Jag and the chick in the pink dress are all but forgotten.

CHAPTER TWENTY-SIX

One and Only

Bishop

I haven't been married for two fucking hours and it almost turned ugly in that club. I had no interest in that woman. I was just being polite to a fan.

When she placed her hand on my thigh and tried to kiss me, I lost my shit. First, I don't kiss just anyone. Second, she wasn't my type. Third, and most importantly, I'm married to the one and only woman I want in my life.

"I'm sorry, baby," I slur as I stumble around to strip from my clothes.

"For what?" she laughs as she kicks off her heels and comes to help me get my shirt off.

"I had way too much to drink," I mutter.

With my shirt gone, she places her warm hands on my torso. I look down at her and still can't believe she's mine. I'm married to the woman who brought the music back to my heart.

She is the music. She is my heart. I usually have all the words, but I just can't find the right ones to tell her that.

"Let's get you out of the rest of this, big boy. Then, we'll get you to bed," she says.

"It's our wedding night. I should be making love to you," I say as I caress her face.

"We have all our lives for that. I'll give you a pass for tonight," she chuckles.

"No," I say determinedly. "That's not going to be good enough for me."

I cup her breasts in my palms and start to pinch her nipples. Her lips part and her eyes fill with lust. She frees my belt buckle and works to get my jeans undone.

I go to kiss her but stumble a little. Saga laughs at me, guiding me back toward the foot of the bed. She tugs my pants down my legs before pushing me to sit down.

My cock is standing at attention now that it's free of its confines. Saga drops to her knees and cups me with her small hands. I twitch in her warm palms, precum already dripping from my tip.

I lick my lips. "Babe, you don't have t—"

My words are cut off as she licks through the moisture on my angry crown. Her eyes light up as I don't take the lead and deny her this pleasure. I've never told her, but I vowed the next woman to suck my cock would be my wife. I grow harder knowing that I kept that vow.

"Were you saying something?"

"Shit. Yeah, but I don't know what," I say, shaking my head to clear it.

She takes me to the back of her throat and I can't think of a single word I was trying to get out. My mouth falls open. Saga's sucking me like I owe her something. Those full lips look so damn sexy around me.

She makes a choking sound, but she doesn't come up for air. I shift my legs back and forth on the sides of her body, grabbing the bedspread beneath me. When she comes up for air, her saliva spills down my shaft.

She spits on my tip for good measure. Lifting her eyes to look through her lashes, she gives me a devilish smile. She works me with her hands, licking her wet lips. I lean in and kiss her soft, swollen mouth.

Saga has other plans. She breaks the kiss and goes back to sucking me until I'm calling out her name. I don't know what's better—the feel, the sound, or the sight of her giving me head. They all have me coming down the back of her throat.

"*Mmm*, delicious," she purrs after swallowing.

I fall onto my back. "I think you just killed me," I push out.

"No, but we can try again," she says.

"I'm scared," I chuckle as she straddles my waist.

I place my hands on her hips, holding her to me. I don't want to let go. A part of me fears waking up and she'll be gone, or she's just the best damn dream I've ever had.

CHAPTER TWENTY-SEVEN

Should We Cancel?

Saga

He's been snoring like a buzz saw. I gave up on sleeping hours ago. Instead, I've been staring down at my husband, watching him sleep.

He's magnificent. Those big arms cradling the pillow beneath his head, his full lips slightly parted, the loose strands of hair that have fallen into his face, I think I've captured an angel in my bed.

I'm so focused on him I jump when my phone rings. I curse under my breath when I remember I never called Isha yesterday. So much happened it totally slipped my mind.

"Hey," I whisper as I try to tiptoe out of the bedroom.

"Why are you whispering?" she says.

"I don't want to wake Bishop." I regret my words two seconds after they're out of my mouth.

"I knew it," she squeals. "You kept saying it was just rumors. Nothing was going on. I could see it in those pictures. You two look so hot together.

"You're screwing him. You're totally screwing him and now I'm so pissed I didn't take the time off to help you drive to California," she rambles in my ear.

"Isha, it's way too early for this. Can you dial it down two or three notches maybe?" I sigh and flop onto the couch.

"I was actually calling with a purpose. *A*, to check on you. You didn't call yesterday. I tried to give you time since you're now in a different time zone from me, but I was so exhausted I passed out before calling you," she says.

"Yeah, yesterday was crazy. Sorry about that. What else did you want?"

"That would be *B*, the plane ticket to come out and see you. You were supposed to be settled in with your parents by now. I'm just checking to see if I should cancel," she says.

"Oh shit," I gasp.

"What's wrong?" Bishop's sleep-filled voice fills the room.

I look toward the bedroom to find him with a sheet around his waist. His hair is hanging loose as he pushes it back out of his face. My mouth waters as I watch his muscles move with the action.

"Saga," Isha calls, snapping me out of my trance.

"Um… hold on, Isha," I say. "Babe, I was supposed to be back in Cali by now. Isha has a ticket to come out and see me. She bought it before I left New York."

He nods. "We'll be back in a few days. She's welcome to stay at the house with us. If she arrives before we do, our housekeeper will make her feel at home."

It hits me, I really got married last night. The way he talks about his home as mine with such ease is a dose of reality. I'll be living with him when we arrive in California, not in my parents' home.

"You don't have to cancel. I'll call you later with details," I say to Isha.

"Oh my God. Do you think I can meet Bishop and the band?"

"I'm pretty sure that'll be inevitable," I chuckle.

"*Hell yeah*. You're my best friend in the world. Scratch that. You're my favorite person in the universe," she hoots.

"Love you too. Talk to you later."

"Oh right, you probably want to screw his brains out again. Call me as soon as you come up for air. I want to know what all has really been going on," she sings before hanging up.

Bishop takes a seat on the couch, tugging me into his lap. I snuggle into him, placing my head on his shoulder. His heavy hand on my side brings me so much comfort. A sigh falls from my lips.

"I'm starving and thirsty as fuck," he grumbles into my hair.

"Want me to order in?"

"No, I want to go out for our first morning as husband and wife. You've been held up in hotel rooms and on the bus enough," he says.

"And here I thought you were ashamed to take me out," I tease.

"A load of bull," he snorts. "You're the one who tried to deny us. I'd tell the world about us if I didn't think I'd totally piss you off."

"Things change. You might want the world to know you're married so I don't have to beat the snot out of anyone for trying to put their lips on you."

He throws his head back and huffs. "You saw that shit?"

"Yup."

"I wasn't sure how much you saw, but I wasn't interested at all. It's only you—"

"I saw it all. You mushed the shit out of her," I laugh.

"If you heard the shit she said before trying to kiss me, you wouldn't blame me," he says in disgust.

"How about this? We tell our families and then we can tell the press," I offer.

"That's fine with me," he says. In one swift motion, he's up with me in his arms, heading into the bedroom. "A shower and food. Then I think I want to spend the day spoiling my wife."

"Not complaining at all."

CHAPTER TWENTY-EIGHT

The Press

Bishop

"We'll take the bag and shoes with us. The rest you can ship to this address," I say as they ring up our purchases.

Saga still looks uncomfortable with all the money I've spent on her. I pull her close by the waist as she chews on her lip. She looks up at me with those big brown eyes.

"Stop worrying. Think of it as my wedding gift to you," I lean to say in her ear and kiss her neck.

"It's so much. I thought you meant we were going to get things I can afford. I wouldn't have purchased any of that on my own. Those are Christmas gifts from my parents. Things I wouldn't dare buy myself," she whispers back.

"Your husband is a wealthy man, Saga. He can afford to give you anything you want. Which means you can afford anything you want," I chuckle back.

She rubs her forehead. "This is going to take some time to get used to."

"We have a lot to get used to and a lifetime to do it in. One step at a time, gorgeous."

My phone vibrates in my pocket. I pull it out and frown at the text from Jag. He's been blowing me up since last night. I was too drunk and focused on my wife to answer then. Today, I've just been ignoring him.

Jag: Where are you?

Me: Shopping with Saga.

Jag: Where? We need to talk.

Me: We'll talk when I get back.

I reply and shove the phone back in my pocket before I can see if he responds. I'm not really interested in anything he has to say at the moment. I sign for the purchases and grab the bag with the things Saga wants to take with her.

"I'm starving again," I say as my stomach starts to grumble.

"Why do I feel like I'm going to spend most of my time feeding a hungry husband?" she laughs.

Wrapping an arm around her, I pull her body in front of mine and lean into her ear. "I have a staff to cook for me. You'll be feeding me, but not food," I say for only her to hear and flick my tongue against her lobe.

"Bishop Love. Is it true? Did you and Saga Walden get hitched?"

I look up and freeze. We're surrounded. I look around for Dwayne. I asked him to give me and Saga a little space to be normal. He was dealing with some shit and seemed a bit distracted anyway.

The last time I saw him, he was pacing and talking on the phone. I wasn't concerned. With the shades and baseball cap, not many people recognized me. However, now he's too far away.

Pushing Saga's body behind mine, I start to retreat back into the shop. That is until I hear words that turn my blood into hot lava. I can feel my face turning red.

"You were seen with someone else last night. We have photos of a girl in a pink dress," one reporter says.

"How does your wife feel about that? You guys haven't been married longer than twenty-four hours and you're already falling into your old ways," someone calls out.

It's happening again. This is how it starts. The fame was just one of the things that drove a wedge between me and Bev. The press made her doubt everything about me.

"What old ways? What the fuck do you know about me? My wife was with me. That fan tried to push herself on me. You're so quick to make shit up—"

"Bishop," Saga barks my name, shutting me up.

I close my eyes, realizing what I just did. *Fuck.* Our families are going to know we're married within the hour.

I turn my back to the cameras and gently push Saga into the store. She looks up at me with such worry and disappointment. I'm fucking crushed I broke her trust.

"I'm so sorry. I… I wasn't thinking. Shit, baby. I'm sorry," I say.

"I'm going to have to leave. I need to get to my parents before this blows up," she says.

"We can FaceTime them. They'll understand."

"No, they won't. My father has dreamed of walking me down the aisle since I was born. Finding out I'm married through Messy Maga or some gossip site or… oh my God. You're Bishop Love. This will be on the freaking news," she starts to freak out.

"Baby, come here," I say soothingly, pulling her into my arms. "We'll figure it out. I'm so damn sorry."

"I'll call them now. When we get to the hotel, I'll make arrangements to head to LA," she says.

My heart sinks. She's not hearing me. I feel like she's slipping away from me.

"I'll cancel the last shows," I say, pulling my phone out.

"No, you can't do that," she says, pulling away from me. "Your fans have waited all this time for you. I'll be fine. I'll see you in Cali."

I swallow hard. "Just promise me we're in this together."

She gives me a weak smile that fades as her phone rings. She answers and the tears start to fall as she listens. When I go to reach for her, she turns and walks away.

I can't live this again.

Saga

"You okay?" Dwayne asks for the hundredth time from the driver's seat of the rental.

Bishop insisted that Dwayne drive me to Calabasas. I could have made the trip on my own. I might have preferred it.

"I'm as good as I can be," I say.

"I had no idea you guys took off to get married. I thought… well, you know. I thought he wanted me to disappear so you guys could hook up or some shit," Dwayne says.

"This was supposed to be a happy time. Why do I feel like shit?"

"Your parents laid into you, huh?"

I rub my throbbing temple. "Much worse than that. I knew my father would be upset, but… he called me irresponsible. That cuts so deep coming from my dad."

"Our parents always want the best for us, but that doesn't mean they always know what's best for us. Take it from someone who tried to please his parents until it nearly ruined my life," he says.

"It's like I know I'm a grown woman, but when my parents start in on me, I forget that. I spend so much time not wanting to disappoint them," I murmur.

"Well, just remember you have a husband now. Bishop is a good guy. The whole social media thing… there's more behind it. Just be patient with the situation and know he'll do anything for you," he says.

My curiosity is piqued, but I get the feeling he's not going to say more than that. Bishop's face when I left comes to mind. He looked heartbroken. As if he won't be on his way here after the last show.

"I miss him," I think out loud.

"I'm sure he's missing you too," he replies. "My cousin is crazy about you. He'll make this right."

I don't reply. I don't know if this is up to Bishop to fix. I need to sit and talk to my family. This isn't the way we do things and they're pissed at me.

But are they right? You married a guy you barely know.

I don't know what's right anymore. Maybe this space is what I need to get my head right, some time to get my thoughts together.

Time without my husband.

CHAPTER TWENTY-NINE

We Raised You

Saga

I sit in my parents' home on the sofa, feeling like a small child. My head hangs low, my eyes downcast as I try to fight back the tears. It's like my time with Bishop never happened and I feel defeated.

I'm disappointing them. I lost my job and said nothing. I got married and again said nothing.

This isn't like me. This isn't us. I've always done my best to make my parents proud of me.

"I don't understand," my father says while pacing. "We raised you better than this."

"Better than what?"

"Better than running off and marrying someone you don't know," he barks.

And just like that, I'm snapped back to the present. The grown woman who's learned to take care of herself. I'm more than capable of making decisions and this one was mine to make.

I ball my fists at my sides and bite my tongue. I won't disrespect my parents. I'll let him have his say.

"Saga, how much do you know about him? You told us yourself you two just started seeing each other. How can you possibly be married?" my mother says.

"We—"

"He couldn't even come to me like a man," my father cuts me off. "Where's the ring? You ran off and married some bum who can't even provide for you?"

"Hold on," I bite out. "I didn't marry a bum. We were waiting to get to LA to go ring shopping. Bishop can provide for me just fine. You haven't even met him—"

"Exactly. He's married to my baby girl and I've never met him." Daddy seethes.

"I'm not a baby. Heck, I'm not even the youngest. Come on, Daddy," I say.

"He's not good enough," my father clips out.

I jerk my head back. "Why not? Because he's a musician? Or is it because he's white?"

"What did she just say to me?"

"Andre." My mother tries to calm him.

"No, don't Andre me. Girl, you have no idea the things we sacrificed to give you the opportunities you have. They say money talks, but there are days that our skin speaks louder.

"I've invested time and wisdom into each one of you. Opened doors that were closed in your mother's face and mine when we were coming up no matter how wealthy we were.

"You come in here with an attitude because you decided to jump on a tour bus and married some entitled singer. I want what's best for my child, white, brown, or purple. You went about this wrong."

"Those are the facts, Saga Marie. You did this wrong," he fumes.

"Wrong for you," I say, calling on my courage to stand up for myself. "But it felt right for me. I can't tell you how I know, but I know my husband is the one. I know I'm right for him and he's right for me."

"You've turned your nose up at every young man your father and I have ever introduced you to, and suddenly this one is the one after a few weeks?" My mother says.

"Yes. Just like I knew they weren't the one, I know Bishop is," I reply.

"But what do you know about him?" my mother says while wringing her hands.

"That he loves me. That he's willing to protect me. He makes me laugh and smile. He has written the most beautiful songs for me—"

"His music is trash. It's raunchy filth," my father barks.

"His old music is racy, but this is different," I plead.

"Filth," my father repeats. "My lawyers are going to work to get you out of this mess. I want to know what happened at your job. That's where this all went off the rails."

"I was fired for not sleeping with my boss and then he had me blackballed," I say tightly. "And I couldn't be happier for it. I've met the love of my life and I'm married to him."

Even as the words fall out of my mouth, I don't know where they come from. I hadn't planned to come here and stick up for my husband or my marriage like this, but the more I sit and listen the more I know it's what I need to do.

"I'll own that company by the time I'm done," my father bellows.

"Daddy, it was time for me to make some changes in my life. Screw Carmichael, Pike, and Jeffreys. I'm moving on with my life," I say.

"You're making light of all this? I don't understand you," my father says and shakes his head. "I told you naming the girl Saga was going to be trouble down the road. Look at this."

"I'm not a girl. That's the problem. You guys still see me as the girl who left your home thirteen years ago," I say.

"Well, since you're grown, let's see you get yourself out of this mess when it blows up in your face," my father says.

I feel like I've been punched in the chest. I don't know what I thought would happen after coming here. However, I didn't think it would be more of this. The phone conversation had been hard enough.

"You're right. You raised me. You raised me to be fair and loving." I stand and collect my things. "You raised me to make the best decisions for me. I love you both. Have a good night."

"Saga," my mother calls as I start out of the room. "Saga. Where are you going?"

"Home," I call back and keep moving.

Bishop

My heart wasn't in that performance tonight. All I could think about was finishing the last two shows so I could head home to my wife. I fucked up royally.

"Hey, baby," I say into the phone.

"Hey," she says, sounding so broken.

I press a hand to my face, trying to get my tired brain to come up with a way to make this better. I'm so angry with myself. It's been so long since I let the press push my buttons.

"I need you to know why I lost it," I say.

"It's okay. You don't have to explain," she says. Then I swear I hear her sniffle.

"Are you crying?"

"It's been a long day."

"I'm coming home. Fuck this tour," I say as I stand and start throwing things into my bag.

"Bishop, you need to finish the tour. I'm fine. Dwayne said he'll stay at the house with me until you get back. Isha will be here tomorrow. I'll be okay," she says softly.

I shove a hand in my hair and tug. This is such a clusterfuck. It's only a few days, but I want to be with my wife.

"The press has been the worst part of this gig. I love the music. The fans—for the most part, they're amazing, but the press… Bev… she said she cheated on me because I cheated first.

"She believed everything they said. I guess when those reporters started talking that shit, it just triggered something. I don't want to lose you," I say.

I'm met with silence. I drop down onto the bed and put my head in my hand. I don't know what I was expecting, but silence wasn't it.

"I think you're forgetting our beginning already. They took innocent moments and spun the stories they wanted. I was there the other night. I know what happened," she says, breaking the silence.

She continues. "Even if there's a time that I'm not there, I've learned to trust you in ways I don't trust many. I got on a tour bus with you three and a half weeks ago and then I said I do. That's a lot of trust, Bishop."

"Yeah, you're right."

I blow out a breath and scrub my hand down my face. Saga deserves so much better than this. I haven't been her husband for forty-eight hours yet and I'm fucking up.

"How was your show?" she asks.

"It sucked. My muse is gone. I couldn't get into it."

I lie back on the bed and stare up at the ceiling. I'd do anything to turn the clock back. I just need to go back to standing outside of that shop.

"I'm not gone. I'm right here in your enormous bed."

"I wish I were there with you. I bet you look sexy as fuck on my black sheets. I can't wait to stain them with your cum," I say as I think of her lying in my bed.

She laughs. "I stumbled across the linen closet. Babe, all your sheets are black."

I release a real laugh for the first time since the last time she was happy and secure in my arms. She makes everything so easy. Even as she's hurting, she's making this better for me. I love her all the more for it.

"We can change anything about the house you don't like."

"It's huge. Lots of room for a little family," she says hopefully.

"I'm ready whenever you are."

"Really?"

I smile at the excitement in her voice. I also hear the hint of surprise. This is all uncharted territory. Yeah, I've told her I want to be a father, but we never talked about us having a family or when we'd want to do that. Things most couples talk about before getting married.

"Yeah, babe. I want gorgeous babies with you as soon as you're ready. I hope they take solely after you. You're perfect," I say.

"How about little boys that look like you and girls that look like me? Even trade," she says sweetly.

"I don't care as long as they're with you, I'm happy."

I try to picture us lying in my bed together. Her belly swollen, our home filled with kids. I want all of that with her.

"Bishop?"

"Yeah, baby."

"I hate this." This time, I can hear her sobbing. "I know I'm doing the right thing. I know what I feel. I… I'm sorry. I'm going to go to bed."

"It's okay. I want you to talk to me. I love you. It's going to be okay."

"Okay. I have a headache. Can we talk later?"

"Yeah, sure. If you need me, call."

"Okay. I love you."

"I love you too. Sleep tight, gorgeous."

I hang up, feeling lost and sick. I stare at my bag, contemplating leaving anyway. It's only one show. We haven't canceled a concert in years.

"Fuck," I mumble.

If I do cancel, it's not going to go over well as this news of my marriage gets out. Fans will feel some way about it. That can go bad in so many ways.

I'm going to have to force myself to stay. I rub at my chest, trying to relieve the ache. I groan and sit up, pulling up the number I need to call to work through my thoughts.

"Hello," my mother answers, sleep clinging to her voice.

"Hey, Mom, it's Bishop."

"Hey, honey. Congratulations. I wanted to call you earlier, but your father said you were probably busy with the tour or stealing time to spend with your new bride."

"Thanks. That's sort of what I want to talk to you about."

"Ut-oh. What's going on?"

I blow out a breath and think of how to start. "I fucked up. Saga and I wanted to tell our families first. Then we were going to announce it to the world.

"It's just… when that reporter started talking shit, I lost it. All I could see…," I trail off and close my eyes.

"Bishop, honey. I know how bad things got with Bev, but we all saw that coming from a mile away. You loved her, so you thought she was someone she wasn't.

"I've kept my mouth shut because I know how much you were hurting. I didn't want to add to that. But let me tell you something. Bev wasn't a nice girl.

"I hate to speak ill of the dead, but she was conniving and had a wandering eye. Jag had come to me and your father a few times for advice on what to do about her. He saw she was going to break your heart."

"Really?" I raise my brows in shock.

"Yes, dear. He has always wanted to protect you as a friend as well as your manager."

I work my jaw as I take her words in. I've been so angry with Jag for butting in where Saga is concerned. I still don't think it's his business, but hearing he saw Bev for who she was and tried to shield me from that chaos causes me to pause.

I shake my head. I have enough on my plate. For now, I need to deal with this situation with Saga.

"Saga is different. I feel it in my bones. She's right for me. She's the one.

"I'd never forgive myself if the media placed a wedge between us, but that's the problem. I think that fear is only in my head. She took finding out about Bev and what happened so well. I'm the one who flew off the handle and put my foot in my mouth."

"It sounds like you need to finally give yourself grace. Saga wasn't a part of your past. You were.

"You're the one who needs to heal from all of that to move forward. If not, you will only see her as Bev when she sounds like anything but," Mom says gently.

I pull a hand down my face. "I know you're right. I have been healing. Because of Saga, I've been healing piece by piece. She smiles and the entire room lights up. When I look at her, music just flows through me, begging me to get it down.

"Since she walked into my life, each note has become a love note. She's everything to me. So much so that I know I can let go of the past. I'd choose her over it all any day," I breathe.

"Oh wow. Okay, so why do I hear a but?"

My mother knows me so well. I know how much I want Saga, but I'm not going to fool myself into thinking we'll get to move forward without a fight.

"You were right. Her parents aren't happy about us. She's so fucking upset. It's gutting me." Mom sighs heavily. "What? What aren't you saying?"

"Your father called Andre to ask him over for drinks to celebrate. He immediately realized Saga's parents have no idea you're our son. Andre vented to him as a friend and your father thought it best to stay quiet for now. I had a feeling this was the real reason for your call, but I didn't want to say anything if it wasn't," she says.

"Go on, say I told you so," I mumble.

"Why would I ever say that? You're my son. I love you and I want to see you happy.

"Saga must really love you; she has never gone against her father's wishes from what I know. I've told you how much he dotes on her and how highly he speaks of her.

"Honey, it will all work out. Your father and I were just as shocked and startled to hear you two were married, but we were both equally happy for you, if not more. I, for one, can't wait to meet her."

"Can you tell me more about her father? Maybe then I can understand how to fix this."

"Oh, Bishop, that's a conversation for your father, not me."

"What's going on?" I hear my dad ask in the background.

"You were right. Andre isn't taking things well. Saga is upset and Bishop wants to make things right. He wants to know more about Andre to know how to handle things," Mom explains.

"I'll talk to him. Give me the phone," Dad says.

"Hey, Bishop," Dad says tiredly.

"Hey, Dad, sorry it's so late."

"Don't worry about it. Congratulations, by the way. I'm proud of you, son."

"Thanks, Dad."

"How can I help?"

"I need to know how to get my father-in-law to like me so my wife will stop crying. Her family means everything to her."

"I wish you would have asked before you got married, but we're here now. Dr. Walden is upset because he doesn't know who you are. My friend would have gotten over a lot, but not knowing who you are is going to be the hurdle you have to overcome now."

"I need to show him who I am. Got it. What else can you tell me?"

I spend about another hour and a half learning who my father-in-law is from my father. I take notes and try my best to figure out how to right my wrongs because one thing I know for sure. I'm not losing my wife over this.

CHAPTER THIRTY

True Friends

Saga

"You suck," Isha pouts as she sips at her wine cooler.

"It was all spontaneous. It felt right, so I went with it," I say.

She gives me a mischievous smile. "It was the sex, wasn't it?"

"You're a nut," I chuckle, tossing the cap to my drink at her.

I love this woman. She's made me laugh all day since she arrived. I needed that to keep from crying nonstop.

"So what's the story with the giant who picked me up?"

"I was waiting for that question. I saw the way you were looking at him," I chuckle. "Honestly, I don't know. I think he's married, but I heard something about a divorce. I really don't know," I reply.

"Damn, it's always the fine ones who are taken," she frowns and crosses her chest with her arms.

"Like I said. I don't know. I could be wrong." I shrug.

"It's cool. I won't be here long. I was just curious," she says. She looks me in the eyes. "Don't freak out. I know you and Bishop said I could stay as long as I want, but I'm not trying to cockblock you. You guys are newlyweds."

"It's fine. There's plenty of room here."

"Yeah, I'm not about to be here with you and your new husband. I already booked an Airbnb. We can hang whenever you're free, but I'm going to get out of your hair."

"Isha." I pout.

"I'm thinking about making some changes. I need the time and space. Don't worry about me."

"Fine. When are you leaving?"

I'm more anxious about the answer than I let on. I thought I would have her here to distract me until Bishop gets back. He still has to go right to work on recording when he does return.

I was hoping I'd have Isha here to keep me company. Under different circumstances, her actions would be my own. Still, I wish she was staying.

"In the morning. Your bodyguard said he could drop me off," she says with a wince.

"My car is in the garage. You can take it," I offer.

"I'll think about it," she says.

We fall into silence. I pick at the label on my drink. My mind wanders to my parents, but I quickly close the door on that so I don't burst into tears.

"I'm happy for you," Isha says, drawing my attention from my thoughts.

"Thanks."

"It's all going to work out. Parents don't always know what's best. Mine aren't too happy with my latest choices, but I'm grown. It's my life. I'm doing what makes me happy," she says.

"What's going on?"

"I—"

"Hey, Saga," Dwayne's voice booms through the house. "Bishop is freaking the fuck out. Where's your phone?"

"Oh shit." I giggle. "Hold that thought."

"Go see what your man wants." She snickers.

Bishop

"Did Isha get settled okay? Dwayne said her flight was delayed, but he found her," I say nervously into the phone.

I pace my dressing room as I talk to my wife. I was losing my shit when she wasn't answering her phone. I thought she decided to take off and leave me after all.

"She's fine. We were just talking. She's going to an Airbnb in the morning," she says sadly.

"Babe, she can stay with us. She doesn't have to leave."

"I told her that. She wants to go. Don't worry about it. What time is your show?"

"In an hour. I just needed to hear your voice. I've been thinking about you nonstop."

It's the truth. I can't get her off my mind. I've been distracted all day.

I want to be there with her. The need to look her in the eyes and hold her in my arms is so strong I feel sick to my stomach from not being able to.

"Call me when it's over. I'll wait up."

"You sure?"

"Yeah, I want to talk to you," she says. "I miss you."

"I miss you too, babe. I'll call you as soon as I get off the stage. Love you, baby."

"Love you too. Break a leg."

I chuckle and hang up. I turn as the door to my dressing room opens. It's Jag.

"We need to talk," he says.

"Talk."

"You went behind my back and got married?" He seethes.

And this is where I get pissed off. There is a thin line between having my back and acting like he's in charge of my life. Jag's been taking shit too far.

I'm taken aback by his questioning me. I jerk my head back and frown. I don't remember when he became my boss.

"First, I can do whatever I want," I say.

"No, Bishop, you can't. This is why she's gone and you're still here moping through your last shows. If you would've told me, I could've covered your ass," he says.

"Why would I tell you when you've done nothing but give us shit? I don't even think Saga likes you." I snort.

"Whatever, I had to know she wasn't here to take you for a ride. You didn't give me a chance to do that either," he grumbles.

"I've got this. She's my wife. That's not going to change."

"Yeah, yeah, yeah. I got it. I'm here with a peace offering. I fucked up. She doesn't like me. I haven't done much to help with that.

"You have an hour, so make it fast," he says and opens the door for an older guy and a young woman to walk in.

"What's this?"

"Gómezes is the best jeweler I could find on short notice. Get your girl a ring, for fuck's sake. Bullshit-ass band she's walking around wearing," he mutters.

I grin. Jag's an asshole, but he means well. I stand and go to pull him into a hug.

"Thanks," I say.

He pulls away and slaps me on the shoulder. Years of friendship allow us to put this under the bridge.

"I'll fix the shit I've done," he says.

"She's stubborn. You're going to have to work pretty hard," I chuckle.

"Yeah, I know. I love you, bro. I just want to see you happy."

"As long as I have her, I'm the happiest man in the world."

CHAPTER THIRTY-ONE

Reality Bites

Saga

I haven't stopped sobbing for two days. My parents are still so mad at me. My sister thinks I'm crazy and my brother is hardly talking to me. Isha has been back and forth to check on me and to hang out, but I don't want to be a burden.

I feel alone and lost. This house is strange and huge. It doesn't feel like home to me. I thought I would stay with my family until Bishop returned, but not after what happened and what was said.

"Saga," Bishop's voice booms through the house.

I jump up from the bed where I've been buried in the covers, crying my eyes out. I nearly trip over the too-big T-shirt I have on. I pulled it from Bishop's closet because it smelled like him.

"Saga," he calls again.

I run out of the bedroom just as he jogs to the top of the stairs. I'm in his arms, wrapped around him as soon as he's in my sight. Having his arms around me is the first time in days that I've felt peace.

"They hate me," I sniffle.

"I'm going to fix this. I promise you," he says into my hair.

"I don't think you can," I sob.

"You don't know me well enough then. I'm going to make this right. I love you so much. I'm not going to lose you."

"I missed you," I say into his neck.

Being apart didn't make me love him less. If anything, I've fallen more in love with him. He's been calling nonstop. Instead of riding on the tour bus to get here, he flew in to get to me sooner.

I inhale his scent and break down completely. Something that feels so right shouldn't be called wrong. Yeah, we could have taken our time and waited to get married.

However, there's a part of me that feels like we were always meant to be together. Something just got crossed along the way to take us off the path we were supposed to be on. Now everything is right where it should be.

"I see you're wearing my shirt," he says as he places me on my feet on the bed to stand up in front of him.

I give a sheepish smile. "I wanted to feel close to you."

He buries his face in my stomach. I wrap my arms around his head as he embraces me. It feels like we've been a part for years, not days.

"My parents want to meet you," he says. "My mom is pissed she didn't get to help plan a wedding, but they're happy for us."

"Of course, I'm the one who makes this more complicated," I huff.

"Your dad isn't wrong. I should have done so much differently," he says, reaching into his pocket. "Like giving you this."

He opens a ring box and reveals the gorgeous ring inside. It's huge. I cover my mouth with my hands and drop to my knees on the bed.

"It's so beautiful," I gasp.

"Not as beautiful as you," he says, pulling the ring out of the box and placing it on my finger.

"Thank you," I say, leaning in to kiss his lips.

What starts as a soft kiss turns hot and heavy real fast. I tug the hem of my T-shirt up to pull it over my head, but he stills my action. I look at him in confusion.

"I came straight here from the last show. I need a shower and something in my stomach," he says with a smile.

"Oh."

"Don't worry. We're going to fuck. I've missed you and that sweet pussy. Shower, food, and you for dessert. Let's go," he says before tossing me over his shoulder and heading for the bathroom.

Bishop

Saga's sitting perched on the kitchen island in front of me while I sit between her legs on a stool. She has on another one of my T-shirts. It's hanging off her shoulder, revealing that gorgeous smooth skin.

She looks at her rings and beams as she chews on her pizza. I love that smile on her face. There's still a little sadness in her eyes, but the smile on her lips is undeniable. I think I love seeing that smile in my home more than anything.

"So your mom is throwing you a birthday party?" she says around a bite of pizza.

"Yeah, she invited your family, but I think we need to sit down before that to sort this mess out."

"You want to have everyone here? At your house," she says cautiously.

"Here, at our house," I say, running a hand up her thigh.

"My stomach hurts just thinking about it. My dad has said some harsh things. Maybe we should let things cool down a little longer," she says, chewing on her lip.

I shake my head. "No. I have to fix this. If your father comes here, he'll see my life up close. You said his biggest concern is me being able to provide for you. He also feels like he doesn't know me. This is a way for him to get to know me."

"Yeah, but I don't know," she says.

"Leave this to me. I think I can handle your dad."

She side-glances me and twists her lips up. I give her my best charming smile. She rolls her eyes at me.

"That's not going to work with my dad. He'll eat you alive," she chuckles.

"Maybe… I have an idea. We'll take a little time. Long enough for me to pull everything together. This will work," I say.

"I know that look," she says.

"Then you know I've got this. Trust me."

She eyes me warily for a beat before placing her pizza crust down and leaning in to wrap her arms around my neck. She places a soft kiss on my lips, then my cheek. Grasping her thighs, I tug her closer.

"I trust you. More than you know," she says.

"All we have to do is show them this," I say, brushing her hair out of her face. "How can anyone see us together and not get that we belong together?"

"Good question," she says against my lips.

"I think I'm ready for my dessert. How about you?" I croon.

"I've been ready."

I crush our lips together and kiss her deeply. I don't know how to just take a sip of her. I need her in gulps. It's as if I'm trying to get to that spark that ignites between us.

I drag my lips from hers to nip and lick her chin, moving to her neck. I lift to my feet and tug her closer still as her fingers thread in my still-damp hair. I reach for the hem of the T-shirt she has on and she lifts her hips so I can get it up and over her head.

"We're going to fuck on every surface in this house. I've been waiting to find you to make this house a home," I say while looking at her naked body perched on the kitchen island.

"Come here," she says, tugging my head to her breast.

I wrap my lips around her waiting peak, sucking hard. She lifts her hips, but I place my hands on them to pin them to the cool marble. Sliding one hand to her inner thigh, I slip two fingers into her heat.

"That's my baby, ready to come for me already," I say against her breast. "Give me."

"It's yours," she gasps as she comes around my fingers.

Removing my fingers from her center, I flip her body until she's on the counter on her knees. Reaching for the shirt I peeled from her body, I double the fabric and place it under her for a cushion. Leaning in, I inhale her scent, smacking my lips.

"Settle in, baby. I'm going in for a full course," I murmur.

Her screams begin to fill the air as I dive in. It's a good thing I sent Dwayne home. I promise she's not going to have a voice when I'm done.

"Yes, baby, yes," she cries out.

I growl into her as she gushes into my mouth. Saga will never know how crazy her screams and wet pussy drive me. I part her cheeks with my hands and work my tongue in a rapid motion.

When I feel her on the verge of coming, I shove two fingers into her and slap her ass with my free hand. The scream that pierces the air blows through my chest as well. It sinks in who I just made come.

"My wife," I say in a heavy rumble.

I need to feast on her again as that realization sets in. I shove my sweats to the floor and palm my cock, stroking while I eat her up. She tries to sink down onto the counter, but I'm not having that.

I band an arm around her waist to hold her up, fastening her to my face. Her legs tremble beneath her, bringing a smile to my lips. I turn my attention to her tight ring, dragging my tongue there.

"I want to have you here," I groan.

"What?" she pants and turns to look at me.

"I want to take you here."

"Wait, wait. I… I'm a virgin there," she says with big eyes.

Oh fuck yeah.

My heart starts to pound with the thought of being the first to have her fat ass. My teeth sink into my lower lip. I squeeze my dick in my palm.

"You're going to give it to me," I say in more of a command than a question.

The pinch of her brow tells me she's worried and unsure. I knead her cheek. My eyes are locked on hers, beckoning her trust and surrender.

"Yes," she whispers.

"That's my girl," I say. "Don't move."

Kicking my sweats from around my ankles, I take off for the bedroom upstairs. I've never moved so fast in my damn life. I grab the lube from my bedside drawer, snatch a few condoms and head for the closet. With a few towels in hand and the rest of my haul, I run back down the stairs.

When I get back, she stares at my erection with her lip trapped between her teeth. I move behind her and kiss her ass. I slow down to lick and caress the globes.

"I'll be gentle. I promise I'll take care of you," I say to ease her worry.

"Okay," she says breathlessly.

I pour the lube and let it drip between her cheeks. My mouth is back on her pussy as I work the lube into her pucker. She starts to relax under my touch, moaning and grinding her hips.

"That's it. Stay right here with me," I murmur.

She moans and pushes her pussy into my face. I take my time getting her ready while I tease and torture her core. She's dripping wet with anticipation and so am I.

When I feel like we both can't take anymore waiting, I reach for a condom and bite it open. I roll on the condom and pour more lube on my latex-covered erection.

"Come here, Saga. I need you," I say, plucking her from the counter and setting her on her feet.

Placing a palm on the center of her back, I bend her over the countertop. She grasps hold of the edges of the counter. My head is buzzing with need.

I start to push in slowly and her body tenses. I grasp beneath her chin and tilt her head back. We lock eyes and I wait for her to relax.

"That's it," I grunt.

I push farther in and her lips part. Her nostrils flare and she lifts her palm to cover the wrist of the hand I have holding her face. I still and wait for her to acclimate. She gives a small nod and I push all the way in.

"Bishop," she cries out.

I cover her mouth and swallow her moans. I reach for her clit, working her nub as I set a slow pace. Soon I'm moving with ease and start to pick up my pace.

"Damn," I grind out as her ass claps against my pelvis. "This is my ass. You feel so fucking good."

Her eyes cross as she screams some nonsense. I grin and pound harder. I'm going to come. It rises from my toes to the base of my spine as my balls draw up.

I release her face to grasp a hold of her waist. My eyes fall to her ass, her cheeks clapping around my cock as I drive forward. Saga claws at the countertop, but can't find purchase.

I grab a handful of the front of her hair, and with my other hand, I start to finger her and pound at the same time. She loses it. When she gives an open-mouthed, silent scream, I roar with satisfaction, releasing into the barrier between us.

I've snatched her fucking voice and I have no remorse about it. I'm seconds from beating my damn chest. Dipping my head, I suck on the skin of her shoulder before giving it a little nip.

"Oww," she says hoarsely and wiggles her ass. "Bi…"

She can't even get my name out. Her voice is officially stripped. I slap her ass and chuckle.

"Come on, baby. There's more house to bless."

CHAPTER THIRTY-TWO

Settling In

Saga

"Have you decided which rooms you want to change?" Bishop murmurs against the top of my head as we lie in bed.

We've only moved to shower and brush our teeth this morning after we returned to bed for a lazy day in. Bishop will have to head into the studio tomorrow. I'm soaking in all the love and attention I can get.

Resting in his arms has gone a long way to soothe my emotions. I run my hand across his bare chest and inhale. He's so warm and comforting.

I clear my throat, before trying to speak through my horse voice. "Can I be honest?"

"Of course."

"It hasn't felt like home, so I didn't think much about it."

He's silent for a moment, but I swear I can hear him thinking. He runs his fingertips up and down my spine, pulling me further under his spell.

"You don't like this place? We can look for another."

"No, that's not what I'm saying."

"You said it doesn't feel like home. I want our place to feel like yours."

"It didn't feel like home when I got here. Not until you got back. Where you are is my home. Now it feels right. Let me think about if I would change anything. I'll let you know."

"That's fair. I just want you happy. Say the word and I'll make it happen."

"Thank you."

"For?"

"Always making sure I'm taken care of. Since the day we met, you've been looking out for me. I think that's what made me fall in love with you. You didn't know me, but you did everything in your power to make sure I was all right."

"I'd do it again in a heartbeat."

"I love you."

He tips my head back and takes my lips in a devouring kiss. My toes curl and I start to get wet all over again. After last night, I would think I couldn't or wouldn't want more sex, but the exhaustion is forgotten as my body softens for him.

"I love you too," he breathes against my lips as he breaks the kiss and pushes into me.

"Bishop," I moan through my raw voice.

"Fuck, I can't get enough of you," he groans.

I wrap my legs around his waist and dig my nails into his back. Suddenly, it's like our time together all starts to play in my head. The first time I looked into his eyes, the talk we had that first night.

All the talks in between. This man has charmed me and broken into my heart with his lyrics, but most of all, with his attention to what I need. Like now, he's gentle as he rocks me to my climax.

It's not rough and demanding like last night. His movements are slow and sensual. Each kiss he places against my skin speaks its own love language. A language I've become accustomed to and now crave.

"Yes, yes, oh my god," I cry out as best I can.

Bishop

As much as I want to lie here and hold Saga in my arms all day, I need to get up and feed us both. She's passed out again, looking absolutely gorgeous in my bed.

Earlier when she said this didn't feel like home, I started to think of all the neighborhoods I wouldn't mind raising a family in. I was ready to move into her dream home if that's what it took to make her happy.

Hearing her say home is where I am made my heart swell. I feel the same way. I can't stop smiling as I pull on a pair of sweats and head downstairs.

"Hey, Chan," I say to my chef, Chandler.

"Bishop," he croons. "What's going on, man? It's good to see you back. I see congratulations are in order."

"Thanks, bro. Have you met her?"

"Not yet, today's my first day back."

I nod. I didn't want to overwhelm Saga with my staff, so I asked my house manager not to have them all come in until I returned. I'm sure Dwayne took care of her food while I was away.

"You want anything special?"

"The usual will be fine," I reply, taking a seat. "I think she'll like those apple tarts you make. Can you make some of those for her?"

"The ones with the caramel dipping sauce? Sure, no problem. Those go nice with the sage sausage."

"Sounds great." I rap my knuckles on the countertop. "I'm headed down to the studio. I want to get something down."

"No worries, I'll bring your plate down."

"Thanks."

I stand and start to hum to myself as the music fills me. It's been silent in my head since the day Saga left the tour. Now I can hear the music clearly. The colors are back in my head.

CHAPTER THIRTY-THREE

Life Changes

Saga

I can't help snickering at Isha as she ogles Dwayne as he leaves the kitchen we're sitting in. She begins to fan her face and shakes her head. When she turns toward me, she pulls a face with her mouth hanging open.

"What?" I ask through my laughter.

"You can laugh all you want, but did you see that? God, he smells so good. How are you that damn big and walk with all that swag?

"Ugh, the man is just comfortable in his skin. And that ass… phew. He's fine, fine."

I can only smile. I only have eyes for my husband, but I do know his cousin is an attractive man. I find it funny because I've seen the way Dwayne checks her out when he thinks no one is looking.

Isha is very pretty with her natural carrottop and nutmeg skin tone. She has the prettiest hazel eyes that almost give her a cartoonlike appearance. I've always admired her wild long curls, although she hates them and keeps them in a gelled-up bun most of the time.

I can totally see why he's been checking her out. Isha remains fit from work and her personal workouts. Then, my friend also has a welcoming personality. It wasn't hard to become and remain friends with her.

"Did you find out more about his situation?" I ask.

Dwayne picked her up to give her a ride to the house. I wonder if she pried during the drive. It's clear something happened between her and Emory, her on-again, off-again boyfriend back in New York.

She hasn't said anything yet, but I know she will when she's ready. She's always been this way. I get the feeling this trip was right on time.

She turns to me with wide eyes. The expression says she has all the tea. Giving me a look as if to say, *Can we go somewhere private to talk?* she hops up from her stool.

I grab her hand and lead her upstairs, dragging her into the walk-in closet I had been organizing when she arrived. Pushing aside the boxes Bishop had picked up from my sister's, I take a seat on the floor in the center of the closet. Isha sits cross-legged across from me.

"Okay, so he's not *single* single. He's in the middle of a divorce. He's a daddy.

"The kids are cute and the proud look on his face as he showed them to me—God, my ovaries were pulsing. He's a nice guy."

"*But*," I drag out, hearing the word in her voice.

"I think I like him and would like to get to know him," she murmurs.

I lift a brow because I still hear that but lurking as she speaks. She's beating around the real issue here. Now that we're talking, I can see the interest she truly has.

She sighs. "He's going through a lot. I'm going through a lot." She scoffs. "I'm not sure I've figured my shit out. He's been so nice to me, but… it's not like he's asked me out or anything. He just looks at me like he wants to eat me."

I burst into laughter and fall over. She shoves at me and pouts. I try to sober up and pull her into my embrace, then rock her back and forth.

"You know you want to be eaten," I laugh. "Are you thinking about moving?"

I don't miss that she's interested in a guy who lives in Cali when she lives in New York. I know Isha and she's not the long-distance type.

She pulls from my embrace and looks me in the eyes. "I'm just saying. If I did live in California, I wouldn't mind running into him when he gets his shit settled. He makes cute babies, after all."

"I would love to have you here. What's going on with your job?"

She shrugs and looks down in her lap. "It's time for a change in all areas of my life. My best friend, who never takes chances, stepped out of her comfort zone and it's paid off. I'm following in her footsteps.

"I'm not going to end up with a rock star, but I could end up happy. I deserve that, right?"

I'm caught off guard when the tears begin to spill onto her cheeks. Her lips tremble and she looks up as if trying not to allow the rest of the tears to fall. I reach for her hands and take them into mine.

"Isha. What's going on, hon?"

"I never should have dated someone I worked with. Emory and I are *over* over. He's been fucking Jenny from the marketing team. They're engaged now.

"Do you know how hard it is to walk into work and see that shit? They're all booed up and he couldn't commit to me to save his own life. Like, what does she have that I don't? Why string me along to play with my feelings like this?"

"Oh, Isha. It's his loss. Now she has to deal with that childish bullshit. Not you. You deserve way better."

She purses her lips and shrugs. "I'm thinking about moving here to be close to my bestie. You're all I have. I don't want to be alone."

I cup her face. "You will never be alone. I'm always here for you. My shit isn't together, but I'll do anything I can to help you out."

She wraps her arms around my neck and holds me tight. I know things have been hard for her. She won't tell me why, but her relationship with her mom and stepdad is strained. They bump heads so much that she doesn't talk to them much.

I think that's why we bonded so quickly when we met. I would love to have her here with me. I haven't even thought about what I plan to do next.

"We'll figure things out together," I say as I give her a squeeze.

Bishop

I climb the stairs with a mug of tea in my hands. My vocal cords are tired from all the stacks I've done for the songs we recorded today. Recording an album is a lot harder than people realize.

My body is exhausted. Going from touring straight into recording is taking its toll. A smile comes to my face, knowing my wife is at the top of these stairs, resting in our bed.

I pick up the pace and start into a jog to get there faster. It feels good to have someone waiting for me. Although I was disappointed to miss dinner with her.

"Hey, baby," I croon as I enter our room.

"Hey," she sings back.

She's in our bed wearing one of my shirts again. It's one of my tank tops. Her hardened nipples are pushing at the thin fabric, bringing a grin to my face.

She has a white scarf tied around her head and a huge smile on her face. God, she looks great against my sheets, just as I knew she would. I walk over to the bed and drop a kiss on her forehead.

"Were you waiting up for me?"

She shrugs. "Aw, babe. Your voice. I was waiting up and thinking. Why don't you get ready for bed? We can cuddle. You don't have to talk."

"I'm fine." I give her a wink.

Placing my mug down, I head into my closet to change into a pair of sweats. When I return, she's under the covers and has left my side turned back. I climb in and get settled with my back against the headboard, then I finish my tea as Saga snuggles into my side.

"How was your day? Did you have fun with Isha?" I ask.

"I love having her here. We had fun. She helped me get my stuff unpacked and kept my mind off things. Seriously, Bishop. You should rest your voice, baby."

I lean to peck her lips. "I wouldn't miss this chance to spend time with my wife and ask about her day. I missed you, baby. You've been on my mind all day."

She moves to straddle my lap and cups my face in her little palms. Pressing her forehead to mine, she's silent as we breathe each other in for a bit.

"I love you so much. I could sit just like this for hours. No need for words," she says after a few beats.

"I was thinking the same thing."

"Good," she purrs, then leans to rest her head on my shoulder.

I wrap my arms around her and hold her tightly against my chest. I can't believe I'll get to do this for the rest of my life. As my lids grow heavy, thoughts of how great our lives will be fill my head.

CHAPTER THIRTY-FOUR

Come On, Really?

Saga

I'm still getting used to living with Bishop. His work hours are insane, so we don't get time together much. He promised things would slow down for a little bit once the album was fully recorded.

I feel bad when he comes up for the night and his voice is all sore and tired. Most mornings, he's up and has disappeared down in the basement where his studio is before I get up.

Like this morning, I wake to cool sheets and I'm disappointed I didn't wake in time to watch him get ready. I sigh and stretch in bed before getting up to shower and get ready for my day.

I'm going to spend the day with Isha at her Airbnb. I haven't driven my car yet and I thought heading to see her and going out to shop would be fun. I can show her around all my old stomping grounds.

"Ugh," I growl as I step into the bathroom. "Come on, really?"

I stomp my foot and roll my eyes. I'm still adjusting to living with a man. One of the things Bishop does that drives me crazy is leaving his wet towels on the bathroom floor.

It's gross and annoying. Especially when I stepped on them the first few times as I woke groggy and stumbled across them. I've fussed at him a few times already and he promises to break the habit, but he hasn't done so yet.

"I want to wring his neck," I mutter to myself as I snatch the towels up and go to toss them in the hamper. "See how easy that is?"

I know he has a housekeeper he's used to having around to pick up after him, but the least he can do is put the darn things in the freaking hamper. I shake my head and strip from my clothes to take my shower.

My mind drifts to my parents. I can hear them saying I told you so. If I'd gotten to know Bishop more before marrying him, I could have addressed the annoying habit. I roll my eyes.

If I think about it, that's the one thing we're bumping heads about. I guess my husband has been too busy for us to be in each other's hair. Although, speaking of hair. The man has tons of it and it's always in the sink.

"Stop it, Saga. You're being grumpy," I chide myself. "Yup, you need out of this house."

***

I pull up to the address Isha gave me with a smile on my face. It's a nice house with a great location. My good mood can be attributed to the warm weather and the quiet ride over.

Bishop tried to insist that Dwayne drive me. I get that I'm now married to a famous rock star, but I still know how to drive. I allowed Dwayne to tag along, but I drove myself.

Dwayne had been super quiet during the ride. I'd left him to his thoughts. The truth is, I missed my car.

I'm also super happy that my car seems to be running good as new. I'll have to thank Bishop properly when I get back home tonight. I want him to know how much I appreciate his help.

Since I fussed at him about the towels and trying to force Dwayne to drive, it wouldn't hurt to have a makeup session when he's done working tonight. I didn't miss how annoyed he was as I left.

Isha steps her cute little self out of the house, her attention focused on her phone. I laugh to myself as I take her in. Yesterday must have been wash day. She has her hair in two corn braids on each side of her head, taking ten years off her age.

Not that she looks thirty, to begin with. Her shorts are short but tasteful. They show off her toned legs and look cute with the high-top sneakers and T-shirt she has on.

To my surprise, Dwayne makes a groaning sound beside me. I look to him as he shakes his head to himself as if to clear it, then silently climbs out of the car. Isha is so focused on her phone she does a double take as Dwayne holds the door open for her.

"Hey," she whispers.

"Hey." He nods.

Isha climbs into the car then reaches to run a hand over her hair. Then she turns to me and scowls, widening her eyes at me as if to ask why I didn't warn her that Dwayne was coming along. I reach for one of her braids and finger the pretty curls at the tip beneath the band, holding the end closed.

"You look adorable. Ready to do some shopping?"

"Retail therapy is in dire need. Lead the way, my friend."

I laugh and start the car as Dwayne settles in the back seat, once again lost in his thoughts. I can't help wondering if his mind has been on his family situation. I haven't asked Bishop anything about it because it's none of my business.

"Oh, I love this song. Turn it up," Isha says.

I tune into what's playing. It's one of Bishop's old songs. I can't help biting my lip as I hear his voice croon the sensual song. I get why my father finds his music to be crude.

The old stuff is such a contrast to the new music he's writing. I did notice the difference during the tour. Not all of it was over-the-top provocative, but the majority was pretty close.

Isha and I sing along until her phone pings, grabbing her attention. Looking out the corner of my eye, I see her look down at it and a scowl comes to her pretty face. Instantly her mood changes.

"Are you fucking kidding me?" she growls.

I stop at a stop sign and turn to fully look at her. She's now staring silently out of the window. In the reflection of the glass, I can see the sadness in her expression.

I glance in the rearview to find Dwayne with his gaze locked on her. I don't ask her what's wrong because he's in the car with us. I note to remember to ask later.

I sigh to myself. I knew getting married would change my life. However, I didn't take into account all the changes that would come from marrying a famous rock star.

"Get used to it, Saga. Dwayne will be with you until I hire someone for you full time," Bishop had said before I left the house.

I guess this is my life now.

CHAPTER THIRTY-FIVE

Hot Bullshit

Saga

"Saga Walden-Moran, you've been served," the guy standing on my doorstep says.

I look down at the envelope in my hand with my brows drawn. I'm so confused. Who in the world could be serving me and for what? I haven't done anything to be sued for.

My heart starts to race. Does Bishop want a divorce? I thought things were going great between us. It's been two weeks, but we haven't had more drama than me fussing about his wet towels all over the bathroom.

I'm still staring blankly at the envelope in my hand when the front door opens and Bishop walks in. He stops and looks at me curiously. His eyes taking on concern.

"What's going on?" he asks, closing the door behind him and pulling me into his embrace.

Okay. Not divorce papers.

"I don't know. I was just served. I haven't opened it yet," I reply.

He takes the envelope from my hand and opens it. I watch his face as he reads over the documents. His face goes from confused to red with rage. Pulling his phone from his pocket, he scrolls through then places a call.

"Hey Garry," he says into the phone.

He looks up at me and places the call on speaker. The voice of an older-sounding man comes through the line. I'm still confused as to what's going on.

"The wife was just saying I should have you over for dinner," Garry says.

"I'd love to do that sometime, but this call is for business. My wife is being sued by her piece-of-shit former boss. The same boss who fired her and had her blackballed after she refused to sleep with him.

"I was a potential client of his a few months back. It was around the time she was still an employee. I hadn't met her at the time and still didn't know her when I decided not to use their firm.

"He's stating that she poached me as a client and stole his campaign. The bullshit campaign that was pitched to me doesn't even come close to what Saga has done since I hired her," he fumes into the phone.

"That's some nasty business. Send the documents over to my office for me to take a look. It may look sketchy if we file a sexual harassment suit at this point, but I'm willing to start digging to see what we can do," Garry says.

"On second thought…" Bishop says and takes a pause. "I need to call in a few favors. We'll talk."

He hangs up the phone, his eyes trained on me. I'm ready to scream. I can't believe that asshole Tom is still at it.

"This is so un-fucking-believable," I grit out. "I never slept with Evan. We dated. Never had sex. Tom is such an asshole! The fact that this man is trying to ruin my life because he couldn't get in my pants… I'm so pissed I could light his ass on fire."

He pulls me into his arms and holds me. "I'll take care of it. I don't want you to even think about this another second."

"I feel like everything is coming apart at the seams," I push out.

"Good thing I learned to sew in high school," he says.

"What?" I look up at him. "Seriously?"

"Yup," he kisses my nose. "All the girls were in home ec. While all the other guys were running from cooking and sewing, I was right there with the girls, becoming their best friend."

I stare at him for a moment, then burst into laughter. I can't even imagine a big-ass teenage Bishop in a home ec class, but I can so imagine him doing something like this to be where the girls were.

Smooth.

My husband has been smooth from day one. I tighten my arms around him. I know, in my heart, he'll make this better. I hope he countersues Tom and Carmichael, Pike, and Jeffreys for all they're worth.

I'm done with my past.

Bishop

"You all right, baby?" I say into Saga's ear as she sits between my legs.

I have the fireplace going as we sit on the rug and take a moment to decompress. A bottle of wine is open, but I have a beer for myself. Music is playing softly throughout the house through the surround sound system.

"Yeah, I'm fine," she says as I begin to massage her shoulders.

I'm so proud of Saga. I thought for sure she was going to fall apart after being served with that bullshit lawsuit. The audacity of that motherfucker.

After making the necessary calls, I made it my business to push all thoughts of the bullshit to the back of my mind so I could focus on Saga and her needs.

We have the next few days off from recording. Though most are single, the guys need to spend time with their families. We're not machines and I'm not about to treat them as such.

We'll get it done, but the guys have things to handle just as I need to handle this. Saga's happiness is a priority for me. I've seen the struggles she's been having. It's not just about her family.

Saga is adjusting to the reality of who I am and who she's married to. I should have thought of all this before dragging her to the altar. Although, I wouldn't change a thing.

I love her more with each day. That's why I'm giving our marriage all my patience and understanding. For the most part, she's made all the changes and sacrifices.

The least I can do is remember to pick up a few towels. I'm working on that. It's not something I do in hotels or on the bus.

However, at home, I have a full staff. As I did while growing up and living with my parents. In some small way, the action brings me the feeling of home.

I shake off my musings and focus on my wife. Her head lulls to the side as she rests in my arms. I dip my head and kiss her neck, feeling some of the tension leave her body.

"You want to talk about it?"

"Talk about what exactly? I've been nothing but drama since I've entered your life."

"Don't go there, baby. You know I don't see it that way."

"I thought I would be able to ignore the bullshit. I don't want to be so pissed about any of it, but I can't help feeling angry, violated, and so damn disrespected," she bites out.

"And you have a right to all those emotions. This isn't right and it shouldn't be happening, but there are the assholes of the world. They only care about themselves, not how their actions affect others.

"It's total bullshit, I know, but you can't allow it to ruin your happiness. That's the bastard's objective. He wants to disturb your peace because he can't shut you down and punish you for not giving in to him and his childish behavior," I say.

Saga sits up and turns to straddle me. I hate the sadness I see in her eyes. However, it quickly turns to determination.

"I want to forget about it all. My parents, Tom, New York. Anything that doesn't make me happy like you do, I want to block it all out for tonight," she says while staring into my eyes.

I nod and drop my gaze to her hardening nipples, pushing at the thin shirt she's wearing. It's been too long since I've ravaged her body. Between late nights in the studio and the exhaustion, I haven't been able to give her the attention she needs in that department.

I grasp her by the throat and look down into her eyes. "Are you looking for something like this to take your mind off things?" I say before giving a gentle squeeze and crushing her lips with mine.

"Yes," she gasps as I start to trail kisses down the side of her neck.

She reaches for my shirt and tugs it up over my head. I return the favor and toss the long shirt she's been wearing aside. My mouth runs dry when the sheer black bra and pantie set she has on comes into view.

I can see her stiff peaks through the fabric. This must be from her shopping trip. I noticed all the lingerie bags she returned with. I wasn't able to explore or inquire then, but I plan to explore the scrap of fabric now.

I cup her breasts in my hands as I look into her eyes and squeeze them in my palms. I lick my lips as she releases a moan. She rocks her hips against me as if she can't wait to have me inside her.

I can't wait either, but I'm not going to rush this. Her hair falls into her eye, covering it from my view, but I can't miss the passion and lust emitting from her gaze.

She sucks her bottom lip into her mouth. The way she looks back at me has me rock hard. I'm going to make her come so fucking hard.

"Saga, baby, you're so fucking gorgeous."

"Babe," she whimpers.

I dip my head and capture one of her peaks in my mouth. She laces her fingers into my hair and tightens her grasp. I groan, sucking harder at her sweet, tight bud.

"Damn, you smell so fucking good."

"I want to feel you inside me. I want you."

"You want me to what? Fuck you hard. You want me to take that tight pussy until it can't get wet anymore? What do you want?" I croon.

"Yes, all of that. I want you to suck me, fuck me, and own me. Take my body. It's yours. Only yours."

I slide my hand into her panties and cup her heated sex. She's so damn hot down there. Her heat beckons me to slip a finger into her.

I oblige it with two. She moans and rolls her head back. I can't tear my eyes away from her as she rides my fingers.

I keep pumping as she rocks on my digits. Cupping the back of her neck, I drag her face closer to mine. Before I can shove my tongue into her mouth, she shoves hers into mine. I take it and suck on it as she gushes all over my hand.

Finding her G-spot, I tap it until she begins to whimper and convulse, not allowing her to pull her mouth away from mine. When the tremors rocking her body slow, she reaches to release me from my sweats.

I finally allow her to pull away, but not before I nip and tug at her lower lip as she goes. Saga climbs from my lap and drops to her knees in front of me.

"Come here, Bishop. Stand up for me, babe."

With a grin on my lips, I climb to my feet and stand before her. I cup the side of her face as she looks up at me. The sight of her sends my heart racing.

"You're so perfect," I breathe.

Without a word, she palms me, then covers me with her mouth. I lift a brow at her while biting my lip. As if I'm not giving her what she wants, she grabs my sweats and yanks them down my legs.

Snapping out of it, I kick them the rest of the way off and widen my stance. She gives me an approving smile around my shaft. I groan and palm the back of her head as she works my cock, milking me for all I'm worth.

"Fuck, baby. Just like that. You're sucking me so good."

She backs off with saliva dripping down her chin and a smile on her lips. So fucking beautiful and all mine. I cup her jaw with one hand and my dick with the other.

"Open for me, baby."

Forcing her mouth open, I guide my way back into her mouth. She sucks me greedily. With a dark chuckle, I pull back out before shoving my way back into her mouth.

I repeat the action a few more times before allowing her to take over. Her whimpers drive me insane.

She backs me up the few steps to the couch and pushes me onto my ass. I drop with a slight bounce. Before I can take over, she steps from her panties and climbs onto the couch on her knees and takes me into her mouth again, her ass high in the air.

"*Fuck*," I drag out as the sound of her slurping and sucking fills the air.

I release my hair and drag a hand through it. I tighten my jaw as she rubs my length against her puckered lips. Tilting her head, she sucks on the sides and hums happily.

Suddenly, I buck my hips off the couch as she sucks my balls into her mouth. I slouch down farther in my seat and widen my legs. I groan so loud it vibes through me.

"You like that, baby?" she purrs.

"Fuck, baby. Yes, you're driving me crazy."

She takes me back in deep, causing me to pump my hips. I drop my gaze to her ass and reach to palm her full globes. I knead her cheeks, then slip my fingers into her wet pussy. She hums against me as I work her dripping heat.

"Oh shit," Saga gasps as she backs off to suck in a breath.

I pull my hand free from her heat and slap her fat ass. Then, slowly, I rub the sting away and lean over to kiss the spot. She moans and twerks her ass. Reaching to finger her again, I suck my lips into my mouth as it's all I can do to keep from taking control and fucking her into this couch.

"Come for me, baby. I want to watch you come apart while you're sucking me," I grit through my teeth.

I feel the moment she relaxes her throat to take me all the way down. I have to use all my restraint not to come. Pulling out of her mouth, I roughly push her onto her back and hover over her body with mine.

I kiss her hard as I find her opening with my dick. I rub against her folds for a few seconds before I slide home. Instead of quenching the fire, it's like it consumes me.

I grasp a tight hold of her waist and grind into her as my eyes roll back. I love that she's grinding back on me. I take this pussy down like it owes me something. How I've gone without this in the last few days, I have no clue.

I come over and over and keep pounding. Saga is right with me, begging for more. The love in her eyes as I own her body says she's my other half. We're on the same page, like always.

"I love you," we say in unison as we come together one final time.

CHAPTER THIRTY-SIX

Band & Friends

Bishop

After yesterday, I know we need to do something to get our minds off things. I happened to overhear Saga on the phone with Isha, talking about going to the amusement park.

Let me tell you how much I love my wife because I absolutely hate amusement parks. The walking, my height when it comes to the rides. There is such a thing as being too tall for stuff. Then there are the crowds and the fact that I'm Bishop Love.

It's all a recipe for disaster. I already hate the places, put all those things together and I loathe them, but hearing the excitement in her voice and knowing I'd need to send Dwayne with her anyway, I decided to text the guys and see if they wanted to make a day of it—so here we all are.

"Cheese," Saga sings as she tosses up a peace sign after Fendi tosses an arm around her shoulders and tugs her into him.

I roll my eyes at him. All the guys have been trying to goad me now that they know Saga's my wife. It's not working.

I know Saga has grown to see them all as friends, like big brothers, if nothing else. I couldn't be happier about that. All the guys had been wary of Bev.

The differences I've noticed in hindsight. The red flags were everywhere. I shake my head clear and wrap my arm around Saga's neck to tug her into my side.

"What's up first?" I murmur against her temple.

"Where are the bumper cars? Cotton candy and bumper cars are always first."

Just as she says the words, Dwayne shows up with cotton candy in his hands. Isha needed to find a bathroom. I wasn't okay with her wondering off on her own since pictures have appeared online of her and Saga together.

People now know who my wife and her best friend are. On one hand, it's cool because Isha's social following has increased and she's been getting calls to book private yoga and Pilates classes.

She's been seriously thinking of making California her home. I have a friend taking her around to look at potential studios. I'm happy for Saga; her friend will be here with her.

On the other hand, people knowing who Isha is places her in harm's way. I don't think either Saga or Isha have grasped this yet. I didn't want to startle either of them, so Dwayne discreetly offered to follow Isha and grab some cotton candy.

Each of the guys brought along their security teams. They're all in plain clothes, but they're around. I take a glance around just to settle my nerves.

Fendi pulls his shades down his nose to look Isha over. He, Thrush, and Bop arrived after Isha went to the restroom.

"Hey, I don't think we've met," he croons.

"Hi. I'm Isha, Saga's bestie," she says.

"Fendi," he says smoothly and holds his hand out.

"I know who you are. Nice to meet you in person though."

"Naw, this is all my pleasure."

Bop bumps him out of the way. "Stay away from this guy. He's trouble. Bartholomew, but everyone calls me Bop," he says.

"I did not know that was your real name." Saga snickers.

"Hey, watch it Moran," Bop scolds with a teasing smile.

Thrush holds his hand out. "Nice to meet you, Red. This family outing just got more interesting. Dibs," he croons.

"What? Have you lost your mind?" Fendi says incredulously.

I'm sure wishing he thought to call dibs first. Dwayne hands Saga her cotton candy and then walks off with a frown. I feel bad for him. From our talks, he has a thing for Isha, but he's still in the middle of a nasty divorce—long story. He's not going to drag her into the middle of that and he's not going to ask her to wait around for him either.

Talk about being stuck between a rock and a hard place. I catch Saga's gaze on Dwayne and see the questions in her eyes. I sigh and decide to mind my business for now.

The group makes its way to the bumper cars. We all climb into our cars and the fun begins. Both Saga and Isha have smiles on their faces.

This is what I want for my wife and her best friend. With everything going on with Saga, she's still worried about her friend. This day was more for Isha than Saga as far as my wife is concerned, but I feel they both need it.

My heart swells as Saga's laughter rings out. My guys look relaxed and happy too—baseball caps, shades and all. I guess we all need this.

I glance at my cousin. If only I could help him kick back and relax. Saga crashes into me and laughs like a maniac. I smile wide and shake my head.

"Head in the game, babe. We're not here to play around."

"You asked for it," I warn, only to have Isha run into my other side.

She's laughing just as hard. That is until Fendi and Bop crash into her, their deep chuckles replacing her laugh. She scowls at them both.

"Oh, you're gonna pay," she growls.

Just then, Thrush rear-ends her. I shake my head and take off for my wife, she's not getting away so easily. We go through and do the bumper cars at least two more times.

After, we mill around and play a few games, winning stuffed animals for Saga and Isha. Dwayne won the biggest stuffed animal and took the smaller ones the other guys won for Isha so she could hold his.

I'm not sure what he did with the others, but I think he may have tossed them in the trash. Things are going to get interesting around here for sure.

Saga

"I can't believe you didn't tell me how much you hate amusement parks," I say as we enter our bedroom.

My feet are killing me, but I had so much fun. This was the best day ever. I flop face down on the bed and groan.

"You wanted to go. I wasn't going to whine about it because I can't stand the places. My feet are killing me, but it was fun," he says.

"I was thinking the same thing," I say into the mattress.

Bishop chuckles. He's moving around, but I can't find the energy to lift my head and look at him. I know I need to get up and strip my clothes off, but I can't find the energy to do that either.

I think I doze for a second as Bishop comes and pulls my shoes from my feet. He reaches beneath me to unfasten my jean shorts and pulls them from my body.

Next, he takes my panties off. Then he lifts me from the bed and carries me into the bathroom. I smile when I hear the water running in the bathtub.

Bishop sets me on my feet in the bath, then removes my T-shirt and bra. I focus my eyes on him to find he's already naked.

He steps in with me and lowers our bodies into the water. I sigh and melt into his chest as we settle in the warm water. Bishop palms my forehead and tilts my head back to drop a kiss on my lips. I smile against his lips.

"Thanks, baby. Isha really needed that," I murmur as we sit quietly.

"I think we all needed that. It was good to see everyone so relaxed."

"Yeah, I did notice the guys were the most relaxed I've ever seen them. I wish Dwayne could have kicked back a little more."

I didn't miss how tense Dwayne had been today. I'm convinced he likes Isha now. I also didn't miss how she gravitates to him as well.

I mean, she flirted with the band members, but I think that was because they're all natural flirts. I know it was a boost to her ego to have four hot guys focused on her after all she's been going through with that asshat Emory.

He's been calling and texting her since she's been here. I hate that for her. I told her to block him and forget about him. He doesn't deserve her time.

"It was a workday for him. He could only join in so much. Sometimes, it's hard for him to work for me and be a friend."

"I can understand that."

We fall silent again as he holds me in his warm embrace. I smile when he begins to hum "Perfection," the song he wrote about me. He's the one who's perfect.

CHAPTER THIRTY-SEVEN

Karma

Bishop

"She doesn't know where we're going?" Dwayne asks as he pulls out of my driveway.

"No, and I plan to keep it that way. She thinks I'll be in the label's studio for the next twenty-four hours. That will give us plenty of time. My mother plans to come over and keep her busy for me," I reply.

The sun is just rising. The air outside is crisp, but my mood says otherwise. I've wanted to make this trip since the day those papers arrived.

"Works for me. We'll get this done and have you back in no time," Dwayne says.

I don't respond, remaining quiet during the rest of the trip while I stew in my anger. There was no way I'd let this shit slide, and I wasn't going to wait another day to do something about it. A few phone calls and I placed dear old Tom Jeffreys in none other than Vegas.

Seems like someone's luck has run out and it isn't mine. The ride to Vegas is quiet for the most part, Dwayne understanding me enough to leave me to my thoughts. Or it could be that he's been stewing in his own.

I'm grateful when the Vegas skyline comes into view. Any longer and I would probably have broken my knuckles from cracking them in anticipation and impatience. The tension from my anger is already suffocating within the confines of this vehicle.

Once on the strip, I have to chant to myself to keep my cool. Dwayne pulls into the parking lot of the hotel and casino Tom is staying at and an eerie calm falls over the car.

After parking, Dwayne and I head back out to the street and stroll right into the back of the hotel. We nod at the head of security, who happens to be a friend of Dwayne's. It's good to know people and have connections.

We take the service elevator up to the suite housing the asshole who thought it was a good idea to try to slap my wife with a lawsuit. I'm fuming as we walk into his suite as the same security guard lets us in. This entitled piece of shit truly thinks he runs the world.

"What… what's going on?" he asks, squinting at us as we walk over and sit on either side of him as he watches two young women fuck each other in front of him.

Tom has to be in his midforties. Blond with blue eyes, but he looks like a ferret. Not an attractive guy at all in my book.

"Time to go, girls," Dwayne barks.

The two look at him and then at Tom. Tom is too busy looking between Dwayne and myself. He looks like he's about to shit his boxers.

"He didn't stutter. Get your things and go," I say.

The two scramble to get their things and leave. Once they're gone, I take off my shades and push the hood from my head. I turn to look Tom in the eyes.

He relaxes, releasing a heavy breath. "Oh, thank God," he breathes out. "I thought my bookie sent you. I'm only a day late—"

I elbow him across the face, shutting him up. I remember not liking this guy when I went to the New York office. He was a total asshole and the biggest reason I didn't work with their firm.

"Shut the fuck up," I bite out. "You disgust me. You thought you could ruin a woman's life and career just because she wouldn't open her legs to you?"

"She's a gold digger. I introduced her to deep pockets and she was all smiles. I only wanted my turn to sample—"

"Say another word and I'll knock your fucking teeth down your throat," I growl.

He closes his mouth, but his head bobs between me and Dwayne. Dwayne bares his teeth at him. He's not going to find an ally in this room.

I continue. "I'm going to tell you how this is going to go. You're going to drop the suit. You're also going to present Saga with a nice severance package. It will include wages from the date of her last paycheck and cover the next five years."

"I'll do no such thing," he says indignantly.

I pop him in the forehead with my palm. His eyes grow wide and he starts to shrink into himself. Good, he's hearing me now.

I hate talking for no reason. I don't talk just to waste my breath. He needs to hear every damn word I'm about to say.

"I'm not asking. I'm telling you. You're also going to give her direct credit for all the campaigns she has done for your firm to place you guys where you are. As a matter of fact, I'm thinking a charity event.

"You'll give ten percent of every dollar she's ever made you. All that will cover some of the pain and suffering, but I'm not done. You see, originally, I was going to come here and beat your fucking ass.

"Then, I thought about it. I know a much better way to hurt you. You've been blackballed. I have bigger friends than you do, in much higher places.

"Good luck trying to dig your way out of this hole once you pay my wife what you owe her. I want you to know how she felt for six months after you tried to ruin her life," I seethe.

"You… you can't do this," he pleads.

"It's done. Tell your partners that they may want to find a new living. Being connected to you from this point on is like being connected to shit. I'm coming for your livelihood just like you did my wife's," I reply.

"I'll lose everything."

"Karma's a bitch, but I'm letting you off easy. That bruise on your face is nothing compared to what I really want to do to you.

"No woman"—I get in his face until we are nose to nose—"and I mean no woman owes you her body or her time. You're a worthless piece of shit.

"If you ever so much as breathe my wife's name again in your life, I'm going to make sure something so nasty happens to you that they'll have to keep your casket closed at your funeral."

Dwayne pats him on the shoulder and leans in to whisper something in his ear. Tom turns completely white, all the blood draining from his face. I've done what I've come to do.

"I'm feeling gracious, so I'll give you two months to have that money to my wife. I'll have someone get in touch with you about that event you'll be sponsoring. You have a good one," I say, getting up to walk out.

Saga

"Hi, dear. I'm so happy you had some time for me," Mrs. Moran says as she pulls me into a hug.

I return my mother-in-law's embrace, warmed by how easily she's welcomed me into her family and her son's life. My stomach sours as I think of how my family hasn't done the same. I was shocked when she called and said she wanted to spend the day with me.

Bishop and the band had to go into the label's studio for a twenty-four-hour session. Isha had a client, which means I didn't have much planned for today. Besides, Bishop's mom is a sweetheart. It's no hardship to spend time with her.

"I was happy to hear from you. I was hoping to get to know you better," I reply.

She reaches for my hand and gives it a gentle squeeze. "We're going to have so much fun together. I've always wanted a daughter.

"We gave up after Knight. I came to the conclusion that I'm just a boy mom. I didn't have the energy for one more rambunctious little boy. In the end, the chance of having another outweighed wanting a little girl," she chortles.

"I'm sure they kept you on your toes."

"You have no idea. The stories I could tell you. Bishop gave us his fair share of trouble. Grab your things, I'll tell you some stories during the ride."

Excitement fills me. I turn to head for my bag and rush to lock up. We climb into her car and she jumps right into stories of Bishop's younger years.

I laugh so much I have tears by the time we park at our destination. She's told a few stories Bishop has shared with me, but they are more humorous coming from her vantage point. Although I can tell how much she loves her sons.

Her face seems to glow as she speaks of her four boys. They're all grown men now, but I can hear in her voice that they are still her little boys in her heart. I try to imagine my huge husband as her little guy, stealing cookies, inviting his friends over to eat up all the snacks, and holding sleepovers without warning his mom his friends are coming over to stay the night.

"Oh my, I feel like I've been rambling on. I haven't allowed you to get a word in," Mrs. Moran says suddenly.

"No, you're fine. I'm enjoying your stories."

"Enough about the boys and their antics. Tell me about yourself."

We climb out of the car and start for the stores to do some retail therapy. With all I have going on, I can so use this distraction. Bishop also mentioned something about a date this weekend.

I want to find something nice to wear. He's been working so hard. I want our date to be special.

He deserves to kick back and relax. Truly happy to be out of the house and not thinking about my troubles, I walk beside Mrs. Moran.

"Well, I'm the oldest of three. I have a sister and a brother," I begin.

"Yes, I'm aware of this. Please tell me you and Bishop want children. No rush, but I'm hoping for a few grandchildren from you two."

My cheeks warm. "Yes, we want children. We haven't talked numbers, but they are in our future for sure," I say.

"I'm so excited. I miss the days when they were all tiny and cute," she coos.

Again, I can't imagine Bishop as tiny. However, images of a little Bishop in my arms fill my head. I wonder who he will take after more?

"Oh, Mrs. Moran, do you mind if we go into this jewelry store?" I ask as I think of something I think will be perfect for Bishop.

"Saga. It's Tessa. Of course we can. Lead the way," she chirps.

I smile, loving the sparkle in her blue eyes. Like her son, her presence only brings me comfort. She loops her arm through mine and gives it a gentle squeeze with her other hand.

"Tell me you plan to redecorate that drab house Bishop calls a home."

I burst into laughter. I don't have a problem with Bishop's house. Could it use a woman's touch? Absolutely, but it's not so terrible that I want to change everything right away.

I haven't decided what I intend to change, if anything, as of yet. I don't want to come in changing everything even though Bishop has said that I can.

"I'm still thinking about it," I say.

"Please do let me know when you're ready, I have a great designer I think you will love."

"I'll be sure to let you know."

"Are you looking for something in particular?" Tessa asks as I stop in front of the jewelry cases.

I freeze, not knowing how much she knows about Bishop's ex and their relationship. This has been on my mind for a while. Each time I see him reach for the necklace he no longer wears, I can't help but think of the anchor it's become in his life.

"Um, well, Bishop had this necklace. He took it off during the tour, but I get the feeling he misses it. I want to see if I can replace it with something that gives him happy thoughts," I say.

I know he's not missing his ex. I get that it was familiar. He created the habit of wearing it. I want to give him new memories to hold on to with something from me.

"Ah, the guitar pick. I did notice he hasn't been wearing it."

She tilts her head to study me. I can't help wondering what she's thinking. I try not to nervously fidget under her watchful gaze.

"I think I see for myself why Bishop fell for you," she finally says with a wide grin on her face.

I return the smile and then look down at the jewelry, not knowing what to say to that. A clerk comes over to help us right as my gaze lands on the perfect pendant. My face lights up and I point to it.

"I'd like that one, the music note," I breathe.

"Oh, that's perfect. He's going to love it," Tessa gushes.

The clerk pulls the pendant from the case for me to take a look at it. The clef note has a microphone running through it and the bottom has a heart dangling from it on its own tiny chain.

"I'll take it and a chain for it, please," I say.

"Would you like it gift-wrapped?"

"Yes, please. Thank you."

"I'll be honest with you. I was happy to see that necklace gone. I had hoped it meant he was healing from the past. I mean, he's with you now. I had hoped he wouldn't allow the past to haunt his present.

"I could hear a change in him, but seeing it gone gave me hope. This gift is a good thing. You are good for him. I have all faith in Bishop and his ability to win your family over," Tessa says.

I blink to hold back the tears. I'm so over crying. However, I can't deny how much it hurts that it's my family causing all the tension.

"Come, let's get some lunch and then we can resume shopping. There's a lovely place around here I like to do brunch at. Their mimosas are to die for," Tessa says as I'm too emotional to speak.

"That sounds nice," I manage to choke out.

The clerk returns with my purchase. After, we head out to lunch. I'll admit, my time with Tessa does lift my spirits. I'm going to love having her as a mother-in-law.

CHAPTER THIRTY-EIGHT

I know You

Bishop

I look down at my watch after rolling the sleeves of my dress shirt up over my elbows. I blow out a breath and roll my shoulders back. Looking down at my black slacks, I chide myself for not wearing a full suit.

It's too late to change now. We need to go. If only my wife would come on already.

"Saga, baby, let's go," I call through the house as I pace at the foot of the stairs, waiting for her to come down.

I'm learning my wife takes way too much time getting ready. I don't complain because she always looks great when she's done, but tonight is different because I'm nervous about this date and I want to get there on time.

"This has to go perfectly," I mutter to myself.

I feel like I've been neglecting her to get this album done. Everything is going as planned as far as my in-laws go, but now I need to turn my attention to my wife. Saga hasn't been in the studio for the recording of the album much.

The label doesn't want us sharing on social media. They're planning a documentary and have their own crew who has been coming to record for that. It's given Saga time to settle into her new home, but I don't get to spend as much time with her as I would like.

We're close to wrapping up the album. Everyone has been pushing to get to the finish line. I'm exhausted.

However, tonight is about us. A chance for me to remind Saga of why she chose me. This will be a reminder of why she's fighting for us to stay together. I want her to know I haven't forgotten her or our love.

"You don't have to shout through the house for me. I was already coming down. Why are you so impatient tonight?" Saga says.

I turn to respond but freeze and nearly swallow my tongue. She looks amazing. There's a glow to her skin and a sparkle in her eyes.

The dress she has on makes me want to change my mind about going out and instead carry her sexy ass right back upstairs to have my way with her. The gold sequin fabric falls to her upper thighs, showing off her toned, shapely legs. The neckline of the dress dips low between the valley of her breasts.

Her feet are in a pair of gold-sequined heels that scream, *fuck me*. I promise here and now that I'm going to answer them before the night is over. I can't wait to have them locked around my head.

"You look amazing," I breathe, sure she can see the lust in my gaze.

She does a turn, revealing her bare back and lush ass. My cock twitches in my pants, demanding I take her now. My wife is so fucking gorgeous.

"I was hoping you would like it," she says, looking back at me over her shoulder.

I walk over, pulling her back to my front, splaying a hand over her belly, allowing her to feel just how much I love it. The way she looks up at me says a million words on its own. Dipping my head, I take her sexy lips.

I groan as she allows me to shove my tongue into her mouth. I'm happily taken by surprise as she sucks on it. Not missing a beat, I deepen the kiss, unable to resist.

Then I reluctantly place my hands on her hips and give a tight squeeze as I break the kiss. If I don't back away now, we're not going anywhere. The thought does cross my mind to reschedule, but I promised my wife a date tonight, and I'm not breaking that promise.

I place a peck on her nose and then nip her lower lip. With knitted brows, I search her face. My chest tightens.

"From craving a grease burger to finding the love of my life, you were the last thing I expected, but everything I needed," I murmur against her lips.

"I almost didn't go inside. Now I'm glad I did."

I suck in a sharp breath. "Come on. We need to go."

Taking her hand, I lead her out of the house. My nerves shoot through the roof. This is our first real date since being back in California.

This can go great or go completely wrong. I'm always under more scrutiny when I'm back home. Being sighted is almost unavoidable, no matter what we try.

I send up a silent prayer. Please don't let them ruin us, or this time. Keep the paparazzi away from my life, at least for a time.

Saga

I snuggle into Bishop's side as we ride in the back of the SUV. I'm wrapped in a cocoon of his scent and heat. There's no other place I'd rather be.

He looks so handsome and sexy in his black dress shirt and slacks, his hair brushed back neatly in a man bun. It's a far cry from the jeans and T-shirt I'm used to seeing him in. That or a thermal and jeans.

"Where exactly are we going?" I ask to break the silence as I realize I don't know where we're going.

Bishop kisses the top of my head. Then he tightens his arm around my waist. I peek up at him and smile.

"It's a surprise. Don't worry. You'll enjoy it." He shoots me a wink.

Him and his surprises. I won't lie and say it doesn't make me all giddy inside to know he's planned something special for me. I loved our date in Atlanta.

"Ah, but are you sure? I mean, do you really feel you know me that well to be sure I'll like it?" I tease.

I feel bad as soon as I see the panic fill his eyes. Cupping his face, I press my lips to his. It takes a moment for him to return the kiss and take over.

It dawns on me how tired Bishop must be because he knows how well he knows me. I look closer at him. It's written all over his face.

He's so tired, and still, he's trying to do this for me. I love him so much for it, but I'm concerned as I look into his tired eyes. This date could have waited.

"Babe, maybe we should reschedule. You need to rest," I say.

"I can rest after we have this time together. This is important to me."

"It's not like I'm going anywhere. If you wear yourself out, then what? I want you healthy, Bishop."

He places a kiss on my lips. "I'm fine, baby. Tonight is what we both need. I'm doing this for us."

I side-eye him. I want to spend time with him too, but we could have done that at home. Not wanting to argue about it, I purse my lips.

Bishop gives me that cocky grin I know him for. "I pay attention to detail. I know you're going to love it. I know you, baby," he says.

I laugh. "Yeah, you do. You're beginning to know me better than I know myself," I purr.

Seeming to shake the moment off, he cups the back of my head and tugs me in for another kiss. We get lost in each other, tongues dancing. I tangle my fingers in his hair and open for him to kiss me deeper.

"I love you." He looks down at me with so much love in his eyes.

I can't help looking back at him with the same. My thoughts go to the necklace and pendant inside my bag. I can't wait to give him the gift.

"I love you too," I say and lean to kiss him again.

He places a hand on my thigh and gives it a squeeze. Disappointment fills me when he pulls away to look over my head out the window.

"We're here."

I turn to look out of the window. The sign for the property comes into view and a smile takes over my face. I turn to Bishop and look him in the eyes.

He does pay attention to details. Without question, he knows me so well. I mentioned loving this brand of wine and wanting to try their new line of brandy.

He's brought me to their vineyard and inn. I've read somewhere that they provide the ultimate exclusive experience here. Romantic dinners and tastings.

"This is so me," I squeal and hug my arms around myself. "Oh my God, Bishop, you do know me so well."

He kisses the back of my head and I melt right on the spot. How did I get so lucky? I think I fall deeper in love with him as we sit here.

CHAPTER THIRTY-NINE

Something New

Saga

I. Am. In. Heaven. This is the best date ever from the private chef, who I get the feeling Bishop brought in himself to the wine tasting and tour of the vineyard to this romantic hayride.

I sit between Bishop's long legs, a blanket wrapped around us. The evening is quiet other than the sound of the carriage wheels and the hooves of the horses. I look up at the stars, feeling like I'm in a dream. Bishop tightens his arms around me.

"Tell me what you're thinking," he murmurs into the top of my head.

"This is really my life. I never would have thought I would say that a few months ago. I was so afraid I'd never find my way back to me," I say softly.

"You're here now and you'll never have that fear again."

"I know. It's still surreal."

"Are you happy?"

I snuggle deeper into his embrace. Then I look back at him. He gives me a sleepy smile.

"Yes, I'm very happy. I'll be happier when I see you rested."

He pecks my lips. "Stop worrying about me. This is relaxing and I'm enjoying myself. I have my woman in my arms, we're on a date, and she's happy. I'm good, baby. Promise."

"Oh, I have something for you," I say, feeling like this is the perfect moment to give him my gift.

"For me?" he says, lifting a brow.

"Yes, for you. I have a gift for my husband. Where did my clutch go?"

With a chuckle, he reaches for my bag and hands it to me. I give him a smile and open my bag to pull the box out. My heart races with excitement.

I turn to face him and hand him the box. His brows are knit as he takes it from me. I bite my lip as I watch him pull the wrapping off and open it.

His blue eyes light up immediately. I let out a sigh of relief as he breaks into a huge smile. He lifts his gaze to mine as he pulls the chain and pendant from the box.

"I love this, baby," he says, his voice full of emotion.

"Really?"

"Yes," he croons.

He drops the box and leans in to capture my lips, palming the back of my head as he devours my mouth. He kisses me with so much passion my toes curl. When he pulls away, I'm breathless.

"It's not too much or too feminine? Maybe they can remove the heart," I say nervously.

I've been agonizing over my choice for days. Thinking it wasn't as perfect as I first thought. I probably shouldn't have gone with the first one I saw.

"Baby, this is perfect. I wouldn't change a thing. This feels like a fresh start. Like a good omen, I'm letting go of the past and stepping into a new future with you.

"Every time I feel the weight around my neck, I'll think of you. I'll be wearing our love. You just gave me a part of you to always have with me. I love it and I love you. This means so much to me, baby," he says fiercely.

"Give it to me. Let me put it on for you," I say excitedly.

He hands me the necklace, then drops his hands to my waist as I get to my knees to place it around his neck. It settles into place and it feels like a piece of us settles with it. I finger the pendant and smile.

The hay begins to bite into my knees, so I turn to sit back on my bottom. Bishop reaches for my chin and lifts my head. When our eyes meet, he gives me this look I can't even describe. It's filled with love and something else. Passion... awe... adoration.

I can't pin it exactly. When he crushes his lips to mine, I feel all of those things and so much more. He shifts to toss the blanket over me.

The next thing I know, he's squeezing my breast and has a tight grasp on my thigh. I spread my legs for him, feeling the need in his kiss.

"Bishop," I cry out as he pushes my panties aside and thrusts two fingers into me.

I arch my back and whimper. He swallows my cries as he consumes my mouth. I'm so wet for him.

He groans as I coat his fingers in my juices. I should protest as we are out in the open and the carriage operator is only a few feet away. However, I can't find it in me to care or ask my husband to stop.

I want him and I want him now. A thrill shoots through me. Once again, Bishop has me stepping outside of my comfort zone.

Again, this is something a Walden girl would never do. I throw caution to the wind and go with it. If I worry about every little thing, I'll end my life, finding that I've never lived.

When I'm with Bishop, I always feel alive. I have bigger dreams when I'm with him. Not because of who he is but because he allows me to be me.

With Bishop, I look at what's necessary to get there, not how. I never question if it's possible, but how soon. I love him and the freedom his love brings.

"Yes, yes," I cry into his mouth.

"Shh," he breaks the kiss to hiss in my ear. "You want me to fuck you; you have to be quiet."

Do I want him to fuck me here? Oh, who am I kidding? Yes, I want him.

The sound of him releasing his belt and unfastening his pants fills the air. I reach to wiggle from my panties. They're of no use to me now anyway.

Bishop has me soaked and my panties are bound to be ruined if I fixed them back into place. I turn, making sure the blanket keeps us covered. Hiking up my dress, I straddle his lap.

I sigh and drop my head back as I sink down on him. He fills me so completely. My eyes cross and I have to bite my lip to keep from moaning.

Bishop cups my face, bringing my lips to his. I love the way he's kissing me. It's as if he can't get enough of my mouth. He moves one hand to my ass, guiding me as I ride his hard length.

"Do you see how hard you make me?" he breathes into my mouth, his warm breath sending a shiver through me.

"Yes," I whimper back.

"I don't know what I was doing before I found you. It wasn't living and I wasn't happy."

"I'm here now, baby."

Bishop

I groan and thrust up into her, covering her mouth with my hand. Her eyes grow wide as she stares into mine. She feels so fucking good I have to grit my teeth to keep from groaning or growling out.

"I love you so fucking much, baby. You know that?" I whisper-hiss in her ear.

She nods feverishly. When I opened that box and saw that necklace, I was done for. I wasn't expecting the gift or the emotions that hit me.

She knows why I removed the old one. I get her intention in giving me this one. Saga has covered all my wounds and brought me the healing I never thought I'd find.

"I didn't know how ready I was for you to come into my life," I admit as she continues to ride the shit out of me.

I feel the vein that pops in my neck. I'm getting close, but I need her to go first. I push a finger into her ass and rock her harder on my shaft.

She licks my palm, causing me to smile and wink at her. Her eyes roll back in her head as her tight pussy squeezes around me. Her thighs tremble against me and her juices gush around my length.

"That's my girl, come all over my shit. Let that little pussy coat me in that sweetness," I croon.

I release her mouth and take it in a searing kiss. I want my tongue plunging into her mouth as she comes for me. I thrust up a little harder and faster, wanting to come with her.

She begins to come right as I shoot my load into her tight heat. My eyes roll back into my head. The weight of the chain around my neck grounds me, washing over me with my climax, calming my soul.

In this moment, I know I'm ready for something new. In my personal life. In my career. It's time to make some changes happen because I want to spend all the time I can with this woman in my arms.

"I didn't think I could love you more than I did, but I do," I breathe.

"I was thinking the same exact thing," she pants.

Changing

Saga

My stomach has been queasy all day. I trust Bishop, but I have no idea what's going to happen tonight. It's been a month since the disaster.

Bishop's solution to our problem is complete. A listening party. This was his big idea.

My family will be arriving at the home I share with my husband tonight to listen to his completed album. I don't know how this is supposed to fix anything, but Bishop has been so sure of himself all week.

I trust my husband.

If I can keep reminding myself of that, maybe I'll be able to get my stomach to release these knots. The anticipation is exhausting. I just want to curl up in bed and sleep until the moment of doom.

"Are you all right?" Bishop asks as he enters the room.

I'm still in his T-shirt I wore to sleep in, perched on the edge of the bed. I try to answer, but my stomach rolls. I shoot up off the bed and rush into the bathroom.

"Saga," Bishop calls as he follows me.

I can hear his heavy footfalls behind me as I sink to my knees before the toilet. I want this night to be over before it kills me. I can't believe I'm so nervous.

"Babe, tell me what you need," he says once I'm done heaving into the toilet.

He kisses the back of my head and rubs my back. I don't know what to tell him. I've been anxious about tonight all week, but this is the first time it's made me sick to my stomach.

"I think I just need to get my mind off tonight. Maybe I just need to rest or something," I say.

"Why don't you go to the spa and relax for the day? By the time you come home, I'll have everything prepared for this evening. You'll only have to get dressed," he says, combing my bangs off my sweaty forehead.

"I don't know," I moan and rub my belly. "Maybe after a nap."

"If that's what you need," he replies. "Come here."

He scoops me up and takes me to the sink to brush my teeth and wash my face for me. I've never been so cherished and loved by a man in my life. This last month of being married to Bishop has been amazing.

He's forever surprising me with his attention to detail and how he always seems to know just what I need. Sometimes, he knows what I need before I do, just like in this moment.

He steps between my legs as I'm perched on the edge of the bathroom countertop and pulls me into a tight hug. It's the soothing balm that makes my body jelly and my anxiety pop like a bubble. My stomach is still a little queasy, but the comfort of his embrace makes it background noise in an otherwise perfect moment.

"I love you," he whispers into my ear. "Everything happens for a reason. You are my reason. When this night is over, everyone will understand and we'll mend everything that was broken."

"I love you too," I say.

"Come on. Let me get you into bed. I'll make an appointment at the spa for this afternoon," he says and proceeds to carry me off to tuck me in.

The perfect husband. That's who Bishop is. Have we had hiccups in between? Yes, but that's a part of getting to know each other. I'll take the good and the bad because it's making us stronger.

He promised to make this all right. Tonight will be fine. We'll be fine.

Bishop

I watch my wife sleep with a shit-eating grin on my face. She doesn't know she's pregnant. I'm pretty damn sure of it. She thinks it's stress.

I know Saga better than she thinks. I know her body better than she knows. With all the stress she's under with her family, I'll wait to point it out to her.

My phone rings and I curse, jumping out of the bed to rush from the room before it wakes her. I smile when I see it's my mother. She's been instrumental in me getting things ready for tonight. She loves Saga.

"Hey, Mom," I say.

"Hey, honey. How are you? How's Saga?"

"I'm fine," I smile as I think of my pregnant wife. "She's great. Nervous about tonight, but it will all work out."

"Your father had to go to the office to meet with a client, but we're excited to hear the new album and to celebrate your new future," she says.

"This is the last one, Mom," I say what I've been holding in. "I spoke to Irving. A greatest hits album will complete my contract. One more tour and I'm done."

"I saw this coming. You're so happy being married. The look in your eyes when you look at her. You two were meant to be," she says, a smile can be heard in her voice.

"I love her more than I thought I could ever love someone. It's so crazy. It's like from the moment I first saw her, I knew. She was it. I would have done anything for her that very first night.

"Even when she's fussing at me for leaving towels and shit all over the place, I still think she's perfect. You know how much I hate amusement parks, but I went just because it made her face light up," I think out loud.

"That's love for you. It will have you doing things you never thought you would. I'm so proud of you, Bishop," she says.

I find myself pacing outside the door to our bedroom. My head is filled with so much I want to do with my wife and how our future will pan out.

"I need tonight to work out. She misses her family. They mean so much to her. Everything's about to change. I need them to be a part of her life."

I tug a hand through my hair. I haven't had anyone to talk to about all of this. I guess that's why it's all spewing out now.

"It will be fine."

"I should go. I have a lot to do. I'll see you tonight," I reply.

"See you tonight. I love you, darling."

"Love you too, Mom."

Saga

A nap and the spa were just what I needed. I feel so much better. I'm still anxious for tonight, but the queasiness has passed. I'm hoping that holds for the rest of the evening.

I've been doing a lot of thinking while I get ready for the party. My heart hurts that this has torn my family apart, but I'm in love with the man I've chosen to marry. Keyword *chosen*.

I've lived my life worried about making my parents proud. Even when I chose to move to New York, I deliberated for so long. I overachieved at work to show my father I made the right decision for me.

"Saga," I hear called into the room.

I step out of the closet to find my sister looking around. I can't help bursting into tears as I rush to pull her into a hug. She holds me close and rocks me as we embrace.

"Reminisce, what are you doing here so early?"

"I wanted to get a chance to see you before everyone else arrived. Besides, it's not that early. You have thirty minutes before the time that was on the invitation," she replies.

"Ugh, I've been lost in my head. I didn't know I lost that much time," I huff.

"Girl, I thought maybe staring at your husband fried your brain cells. That man is fine. He is putting a hurting on that suit. Like… just wow," she says, fanning her face.

"You've seen him? I haven't seen him since I got back. He's been busy getting this place ready and I've been off at the spa," I say and frown at myself. "I'm a terrible wife. This all has to be hard on him."

"The place looks and smells amazing and he looks as cool as a cucumber," my sister says.

"I hope Mommy and Daddy think so," I say, my shoulders slumping.

"Leave them bougie folks to stew in their old ways. Daddy is always talking about the opportunities he's built for us, but they named us Saga, Reminisce, and Legend," she says and rolls her eyes.

I start to laugh. I love my sister. She's always direct and has always said what's on her mind.

"This is true."

"It's why I had to start my own firm. Top of my class, but my name… people take one look at my résumé and go, *nope*. But seriously, I thought you were crazy for marrying some guy you just met, but you look happy and the way his face lit up when I said your name, he adores you," she says.

"He's pretty amazing. I don't know how he did it, but he got Tom to drop that dumbass lawsuit against me," I say.

"You know I would have eaten his ass up in court."

"Yeah, but I didn't want to get you involved in that mess," I say.

"Fuck him. Look at you. You're glowing."

"I'm happy. I love my new job." I shrug.

"Sounds good to me," she says. "I need to find some of that happiness for myself… is that your dress? Oh my god, it's gorgeous."

I turn to the bed where the gold-and-blue dress is laid out. It is gorgeous. It took my breath away when I first saw it.

"Yeah, Bishop picked it out and had it delivered to the house for me," I reply.

"Then let's get you dressed," my sister squeals.

My heart swells with regret. Maybe Daddy did have a right to be disappointed about me not having a wedding. I feel a little pang in my chest as I think of missing out on this—getting ready for my wedding day with my mother and my sister there to help me.

My sister just zips me up when I have another visitor. My mother steps into the room. She freezes and lifts her hands over her heart and mouth.

"You look so beautiful," she sobs.

I look down at the one-shoulder dress that snatches my waist and flares out into a wide skirt. I feel like I'm on my way to the Grammys. I look back to my mother and the pride I see on her face.

"I was wrong," I blurt out. "Not for marrying my husband, but for taking the moment of the wedding from everyone. That wasn't a thought at the time, but I get how important that moment was to you and Daddy."

"Oh, Saga," my mother says as she rushes to embrace me. "I've only ever wanted to see you happy. Your father was crushed over the wedding and not getting to approve of your choice first, but he'll get over it. I think we both just want the best for you."

"But you both are so angry at me," I sob.

She pulls away to cup my face in her hands. "You will always be our baby. We want to make sure you've picked the right person for you. We may have jumped the gun on throwing your husband under the bus."

"Okay, I'm going to jump in right here," Reminisce says. "You and Daddy were dead wrong. It's embarrassing. If Bishop's family did the same thing to Saga, you would've called them all kinds of racists and bigots—"

"Reminisce," I groan.

"No, Saga. This needs to be said. You guys thought he was some lame musician chasing money. You didn't take the time to find out who he was. I mean, come on. Legend needs to be slapped upside the head for starting this in the first place—"

"Wait, what?"

I look at my sister incredulously. I had assumed my parents found out from the news or something. I had no clue it was my brother who told them.

"You didn't know?" Reminisce turns to me and says. "He was the one who ran to tell Mommy and Daddy you were married to a musician.

"He didn't even tell them that he was a famous rock star, which I know he did on purpose. He knew Daddy would lose his shit if he found out you married some dusty-ass musician who wasn't going anywhere."

I stare at my sister with my mouth open. This is insane. I'm going to kill him. My family wasn't on board when he first met Anita. She's not exactly the wealthy match they wanted for him.

"Not that it should matter in the first place, but I told you guys Bishop has a great career," I say.

"Girl, we're talking about your father," my mother says. "By the time you arrived, he had his mind made up. He wasn't listening to a thing you were saying."

"But you seem to have had a change of heart," Reminisce sasses.

"I'm embarrassed by both myself and your father. We're very good friends with Bishop's parents. We'll be eating crow all evening," my mother says as she blushes.

It takes a moment for her words to fully hit me. I've met Bishop's parents and they never told me they know my mom and dad. I'm completely confused.

"Wait, you know the Morans?"

"Yes," my mother says, palming her forehead. "Your father performed surgery on Fred some years back. They became good golf buddies afterward. That was so long ago. It's crazy. I can't believe you and Bishop have never met."

"Hold on, the Morans? Tessa and Fred?" Reminisce says.

"Yes," Mom mumbles. "You have no idea how embarrassing this is. In my defense, I've never met Bishop before either. He left to pursue his music by the time I met and became friends with Tessa.

"Your father is too stubborn to be embarrassed, but I feel like an ass. Especially as I thought of how hard it was for me when I met my in-laws the first time."

"Wait, I'm still trying to understand how Saga and I have never met Bishop. I know his brothers," Reminisce says and snaps her fingers. "And now I know why he looks so familiar. The long hair threw me off. He does look like his brothers. Oh, this is going to be good."

My sister has that little grin on her lips that I've learned never to trust. My stomach starts to feel uneasy again. This is going to be a long night.

"I don't like the sound of that. Your father and I have made big enough asses out of ourselves. Don't add to this mess, Reminisce. I'm warning you," Mom chides.

Reminisce throws her hands in the air. "I'm here for my sister. Besides, I want to hear this album. From what I've heard online, it's going to be epic."

Mom cups my face and wipes at my tears. "Let's get this face fixed. Bishop is handsome. That suit is very attractive on him."

"What suit? I need to see what you two are talking about," I say.

"Then we better get you together," my sister says.

"And go save your husband from the death glare your father is sure to still be giving him," Mom says and rolls her eyes.

Hope blooms. With my mother on my side, we only have to win over my dad. This night may work out after all.

CHAPTER FORTY-ONE

Everything Broken

Saga

It feels good to have my mother and sister here, at my sides, as we descend the stairs to where the rest of the party has started. I'm chuckling at my crazy sister when we turn the corner and Bishop comes into view. I lose my breath.

He looks phenomenal in the tailored suit that's draping his big body. The top button of his shirt is open, giving him a casual but sexy look. He hasn't shaved in a day or two, which I'm not complaining about. His long locks are loose and hanging down around his shoulders.

"Yup, that was exactly how I looked when he introduced himself," Reminisce says next to me. "Damn, how did I miss that he's a Moran?"

I cast my gaze around my husband and find three other faces that look like his. Their genes are strong. I'll be locking my sons away from all the fast little girls if they take after their father and uncles. My God, these are some fine men.

When I train my gaze back on Bishop, he's staring at me. He has this look in his eyes that says a ton of unspoken things. Some are better left unsaid in present company. My feet are moving without my permission.

"You are more gorgeous than I dreamed," he says, cupping my face.

"You aren't looking too bad yourself," I say and smile up at him.

The soft kiss he places on my lips is so tender it nearly brings me to tears. I'm going to need an emotional detox after tonight. I've been such a mess today. Bishop brushes his thumb across my lips as he looks into my eyes.

"From the first day I met you, I knew you were the one, but I don't think I could've loved you as deeply as I do if I hadn't learned heartbreak first," he whispers.

"Stop trying to eat the girl and introduce us," one of the tall blonds says.

Bishop points a finger. "That's Prince," he says as an introduction.

"Good to finally meet you, sis," Prince says.

"Hi. It's nice to meet you too."

"My twin doesn't have manners. I think I stepped on his head on the way out of the womb," the next brother says. "I'm Lord."

He takes my hand and kisses the back of it. Bishop elbows him, shooting him a glare. I stifle a laugh and shake my head.

"Lord," I look at Bishop. We've talked about our parents' choices of names before. However, putting faces with the names tickles me all over again. "It's so nice to meet you."

"That would leave my youngest brother," Bishop says.

"Hello, beautiful. I'm Knight."

"Watch him, he bites," Lord chuckles.

"This may be true, but this Walden is taken," Knight says, but his gaze is over my head.

I turn to see my sister looking at Knight with narrowed eyes. Oh, there is definitely something going on there. I know that look.

"Saga, you look lovely, dear," Mrs. Moran sings, drawing my attention.

Bishop and his brothers get their blue eyes from their mother. She's tall, with a thin frame. The pale-pink dress she has on enhances her tanned skin.

"Hello, Mrs. Moran."

"You stop that. I told you to call me Tessa. You're simply glowing. Fred, doesn't she look lovely?"

"As always," Bishop's father replies as he comes to kiss me on the cheek.

Now, when it comes to the large, broad frame most of the guys have, you know right away that they get it from their father. As tall as Tessa is, her husband makes her seem as tiny as I am next to Bishop. When I look at Bishop's parents, I can see a mix of them both in their sons.

"My baby does know how to make an entrance."

I close my eyes as my father's voice fills the room. Pain races through me as I think of the words he hurled at me the last time we were in the same room together. When I open my eyes, my father is standing in front of me.

"Hey, Daddy," I whisper.

"Hello, sweet pea," he says. "It's good to see you."

"It's great to see you too."

You can cut the tension in the room with a knife. My father's posture says a lot. Bishop splays a hand on my belly and kisses my temple. I melt into his hold.

"Should we get the evening started?" Bishop says close to my ear.

I turn to look up at him. I'm momentarily lost in his gaze. I shake it off and nod.

"Everyone, I thought we'd have dinner before we start. If you'll join Saga and me in the dining room, we can get the night started," Bishop says.

"I could stand to eat," Knight says with a mischievous smile.

I catch a glance at my sister in time to see her shiver. I don't think anyone else catches it, but I do. I look to my brother and roll my eyes at him. We're going to have a long talk.

I'm going to kick your ass. I mouth to him.

Legend just frowns at me. I'm so pissed at him. We're not kids anymore. When we were younger, he would run home to tell my dad about my boyfriends. It was annoying, but I thought of it as sweet. My little brother wanted to look after me.

This time, he took things too far. If he was going to run his mouth, he should've at least given all of the information. I shake my frustration with my brother off and follow everyone into the dining room.

"Relax," Bishop leans to say in my ear.

I look at him, and suddenly, I find my center. My brother's betrayal and big mouth are forgotten. For now, at least.

Bishop

This is it. I worked hard on the last song on the album. We recorded each song over and over until they were perfect.

Everything had to be just right for tonight. I planned every detail down to a science. Dinner went as well as we could expect. My father-in-law still isn't ready to warm up to me. That was clear from the moment he arrived.

I've watched his jaw work as he listens to the album I've made for his daughter, but those songs are not the ones I wanted him here for. It's this one, the final song, that I need him to hear.

"I decided to play this one live. It's the most important song on the album," I say. "Saga, baby, can you come up here for me?"

Saga's cheeks glow as she stands and comes to a stop by me at the piano. I kiss her cheek before lifting her to sit on the piano top. She gives a little surprised yelp, pulling a chuckle from everyone.

I take a seat in front of the keys and look at my bandmates. They give me a nod. If I can't get everyone to understand how I feel with this last song, I'll never be able to get them to understand.

I start to play while looking into Saga's eyes. I'm overwhelmed with the depth of love I feel for her. It all comes to the surface.

The day you were born somewhere in the ethers, a flame was
ignited
On the other end of that flame was my heart
I've been floating without you
I've been dreaming about you

Someone to love me, someone to get me
Someone who makes me my best
I can't think of life without you now that I've found you
I'm convinced losing you would mean death
With my life, I'd protect you
I'd fall on a sword if it meant you could take your next breath
My heart knows you—
It pounds harder whenever you're near
It beats for you—
No one in the world could know how much I adore you
I hope this doesn't bore you
But I need you to know how much I care

Saga is in tears by the time I get to the chorus. If this song doesn't get through to anyone else, I know it's getting to her. I lift to peck her lips before sitting again to play and sing the hook.

Please don't worry—
I know that you love me
You know that I love you
With our love, we'll mend everything
The sky could be falling, death could be calling
but our love could face anything
I know it all seems broken
but our love is strong enough to heal anything

I reach to wipe the tears from Saga's face. The band plays on. I lift to place my forehead to hers as they play the bridge.

She palms my face and kisses my lips. My restraint breaks and I can't hold back. I deepen the kiss and pour all my love into it. Reluctantly, I break the connection to play the next verse.

Let me make you a promise
Every breath that I take will always belong to you

And when I die, that flame will still burn, so once again, you'll
come back to me
Can you feel me—?
Cause I feel you in my heart, I have from the start
Nothing in this world can tear us apart
This is my love note, my heart at your feet
I want to give you forever and ever
Call on me whenever you need
If the world turned its back on me, I know I'd have you
You get me; you understand all the things unsaid
Someday, we'll start a family, a little you, a little me
You'll be giving me more air to breathe
Do you know I breathe you—?
Just shows how much I need you
I swear my heart will always know how to find you

I have my own tears gathering in my eyes as I look up at my wife. This moment was supposed to be to demonstrate our love to her family, but as I sing the words, they show me exactly how much I love this woman and would die to give her everything she wants.

"I love you," I say to Saga as the band sings and plays the chorus.

"It's perfect," she says. "The perfect end to the album. I love you so much."

I stand, grasping the small of her back and kiss her. It's a hungry, demanding kiss that she returns with just as much vigor. Whistles and hand clapping bring us back to the room with our guests. I pull away and kiss the tip of her nose.

When the band plays the last note, the applause gets louder. I get choked up when I see the misty eyes and some wiping of actual tears. However, it's the look on my mother-in-law and father-in-law's faces that tells me I've done what I set out to do.

"It's going to be fine," I lean to say in Saga's ear.

She looks up at me. "I know. Thank you."

Saga

"Thank you for sitting with me," my father says as we all sit down in Bishop's office.

All my emotions and thoughts rush me. I have so much I want to say. So much to get off my chest. I begin to blurt it all out.

"I'm so sorry. I should've thought about how this would—"

"You're a grown woman. Yes, I would have loved to walk you down the aisle. To see the sparkle in my little girl's eyes as she anticipated starting a new life with a young man I got to know." Daddy pauses to side-eye Bishop.

"But you're more than old enough to make your own decisions. I know I've been hard on you. I said some things I shouldn't have, but watching you two together this evening, I completely understand why you two felt this was the right decision for you," my father says.

"I'm sorry I didn't go about this differently, but I didn't want to lose Saga. I felt like I had to make her mine as soon as I could," Bishop says.

"It hurt that you didn't at least tell us," my father says. "Finding out that you were the son of a good friend of mine… Fred has always been a good friend. I know he raised his boys right. I would have just liked to have had all those facts before my knucklehead son came to toss this all at me, catching me completely off guard."

"We hadn't planned for that to happen. We weren't going to tell anyone until we shared it with our families. The press showed up and things just went downhill from there," I say.

"What's done is done. However, I am sorry for any stress I added to your plate as newlyweds," Daddy says sincerely. He sighs. "I see the way you look at each other. I can't deny the love I see between you two."

"I hope you can see I didn't marry a bum as well," I say teasingly.

"He may have done well for himself," Daddy replies.

"I try," Bishop says with a chuckle.

"Hopefully, your sister will allow me to walk her down the aisle someday," my father says.

"Actually," Bishop says. "We would be honored if everyone would join us for our wedding anniversary next year. We'd like to renew our vows then with all our family."

"We've talked about it. I'd like to have you walk me down the aisle this time. I want Mommy to help me put on my veil and we want our family there to bear witness to our love," I say.

This has been something we've been talking about within the last week. I love the idea. Tonight just confirmed how much I want to follow through with it.

"That sounds wonderful. I get to spoil my baby one last time," my father says. "There's hope for you yet, Bishop."

"I'm not a bad guy, Dad," Bishop replies.

"I don't know if we're there yet," Dad says, but the smile on his lips eases his words.

I crack up. This is the lightest I've felt in weeks. It's as if my world has fallen right into place.

"You know. It's a small world. Saga, you left for New York when Fred and I really became tight and Bishop here had already started to travel the world with his music. It's interesting that you two didn't meet sooner," my father muses.

"I think we met right when we should have," I say, looking up at Bishop.

"I know we did," Bishop says. "You showed up right when I needed you."

"You know, I was thinking that very same thing," I say as I beam at him.

CHAPTER FORTY-TWO

Our Next Chapter

Saga

I haven't been able to stop smiling since our family left. Tonight turned out better than I hoped. I even made up with my brother—at least, I did after placing him in a headlock.

"You look happy," Bishop says as he walks up behind me and buries his face into my neck.

Looking at us in the full-length mirror, I smile at the sight we make. Bishop is the total opposite of my type, and yet he's the perfect man for me. I'd do it all again if I had the chance. Mistakes and all, it was our path.

"I can't help but feel like my life is perfect. I love my job. This place is starting to feel like home now that you're here with me. My family is talking to me again. And I have you," I say.

Bishop locks eyes with me in the mirror. He studies me for a moment. I crease my forehead in curiosity.

"Yet something is missing. I heard it at the end," he murmurs.

"You know me so well," I chuckle.

"What is it?"

"All of this business with my dad and family. It has forced me to think about everything in my life. The choices I made before you. The ones that led to New York and my workaholic life.

"I don't know if I chose my career for me or if that was just one of many things I did to please my father. I'm thinking I want to explore something new. My sister is an entrepreneur. Maybe I should take a page from her book," I reply.

"What do you plan to do?"

I laugh. "That's just it. I'm still figuring that out," I say.

"I've learned that it's never too late to go after your dreams. When you figure it out, we'll make it happen. For now, we'll focus on being happy," he says.

"When do you plan to tell me that you're retiring? I'm going to need to find a new job when you do," I say, watching him for a reaction.

"You have a year to figure things out. The album drops next week and the tour will start in a few months. Once it's over, I'm done. I already have a few people calling to have me write for them," he says and shrugs.

Kissing the top of my head, he continues. "You don't have to worry about a new job. If you want to stay home with the kids, that's fine with me," he says with a twinkle in his eyes.

I laugh. "We have time before I have to decide whether or not I want to be a stay-at-home mom."

"Are you sure about that?"

I stare at him with my brows drawn. Turning in his arms, I look up at him. He just smiles at me like a loon.

"What am I missing? Do you want to start trying?"

"When have we ever not been trying? We sure as hell have never prevented it from happening," he says with mirth in his eyes.

"Okay, this is true," I say and nod. I pause to think before musing aloud. "I don't think I've had my period this month."

"That's my girl," Bishop chuckles, dipping his head to take my lips. Then he breathes against them. "I was waiting for you to figure it out."

"Oh my God! You think? This morning, that wasn't just my nerves. We're having a baby?" I say excitedly.

Bishop starts to sway my body in his arms as he presses his forehead to mine. He pecks my lips gently. I'm smiling from ear to ear.

"I think so. I hope so. Your body has been changing. I noticed last week," he says with a bright smile.

"So begins the next chapter in our lives," I whisper.

"So it begins," he says and presses his lips to mine.

The kiss goes from soft to searing within seconds. I moan into his mouth as he palms my back and presses my curves into his hard body. Anticipation begins to fill my veins.

The sound of the zipper releasing on my dress reaches my ears. I reach to push his suit jacket from his broad shoulders. Bishop peels my dress away from my body, letting it hit the floor in a pool of fabric at my feet.

I palm his face. "I love you," I say as his lips move to my neck.

"I love you so much," he replies huskily.

He tugs his shirt open, buttons pop and fly free. My breasts heave as I lose my breath with want. I will never have enough of this man. He leaves me wanting more even as he touches me.

Reaching for his wrist, I stare up at him as I release his cuff link. I've admired how sexy he has looked all night. Yet, my shirtless Bishop is my favorite. Not just because I get to ogle his amazing body, but because it's when I get to see him most relaxed.

Once I have the cuff links in my palm, he lifts me onto his waist and carries me over to the bed. He lays me down gently and takes his links from my hand, placing them in his pocket. I sit up on my elbows as I watch him release his pants and push them down his thick thighs.

"You are a stunning man," I breathe.

"You are a remarkable woman. I see how close you are to your family. I know you were willing to give that up to stay with me. Your strength is something I hope to match in our marriage," he says.

My cheeks heat. He's right. I love my family dearly and I would have been devastated if they couldn't come to terms with my marriage. Yet, this pull I have when it comes to my husband. It feels right. I would have done whatever kept me in his arms.

"I truly believe we were meant to be," I say.

"I know we were," he says, grabbing my ankles and pulling me to the edge of the bed.

He sucks my toes into his mouth as his eyes stay locked on mine. I never in my life thought this would turn me on. He smiles around my big toe before releasing it.

Dropping to his knees, he begins to feast on my core. I'm clenching the sheets and calling out almost instantly. Bishop chuckles in pleasure. He relishes this torture he places on my body.

Halfway to my first orgasm, he pauses, moving his face to my belly. He starts a circle of reverent kisses across my skin. It settles in that I might be pregnant. We'll need to make sure first thing tomorrow.

"It feels like I've waited forever for you and your mother. You both make me a better man. I will cherish and protect you both with every breath I have," he says against my tummy.

I push a hand through his hair, causing him to lift his eyes to mine. His blues glisten with unshed tears. I think I just fell in love with him all over again.

"We're the lucky ones. You've been there to protect me and fix things for me from the time we first met. Thank you for that," I say.

"Thank you for letting me."

He leans in to kiss me, my flavor on his lips. I moan at the taste, needing him more than ever. Slipping a hand beneath my ass, he moves me up the bed.

Breaking the kiss, he sinks into me slowly. He stretches me in that way that makes me feel complete. The slow work of his hips stirs something deep in my soul.

I cling to him as a firestorm builds inside me so perfectly. His groans become music to my ears. I turn my head and lick the sweat from his bicep.

"Babe," he grunts.

"I need more," I whimper.

He kisses me deeply, only increasing his pace after he's had his fill of my mouth. We're going to peak together. I know it. I can feel it.

It's the moment of all moments. The one where I can feel my soul connect to his. I look into his eyes and the world falls away. I am his and he is mine.

Our hearts sing the final notes to our song.

CHAPTER FORTY-THREE

Resolutions

Saga

I flip through the mail, stopping at the large envelope with my name on it. I place a hand on my still flat tummy. The morning sickness has gotten real.

I think to wait for Bishop to return from his meeting with the label, but curiosity wins out. I tear the envelope open and pull out the folder inside. I skim through the contents and freeze.

It's a severance package and an apology from the partners at Carmichael, Pike, and Jeffreys Advertising and Marketing. Only the letterhead reads Carmichael and Pike Advertising and Marketing, no longer Jeffreys.

I laugh out loud when I see an offer for my old job back. "I'm good," I say to myself.

Shaking my head, I flip through the rest of the documents. There's a spread on a fundraiser that was given. I'm still sitting, flipping through everything, when I feel Bishop's presence at my back. He kisses the side of my neck.

"We can close that chapter now too. You deserve every penny. He will forever remember the consequences of his actions," he says.

"How?"

"I will always keep you safe and taken care of," he replies, placing his hand on my belly. "Both of you."

I turn to look up at him. His eyes are closed off. I know he's not going to give me any further information about this.

"Thank you," I say.

"Your brother is coming to hang out with me today. What are you getting up to?"

"I'm exhausted. I'm going to get in a nap because this little monster in there is determined to drain Mommy of all her energy," I chuckle.

"Then come on. I'll tuck you two in and play you a lullaby before Legend gets here," he laughs back.

"Sounds good," I yawn.

He scoops me up and starts upstairs. My lids are growing so heavy already. I blame the comfort of his big, strong arms.

"Maybe you should write an album for my children's book," I muse sleepily.

"Not a bad idea. We'll talk about it later. That might be fun to do together."

"We make a great team. Go, team SagaBish," I cheer.

"Babe, that still sucks," he rumbles with laughter.

I shrug. "Thought I'd still try."

Placing me into the bed, he strips off his outside clothes and climbs in beside me. When his arm settles over me, I feel like I'm in a warm cocoon.

"What if I didn't get on that bus?" I wonder as my sleepy thoughts bounce around in my head.

"I would've stayed right there at that diner until the next morning when we could've gotten you a tow. Then I would've followed you to the auto shop, where they would've told you the car was busted and I would've offered you a ride again," he says with humor lacing his voice.

"In other words, I would have gotten on the bus one way or another." I snicker.

"Damn right. You were the one, babe. I knew it then and I know it now. No matter what, we were always meant to be right here in the end."

"Yeah, I was fired to get stranded. All so I could be your muse. Not a bad destiny at all."

Anniversary

Bishop

We made it. Our first year as a married couple. Our sons were born three months ago and I couldn't be happier with my life.

That is, until this moment. I can't breathe. Saga looks so beautiful I might faint. She worked her ass off to fit into her gown for the wedding.

I loved her body after she gave birth to our boys, but she wanted to do this for herself. I just can't believe I'm the lucky bastard who gets to call her my wife. She looks like a princess as she walks down the aisle in her gown which sparkles with each step.

Her brown shoulders are bare and her breasts are tastefully held with love and care by the fabric. Even swollen from feeding our sons she looks phenomenal. The fitted waist of the dress belies the fact that she was ever pregnant. Forget about being so three months ago with twins.

"You did good, bro," Lord says beside me.

"I did, didn't I?" I say with a throat clogged with emotions.

I look around at our family. Nothing but smiling faces around us. I still don't know where the fuck Jag is. He got hammered last night and hasn't shown up.

I don't know if I'll forgive him for this one, but everyone else that's important to us made it. We made it. No one thought we would. A year ago, on this day, we had all the cards stacked against us.

"You two have proven me wrong and made me a proud grandfather," my father-in-law says as he hands over my bride. "I want you to always remember this love right here. When life gets tough, remember the love you started with and always work together to find your way back to it."

"We will," Saga says shakily.

Her father kisses her cheek. "Finally. I've walked my princess into her future. I love you, sweet pea."

"I love you too, Daddy."

"Okay, Bishop. She's all yours."

"Thanks, Dad," I say with a teasing grin.

"You're welcome, son," he says and pats my cheek.

I'm thrown for a moment. I wasn't expecting his acceptance. I thought he'd joke that we still weren't there yet.

"See, I told you he likes you," Saga says sweetly.

"Yeah," I say and nod. My throat too full of emotion to say more.

"Shall we sing our vows, Mr. Moran?"

I look at my wife and smile. We made our vows up from the hooks from the album I dedicated to her. It's the perfect mix of who we are and what we mean to each other.

"I was born ready."

ACKNOWLEDGMENTS

I loved Bishop and Saga the first time and I love them even more this go-round. I look forward to bringing the rest of this series to life and introducing you to the rest of the brothers. Book 2 is the reason this series is moving to Amazon to join the Lost Souls so we can get to Kevlar. I hope you are ready.

Thank you to everyone for your support. I enjoyed writing this book so much. I found myself tickled as I counted bars and arranged the music as if it were to be recorded. My music-writing brain fussed with my book-writing brain. I loved every minute of it.

Thank you to my husband, who listened to me rant about this book and what I wanted to do with it both times. It's been fun in my house as he watches me crank out book after book. I've written way more than you've seen. LOL

I will always thank God because I know that this is all possible because of Him. I've been walking by faith and not by sight. Each day is a blessing and another chance to be great. For that, I'm grateful.

On to the Next!! *There is a method to the madness. We're going somewhere.*

ABOUT THE AUTHOR

Blue Saffire, an award-winning, bestselling author of over thirty contemporary romance novels and novellas,—writes with the intention to touch the heart and the mind. Blue hooks, weaves, and loops multiple series, keeping you engaged in her worlds. Every word is meant to have a lasting touch that leaves you breathless for more.

Blue and her husband live in a home filled with laughter and creativity in Long Island, NY. Both working hard to build the Blue brand and cultivate their love for the arts. Creativity is their family affair.

Wait, there is more to come! You can stay updated with my latest releases, learn more about me, the author, and be a part of contests by subscribing to my newsletter at

www.BlueSaffire.com

If you enjoyed *Love Notes*, I'd love to hear

your thoughts and please feel free to leave a

review. And when you do, please let me

know by emailing me TheBlueSaffire@gmail.com

or leave a comment on Facebook https://www.facebook.com/BlueSaffireDiaries or Twitter @TheBlueSaffire

Other books by Blue Saffire

Placed in Best Reading Order

Also available....

Legally Bound

Legally Bound 2: Against the Law

Legally Bound 3: His Law

Perfect for Me

Hush 1: Family Secrets

Ballers: His Game

Brothers Black 1: Wyatt the Heartbreaker

Legally Bound 4: Allegations of Love

Hush 2: Slow Burn

Legally Bound 5.0: Sam

Yours 1: Losing My Innocence

Yours 2: Experience Gained

Yours 3: Life Mastered

Ballers 2: His Final Play

Legally Bound 5.1: Tasha Illegal Dealings

Brothers Black 2: Noah

Legally Bound 5.2: Camille

Legally Bound 5.3 & 5.4 Special Edition

Where the Pieces Fall Book 1 : Lost Hearts Series

Legally Bound 5.5: Legally Unbound

Brothers Black 4: Braxton the Charmer

Broken Soldier Book 2: Lost Hearts Series (Novella)

Brothers Black 5: Felix the Watcher

A Home for Christmas

Doctor Feel Good

Brothers Black 6: Ryan the Joker

Brothers Black 7: Johnathan the Fixer

Coming Soon…
Pieces of Trevor's Heart Book 3: Lost Hearts Series
King of Inferno Book 2: Immortal Iron Brothers Series

Other Blue Saffire Series

Hold On To Me Series
My Funny Valentine
Be My Valentine

Hitter Squad Series
Remember Me

Work Husband Series
Unexpected Lovers
My Best Friend's Wish
The Ones Left Behind
The Last Ones Standing

The Lost Souls MC Series
Forever
Never
Always

The A**hole Club Series
Pit Book 1: The A**hole Club
Ox Book 5: The A**hole Club
Kelex Book 6: The A**hole Club

The Immortal Iron Brothers Series
King of Knights Book 1: Immortal Iron Brothers

Check out Blue Saffire exclusives on the
BlueSaffire.com website
His Miracle Baby
Razor
Dane
Trip
Wounded
12 Rounds
Professor Jones

Other books from Evei Lattimore Collection Books by Blue Saffire
Black Bella 1

Destiny 1: Life Decisions
Destiny 2: Decisions of the Next Generation
Destiny 3 coming soon…

Star

Other books from Royal Blue Gay Romance Collection written by Blue Saffire
Kyle's Reveal
Beau's Redemption